Praise for *BEHIND CLOSED DOORS*

An August 2016 Best Book of the Month
by Amazon, iBooks, and *Real Simple* magazine

An August 2016 Indie Next Pick
and LibraryReads List Pick

An August 2016 Book Club Pick by *POPSUGAR*:
"Perfect for fans of *The Girl on the Train*!"

As seen featured in *The Skimm*'s newsletter:
"It'll have you page-turning 'til the end."

"In B. A. Paris's hair-raising debut, a woman falls in love with a psychopath, only realizing his true nature when she's hidden from the world and suffering unthinkable horrors at the hands of a seemingly perfect man. *Behind Closed Doors* is both unsettling and addictive, as I raced through the pages to find out Grace's fate. A chilling thriller that will keep you reading long into the night."
—Mary Kubica, *New York Times* and *USA Today*
bestselling author of *The Good Girl*

"A gripping domestic thriller . . . the sense of believability and terror that engulfs *Behind Closed Doors* doesn't waver." —Associated Press

"If you're hunting for a thriller to give you chills in August, look no further than this book, which is already a big hit in the United Kingdom." —*Real Simple* magazine

"This dark and twisted thriller will keep you on your toes and have you wondering exactly what goes on behind your neighbor's door."

—*BuzzFeed* (Six Thriller/Mystery Reads That Will Have You Sleeping With the Lights On)

"Newlyweds Grace and Jack Angel seem to lead a perfect life in British author Paris's gripping debut, but appearances can be deceiving. . . . Grace's terror is contagious, and [her sister] Millie's impending peril creates a ticking clock that propels this claustrophobic cat-and-mouse tale toward its grisly, gratifying conclusion."

—*Publishers Weekly*

"Making her smash debut, Paris [keeps] the suspense level high. In the same vein as *Gone Girl* or *The Girl on the Train,* this is a can't-put-down psychological thriller."

—*Library Journal* (starred review)

"Debut novelist Paris adroitly toggles between the recent past and the present in building the suspense of Grace's increasingly unbearable situation, as time becomes critical and her possible solutions narrow. This is one readers won't be able to put down."

—*Booklist* (starred review)

"A frighteningly cool portrait of a serious sadist, *Behind Closed Doors* is a gripping, claustrophobia-inducing thriller . . . Read at the risk of running from every handsome British lawyer who crosses your path."

—*RT Book Reviews*

Also by B. A. Paris

*Behind Closed Doors*

# THE BREAKDOWN

## B. A. PARIS

St. Martin's Paperbacks

*For my parents*

This is a work of fiction. All of the characters, organizations, and events portrayed in this novel are either products of the author's imagination or are used fictitiously.

First published in the United Kingdom by MIRA/Harlequin, HarperCollins.

Published in the United States by St. Martin's Paperbacks, an imprint of St. Martin's Publishing Group.

THE BREAKDOWN

For information, address St. Martin's Publishing Group, 120 Broadway, New York, NY 10271.

www.stmartins.com

Library of Congress Catalog Card Number: 2017002673

ISBN: 978-1-250-12247-6

Our books may be purchased in bulk for promotional, educational, or business use. Please contact your local bookseller or the Macmillan Corporate and Premium Sales Department at 1-800-221-7945, ext. 5442, or by email at MacmillanSpecialMarkets@macmillan.com.

Printed in the United States of America

St. Martin's Press hardcover edition / July 2017
St. Martin's Griffin edition / May 2018
St. Martin's Paperbacks edition / March 2020

10  9  8  7  6  5  4  3  2  1

# ACKNOWLEDGMENTS

Eternal gratitude to my wonderful agent, Camilla Wray, who has made so many things possible, and to the rest of the team at Darley Anderson for being an absolute pleasure to work with. And also for their expertise—I wouldn't be where I am without them.

Huge thanks to my amazing editor, Sally Williamson, for her invaluable advice and support, and for always being on the end of the phone. Thank you too to the rest of the team at HQ for their enthusiasm and professionalism—you're the best! And in the U.S., to Jennifer Weis, Lisa Senz, Jessica Preeg, and all at St. Martin's Press for their continued faith in me.

Last, but definitely not least, special thanks as always to my family—my daughters, my husband, my parents, my brothers and sister—for always being interested in my writing. And to my lovely friends, both in England and France, who are as excited about my new career as I am!

# FRIDAY, JULY 17TH

The thunder starts as we're saying goodbye, leaving each other for the summer holidays ahead. A loud *crack* echoes off the ground, making Connie jump. John laughs, the hot air dense around us.

"You need to hurry!" he shouts.

With a quick wave I run to my car. As I reach it, my mobile starts ringing, its sound muffled by my bag. From the ringtone I know that it's Matthew.

"I'm on my way," I tell him, fumbling for the door handle in the dark. "I'm just getting in the car."

"Already?" His voice comes down the line. "I thought you were going back to Connie's."

"I was, but the thought of you waiting for me was

too tempting," I tease. The flat tone to his voice registers. "Is everything all right?" I ask.

"Yes, it's just that I've got an awful migraine. It started about an hour ago and it's getting steadily worse. That's why I'm phoning. Do you mind if I go up to bed?"

I feel the air heavy on my skin and think of the storm looming; no rain has arrived yet but instinct tells me it won't be far behind. "Of course not. Have you taken anything for it?"

"Yes, but it doesn't seem to be shifting. I thought I'd go and lie down in the spare room; that way, if I do fall asleep, you won't disturb me when you come in."

"Good idea."

"I don't really like going to bed without knowing you're back safely."

I smile at this. "I'll be fine, it'll only take me forty minutes. Unless I come back through the woods, by Blackwater Lane."

"Don't you dare!" I can almost sense a shaft of pain rocketing through his head at his raised tone. "Ouch, that hurt," he says, and I wince in sympathy. He lowers his voice to a more bearable level. "Cass, promise you won't come back that way. First of all, I don't want you driving through the woods on your own at night and, second, there's a storm coming."

"OK, I won't," I say hastily, folding myself onto the driver's seat and dropping my bag onto the seat next to me.

"Promise?"

"Promise." I turn the key in the ignition and shift the

car into gear, the phone now hot between my shoulder and ear.

"Drive carefully," he cautions.

"I will. Love you."

"Love you more."

I put my phone in my bag, smiling at his insistence. As I maneuver out of the parking space, fat drops of rain splatter onto my windscreen. *Here it comes*, I think.

By the time I get to the dual carriageway, the rain is coming down hard. Stuck behind a huge lorry, my wipers are no match for the spray thrown up by its wheels. As I move out to pass it, lightning streaks across the sky and, falling back into a childhood habit, I begin a slow count in my head. The answering rumble of thunder comes when I get to four. Maybe I should have gone back to Connie's with the others, after all. I could have waited out the storm there, while John amused us with his jokes and stories. I feel a sudden stab of guilt at the look in his eyes when I'd said I wouldn't be joining them. It had been clumsy of me to mention Matthew. What I should have said was that I was tired, like Mary, our Head, had.

The rain becomes a torrent and the cars in the fast lane drop their speed accordingly. They converge around my little Mini and the sudden oppression makes me pull back into the slow lane. I lean forward in my seat, peering through the windscreen, wishing my wipers would work a little faster. A lorry thunders past, then another and when it cuts back into my lane without warning, causing me to brake sharply, it suddenly feels too dangerous to stay on this road. More lightning forks the sky and in its wake the sign for Nook's Corner, the little hamlet where I live, looms into view. The black letters on the white background, caught in the headlights and glowing like a beacon in the dark, seem so inviting that, suddenly, at the very last minute, when it's almost too late, I veer off to the left, taking the shortcut that Matthew didn't want me to take. A horn blares angrily behind me and as the sound chases me down the pitch-black lane into the woods, it feels like an omen.

Even with my headlights full on, I can barely see where I'm going and I instantly regret the brightly lit road I left behind. Although this road is beautiful by day—it cuts through bluebell woods—its hidden dips and bends will make it treacherous on a night like this. A knot of anxiety balls in my stomach at the thought of the journey ahead. But the house is only fifteen minutes away. If I keep my nerve, and not do anything rash, I'll soon be home. Still, I put my foot down a little.

A sudden rush of wind rips through the trees, buffeting my little car and, as I fight to keep it steady on the road, I hit a sudden dip. For a few scary seconds, the wheels leave the ground and my stomach lurches into my mouth, giving me that awful roller-coaster feeling. As it smacks back down onto the road, water whooshes up the side of the car and cascades onto the windscreen, momentarily blinding me.

"No!" I cry as the car judders to a halt in the pooling water. Fear of becoming stranded in the woods drives adrenaline through my veins, spurring me into action. Shifting the car into gear with a crunch, I jam my foot down. The engine groans in protest but the car moves forward, plowing through the water and up the other side of the dip. My heart, which has been keeping time with the wipers as they thud crazily back and forth across the windscreen, is pounding so hard that I need a few seconds to catch my breath. But I don't dare pull over in case the car refuses to start again. So I drive on, more carefully now.

A couple of minutes later, a sudden crack of thunder makes me jump so violently that my hands fly off the wheel. The car slews dangerously to the left and as I yank it back into position, my hands shaking now, I feel a rush of fear that I might not make it home in one piece. I try to calm myself but I feel under siege, not only from the elements but also from the trees as they writhe back and forth in a macabre dance, ready to pluck my little car from the road and toss it into the storm at any moment. With the rain drumming on the roof, the wind rattling the windows and the wipers thumping away, it's difficult to concentrate.

There are bends coming up ahead so I shift forward in my seat and grip the wheel tightly. The road is deserted and, as I negotiate one bend, and then the next, I pray I'll see some taillights in front of me so that I can follow them the rest of the way through the woods. I want to phone Matthew, just to hear his voice, just to know I'm not the only one left in the world, because that's how it feels. But I don't want to wake him, not when he has a migraine. Besides, he would be furious if he knew where I was.

Just when I think my journey is never going to end,

I clear a bend and see the rear lights of a car a hundred yards or so in front of me. Giving a shaky sigh of relief, I speed up a little. Intent on catching it up, it's only when I'm almost on top of it that I realize it isn't moving at all, but parked awkwardly in a small lay-by. Caught unaware, I swerve out around it, missing the right-hand side of its bumper by inches and as I draw level, I turn and glare angrily at the driver, ready to yell at him for not putting on his warning lights. A woman looks back at me, her features blurred by the teeming rain.

Thinking that she's broken down, I pull in a little way in front of her and come to a stop, leaving the engine running. I feel sorry for her having to get out of her car in such awful conditions and, as I keep watch in my rearview mirror—perversely glad that someone else has been foolish enough to cut through the woods in a storm—I imagine her scrambling around for an umbrella. It's a good ten seconds before I realize that she's not going to get out of her car and I can't help feeling irritated, because surely she's not expecting me to run back to her in the pouring rain? Unless there's a reason why she can't leave her car—in which case, wouldn't she flash her lights or sound her horn to tell me she needs help? But nothing happens so I start unbuckling my seat belt, my eyes still fixed on the rearview mirror. Although I can't see her clearly, there's something off about the way she's just sitting there with her headlights on, and the stories that Rachel used to tell me when we were young flood my mind: about people who stop for someone who's broken down, only to find there's an accomplice waiting to steal their car, of drivers who leave their cars to help an injured deer lying in the road only to be brutally attacked and find that the whole thing was staged. I do my seat belt back up quickly. I hadn't seen anyone else in the car as I'd driven past but that doesn't mean they're not there, hiding in the back seat, ready to leap out.

Another bolt of lightning shoots through the sky and disappears into the woods. The wind whips up and branches scrabble at the passenger window, like someone trying to get in. A shiver runs down my spine. I feel so vulnerable that I release the handbrake and move the car forward a little to make it look as if I'm going to drive off, hoping it will provoke the woman into doing something—anything—to tell me that she doesn't want me to leave. But still there is nothing. Reluctantly, I pull to a stop again, because it doesn't seem right to drive off and leave her. But neither do I want to put myself at risk. When I think about it, she hadn't seemed distressed when I'd driven past, she hadn't waved frantically or given any indication that she needed help, so maybe somebody—her husband or one of the breakdown services—is already on their way. If I broke down, Matthew would be my first port of call, not a stranger in a car.

As I sit there, dithering, the rain picks up speed, drumming urgently on the roof—*Go, go, go!* It makes my mind up for me. Releasing the brake, I drive off as slowly as I can, giving her one last chance to call me back. But she doesn't.

A couple of minutes later, I'm out of the woods and

heading toward home, a beautiful old cottage with climbing roses over the front door and a rambling garden at the back. My phone beeps, telling me that the phone signal has kicked in. A mile or so further down the road, I turn into our drive and park as close to the house as possible, glad that I'm home safe and sound. The woman in the car is still on my mind and I wonder about phoning the local police station or the breakdown services to tell them about her. Remembering the message that came through as I drove out of the woods, I take my phone from my bag and look at the screen. The text is from Rachel:

*Hi, hope you had fun tonight! Off to bed now as had to go straight to work from the airport so feeling v jet-lagged. Just wanted to check you got the gift for Susie? I'll call you tomorrow morning xx*

As I get to the end I find myself frowning—why was Rachel checking to see if I'd bought Susie a present? I hadn't, not yet, because with the run-up to the end of the school year I'd been too busy. Anyway, the party isn't until tomorrow evening and I'd been planning to go shopping in the morning to buy her something. I read the message again and, this time, the words "the gift" rather than "a gift" jump out at me, because it sounds as if Rachel is expecting me to have bought something from the two of us.

I think back to the last time I saw her. It had been about two weeks ago, the day before she'd left for New

York. She's a consultant in the UK division of a huge American consultancy firm, Finchlakers, and often goes to the U.S. on business. That evening, we'd gone to the cinema together and then on for a drink. Maybe that was when she'd asked me to get something for Susie. I rack my brains, trying to remember, trying to guess what we might have decided to buy. It could be anything—perfume, jewelry, a book—but nothing rings a bell. Had I forgotten? Memories of Mum, uncomfortable ones, flood my mind and I push them away quickly. *It isn't the same*, I tell myself fiercely, *I am not the same. By tomorrow, I'll have remembered.*

I stuff my phone back in my bag. Matthew's right, I need a break. If I could just relax for a couple of weeks on a beach, I'd be fine. And Matthew needs a break too. We had't had a honeymoon because we'd been busy renovating our cottage so the last time I'd had a proper holiday, the sort where you do nothing all day but lie on a beach and soak up the sun, was before Dad died, eighteen years ago. After, money had been too tight to do anything much, especially when I'd had to give up my job as a teacher to care for Mum. It was why, when I discovered shortly after she died, that rather than being a penniless widow, she was in fact wealthy, I was devastated. I couldn't understand why she'd been content to live with so little when she could have lived in luxury. I was so shocked I'd barely heard what the solicitor was saying, so that by the time I managed to grasp how much money there was I could only stare at him in disbelief. I'd thought my father had left us with nothing.

A crack of thunder, farther away now, brings me sharply back to the present. I peer through the window, wondering if I can make it out of the car and under the porch without getting wet. Clutching my handbag to my chest, I open the door and make a dash for it, the key ready in my hand.

In the hall, I kick off my shoes and tiptoe upstairs. The door to the spare bedroom is closed and I'm tempted to open it just an inch to see if Matthew is asleep. But I don't want to risk waking him so instead I quickly get ready for bed, and before my head even touches the pillow, I'm asleep.

# SATURDAY, JULY 18TH

I wake the next morning to find Matthew sitting on the edge of the bed, a mug of tea in his hand.

"What time is it?" I murmur, struggling to open my eyes against the sunshine streaming in through the window.

"Nine o'clock. I've been up since seven."

"How's the migraine?"

"Gone." In the sunlight his sandy hair looks golden and I reach up and run my hands through it, loving its thickness.

"Is that for me?" I ask, eyeing the mug hopefully.

"Of course."

I wriggle into a sitting position and sink my head

back against the pillows. "Lovely Day," my favorite feel-good song, is playing on the radio downstairs and with the prospect of six weeks' holiday in front of me, life feels good.

"Thanks," I say, taking the mug from him. "Did you manage to sleep?"

"Yes, like a log. I'm sorry I couldn't wait up for you. How was your journey back?"

"Fine. Lots of thunder and lightning, though. And rain."

"Well, at least the sun is back out this morning." He nudges me gently. "Move over." Careful not to spill my tea, I make way for him and he climbs in beside me. He lifts his arm and I settle back into him, my head on his shoulder. "A woman has been found dead not far from here," he says, so softly that I almost don't hear him. "I just heard it on the news."

"That's awful." I put my mug on the bedside table and turn to look at him. "When you say not far from here, where do you mean? In Browbury?"

He brushes a strand of hair from my forehead, his fingers soft on my skin. "No, nearer than that, some-where along the road that goes through the woods be-tween here and Castle Wells."

"Which road?"

"You know, Blackwater Lane." He bends to kiss me but I pull away from him.

"Stop it, Matthew." I look at him, my heart fluttering behind my ribs like a bird trapped in a cage, waiting for him to smile, to tell me that he knows I came back that way last night and is just teasing. But he only frowns.

"I know. It's horrible, isn't it?"

I stare at him. "Are you serious?"

"Yes." He looks genuinely puzzled. "I wouldn't make something like that up."

"But . . ." I feel suddenly sick. "How did she die? Did they give any details?"

He shakes his head. "No, just that she was in her car."

I turn away from him so that he can't see my face. *It can't be the same woman*, I tell myself, *it can't be*.

"I have to get up," I say as his arms come round me again. "I need to go shopping."

"What for?"

"Susie's present. I still haven't got her anything and it's her party tonight." I swing my legs from the bed and stand up.

"There's no hurry, is there?" he protests. But I've already gone, taking my phone with me.

In the bathroom, I lock the door and turn on the shower, wanting to drown out the voice in my head telling me that the woman who's been found dead is the one that I passed in my car last night. Feeling horribly shaky, I sit down on the edge of the bath and bring up the Internet, looking for news. It's Breaking News on the BBC but there are no details. All it says is that a woman has been found dead in her car near Browbury in Sussex. Found dead. Does that mean she committed suicide? The thought is appalling.

My mind races, trying to work it out. If it is the same woman, maybe she hadn't broken down, maybe she had stopped in the lay-by on purpose, because it was

isolated, so that she wouldn't be disturbed. It would explain why she hadn't flashed her lights, why she hadn't
asked for my help—why, when she'd looked back at
me through the window, she hadn't made any sign for
me to stop, as she surely would have if she'd broken
down. My stomach churns with unease. Now, with
the sun streaming in through the bathroom window, it
seems incredible that I hadn't gone to check on her. If
I had, things might have ended differently. She might
have told me she was fine, she might have pretended
that she'd broken down and that someone was coming to help her. But if she had, I would have offered to
wait until they arrived. And if she had insisted I leave,
I would have become suspicious, I would have got her
to talk to me—and she might still be alive. And wasn't
I meant to have told someone about her? But distracted
by Rachel's text and the present I was meant to have
bought for Susie, I'd forgotten all about the woman in
the car.

"Are you going to be long in there, sweetheart?"
Matthew's voice comes through the bathroom door.

"I'll be out in a minute!" I call over the sound of the
water running wastefully down the drain.

"I'll make a start on breakfast, then."

I strip off my pajamas and get into the shower. The
water is hot but not hot enough to wash away the burning guilt I feel. I scrub my body fiercely, trying not to
think about the woman unscrewing a bottle of pills and
shaking them into her hand, lifting them to her mouth
and swallowing them down with water. What horrors
had she endured to make her want to take her life? As

she was dying, was there a point when she began to regret what she had done? Hating where my thoughts are going, I turn off the water and get out of the shower. The sudden silence is unsettling so I locate the radio on my phone, hoping to hear someone belting out a song full of hope and cheer, anything to stop me from thinking about the woman in the car.

"... *a woman has been found dead in her car in Blackwater Lane in the early hours of the morning. Her death is being treated as suspicious. No further details have been given for the moment but the police are advising people living in the area to be vigilant.*"

Shock takes my breath away. "*Her death is being treated as suspicious*"—The words resonate around the bathroom. Isn't that what the police say when someone has been murdered? I feel suddenly frightened. I was there, in the same spot. Had the killer been there too, lurking in the bushes, waiting for the opportunity to kill someone? The thought that it could have been me, that I could have been the one to be murdered makes me feel dizzy. I grope for the towel rail, forcing myself to take deep breaths. I must have been mad to have gone that way last night.

In the bedroom, I dress quickly in a black-cotton dress, pulling it from a pile of clothes left on the chair. Downstairs, the smell of grilled sausages turns my stomach before I've even opened the kitchen door.

"I thought we'd celebrate the start of your holidays with a slap-up breakfast," Matthew says. He looks so happy that I force a smile onto my face, not wanting to spoil it for him.

"Lovely." I want to tell him about last night, I want to tell him that I could have been murdered, I want to share my horror with him because it seems too big a thing to keep to myself. But if I tell him that I came back through the woods, especially after he specifically told me not to, he'll be furious. It won't matter that I'm here, sitting in the kitchen unharmed, not lying murdered in my car. He'll feel like I do, scared at what could have happened, appalled that I put myself in danger.

"So what time are you going shopping?" he asks. He's wearing a gray T-shirt and thin cotton shorts and, at any other time, I'd be thinking how lucky I was that he was mine. But I can barely look his way. It feels as if my secret is burned on my skin.

"As soon as I've finished breakfast." I look through the window to the back garden, trying to concentrate on how lovely it looks but my mind keeps tripping over last night, over the memory of me driving away. She had been alive at that point, the woman in the car.

"Is Rachel going with you?" Matthew interrupts my thoughts.

"No." Suddenly, it seems like the best idea in the world because maybe I could tell her about last night, share the devastation I feel. "Actually, that's a good idea. I'll phone and ask her."

"Don't be long," he says, "it's almost ready."

"I'll only be a minute."

I go into the hall, take the house phone—we can only get mobile reception upstairs in our house—and dial Rachel's number. It takes her a while to answer and when she does her voice is heavy with sleep.

"I've woken you," I say, feeling bad, remembering she only got back from her trip to New York yesterday.

"It feels like the middle of the night," she says grumpily. "What time is it?"

"Nine-thirty."

"So it is the middle of the night. Did you get my text?"

The question throws me and I pause, a headache building behind my eyes. "Yes, but I haven't bought anything for Susie yet."

"Oh."

"I've been really busy," I say quickly, remembering that for some reason Rachel thinks we're buying something together. "I thought I'd wait until today in case we changed our minds about what to get her," I add, hoping to prompt her into revealing what we'd decided.

"Why would we? Everybody agreed yours was the best idea. Plus the party's tonight, Cass!"

The word "everybody" throws me. "Well, you never know," I say evasively. "I don't suppose you want to come with me, do you?"

"I'd love to but I'm so jet-lagged . . ."

"Not even if I buy you lunch?"

There's a pause. "At Costello's?"

"Done. Let's meet in the café in Fentons at eleven, then I can buy you a coffee as well."

I hear her yawning and then a rustle. "Can I think about it?"

"No, you can't," I tell her firmly. "Come on, out of bed. I'll see you there."

I hang up, feeling a little lighter, pushing Susie's present from my mind. After the news this morning, it feels a small worry in comparison.

I go back to the kitchen and sit down at the table.

"How does that look?" Matthew asks, swooping a plate of sausages, bacon and eggs in front of me.

It looks like I could never eat it but I smile enthusiastically. "Great! Thanks."

He sits down next to me and picks up his knife and fork. "How's Rachel?"

"Fine. She's going to come with me." I look at my plate, wondering how I'm going to do it justice. I take a couple of mouthfuls but my stomach rebels so I push the rest around for a bit, then give up. "I'm really sorry," I say, putting my knife and fork down. "I'm still full after the meal last night."

He reaches over with his fork and spears a sausage. "It's a shame to let it go to waste," he says, grinning.

"Help yourself."

His blue eyes hold my gaze, not letting it shift away. "Are you OK? You seem a bit quiet."

I blink quickly a couple of times, sending the tears that are threatening my eyes back to where they came from. "I can't stop thinking about that woman," I say. It's such a relief to be able to talk about it that my words come out in a rush. "They said on the radio that the police are treating her death as suspicious."

He takes a bite of sausage. "That means she was murdered, then."

"Does it?" I ask, even though I know that it does.

"That's usually what they say until all the forensics have been done. God, how awful. I just don't understand why she would put herself at risk, taking that road at night. I know she couldn't have known that she'd be murdered, but still."

"Maybe she broke down," I say, clenching my hands together under the table.

"Well, she must have. Why else would anyone stop along such a deserted road? Poor thing, she must have been terrified. There's no phone signal in the woods so she must have been praying that someone would come along to help her—and look what happened when they did."

I draw in my breath, a silent gasp of shock. It's as if a bucket of ice-cold water has been thrown over me, waking me up, making me face up to the enormity of what I did. I had told myself that she had already phoned for help—yet I knew there was no signal in the woods. Why had I done that? Because I'd forgotten? Or because it had allowed me to leave with a clear conscience? Well, my conscience isn't clear now. I had left her to her fate, I had left her to be murdered.

I push my chair back. "I'd better go," I tell him, busily picking up our empty mugs, praying he doesn't ask me if I'm OK again. "I don't want to keep Rachel waiting."

"Why, what time are you meeting her?"

"Eleven. But you know how busy the town is on Saturdays."

"Did I hear that you're having lunch with her?"

"Yes." I give him a quick kiss on the cheek, wanting to be gone. "I'll see you later."

I fetch my bag and take the car keys from the hall table. Matthew follows me to the door, a piece of toast in his hand.

"I don't suppose you could pick up my jacket from the cleaner's, could you? That way I can wear it tonight."

"Sure, have you got the ticket?"

"Yes, hang on." He fetches his wallet and hands me a pink ticket. "It's paid for."

I slip it into my bag and open the front door. Sunlight streams into the hall.

"Take care," he calls as I get into the car.

"I will. Love you."

"I love you more!"

The road into Browbury is already heavy with traffic. I tap the steering wheel nervously. In my haste to get away from the house, I hadn't thought about how it would feel to be in the car again, sitting in the same seat I'd been in when I saw the woman in the car. In an attempt to distract myself, I try to remember the present I'd suggested for Susie. She works in the same company as Rachel, in the Admin section. When Rachel said that everybody had agreed to my suggestion, I'm guessing she was referring to their group of friends from work. The last time we'd met up with them had been around a month ago and I remember Rachel talking about Susie's fortieth birthday party, taking advantage of the fact that she hadn't been able to join us that night. Was it then that I'd come up with an idea for a present?

By some miracle, I find a parking space in the street not far from Fenton's department store and make my way to the tea room on the fifth floor. It's crowded but Rachel is already there, easily visible in a bright yellow sundress, her dark head of curls bent over her mobile. Two cups of coffee sit on the table in front of her and I feel a sudden rush of gratitude for the way she always looks out for me. Five years older, she's the sister I never had. Our mothers had been friends and because her mother worked long hours to support the two of them—having been abandoned by her husband not long after Rachel was born—Rachel had spent a large part of her childhood at our house, to such an extent that my parents affectionately referred to her as their second daughter. When she'd left school at sixteen to begin working so her mother would be able to work less, she'd made a point of coming over for dinner once a week. She was especially close to Dad and had mourned him almost as much as I had when he died, knocked down by a car outside our house. And when Mum had become ill and couldn't be left alone, she would sit with her once a week so that I could go shopping.

"Thirsty?" I try to joke, nodding at the two cups on the table. But my words sound fake. I feel conspicuous, as if everyone somehow knows that I saw the murdered woman last night and did nothing to help her.

She jumps up and gives me a hug. "There was such

a queue that I decided to go ahead and order," she says. "I knew you wouldn't be long."

"Sorry, the traffic was bad. Thanks for coming, I really appreciate it."

Her eyes dance. "You know I'll do anything for lunch at Costello's."

I sit down opposite her and take a welcome sip of coffee.

"Did you have a wild time last night?"

I smile and a tiny bit of pressure lifts. "Not wild, but it was good fun."

"Was gorgeous John there?"

"Of course he was. All the teachers were."

She grins. "I should have dropped in."

"He's far too young for you," I say, laughing. "Anyway, he has a girlfriend."

"And to think that you could have had him." She sighs, and I shake my head in mock despair, because she's never quite gotten over the fact that I chose Matthew over John.

After Mum died, Rachel had been brilliant. Determined to get me out of the house, she began taking me out with her. Most of her friends were people she worked with, or knew from her yoga class, and when I first met them, they would ask me where I worked. After a couple of months of telling them that I'd given up my job as a teacher to look after Mum, someone asked why I wasn't going back to work now that I could. And suddenly, I wanted to, more than anything. I was no longer content to sit at home day after day, enjoying a freedom I hadn't experienced in years. I wanted a life, the life of a 33-year-old woman.

I was lucky. A shortage of teachers in our area meant I was sent on a refresher course before being offered a job at a school in Castle Wells, teaching History to Year 9 students. I enjoyed being back in work and when John, the resident heartthrob of both teachers and students, asked me out, it was ridiculously flattering. If he hadn't been a colleague, I would probably have accepted. But I refused, which made him ask me out even more. He was so persistent that I was glad when I eventually met Matthew.

I take another sip of coffee. "How was America?"

"Exhausting. Too many meetings, too much food." She takes a flat package from her bag and pushes it across the table.

"My tea towel!" I say, taking it out and unfolding it. This time, there's a map of New York on the front. Last time, it was the Statue of Liberty. It's a joke between us—whenever Rachel goes away, on a business trip or on holiday, she always brings back two identical tea towels, one for me and one for her. "Thank you, you have the same one, I hope?"

"Of course." Her face suddenly becomes serious. "Did you hear about the woman who was found dead in her car last night, on that road that goes through the woods between here and Castle Wells?"

I swallow quickly, fold the tea towel in half, then in quarters and bend to put it in my bag. "Yes, Matthew told me, it was on the news," I say, my head beneath the table.

She waits until I'm sitting straight again, then gives a shudder. "It's horrible, isn't it? The police think she broke down."

"Do they?"

"Yeah." She pulls a face. "How awful—imagine breaking down in the middle of a storm, in the middle of nowhere. I don't even want to think about it."

It takes everything I've got not to blurt out that I was there, that I saw the woman in the car. But something stops me. This place is too crowded and Rachel is already emotionally invested in the story. I'm afraid she'll judge me, be horrified that I did nothing to help. "Me neither," I say.

"You sometimes use that road, don't you? You didn't take it last night, did you?"

"No, I'd never take that road, not when I'm by myself." I feel my skin reddening and I'm sure she'll know that I've just lied.

But she carries on, unaware: "Just as well. It could have been you."

"Except that I wouldn't have broken down," I say.

She laughs, breaking the tension. "You don't know that! She might not have broken down. It's only supposition. Maybe somebody flagged her down, pretending they were in trouble. Anybody would stop if they saw someone in trouble, wouldn't they?"

"Would they, though? On a lonely road and in a storm?" I desperately want the answer to be "No."

"Well, not unless they didn't have a conscience. Nobody would just drive on. They'd at least do something."

Her words slam through me and tears prick my eyes.

The guilt I feel is almost unbearable. I don't want Rachel to see how much her words have affected me so I lower my head and fix my eyes on the vase of orange flowers sitting between us on the table. To my embarrassment, the petals begin to blur and I reach down hastily, groping in my bag for a tissue.

"Cass? Are you all right?"

"Yes, I'm fine."

"You don't seem it."

I hear the concern in her voice and blow my nose, giving myself time. The need to tell someone is overwhelming. "I don't know why, but I didn't . . ." I stop.

"Didn't what?" Rachel looks puzzled.

I open my mouth to tell her but then I realize that if I do, not only will she be appalled that I drove on without checking that the woman was all right, she'll also catch me out in a lie, because I've already said that I didn't go home that way last night.

I shake my head. "It doesn't matter."

"It obviously does. Tell me, Cass."

"I can't."

"Why not?"

I scrunch the tissue with my fingers. "Because I'm ashamed."

"Ashamed?"

"Yes."

"Ashamed of what?" When I don't say anything, she gives a sigh of exasperation. "Come on, Cass, just tell me! It can't be that bad!" Her impatience makes me even more nervous so I look for something to tell her, something she'll believe.

"I forgot about Susie," I blurt out, hating myself for using what is just a mundane issue compared to the woman's death. "I forgot that I was meant to have bought her something."

A frown appears on her face. "What do you mean, *forgot*?"

"I can't remember, that's all. I can't remember what we decided to buy her."

She looks at me in astonishment. "But it was your idea. You said that as Stephen is taking her to Venice for her birthday, we should buy her some lightweight luggage. We were in the bar near my office at the time," she adds helpfully.

I let relief show on my face, although the words mean nothing to me. "Of course! I remember now— God, I'm so stupid! I thought it must be perfume or something."

"Not when there's so much money. We all put in twenty pounds, remember, so you should have a hundred and sixty altogether. Have you got it with you?"

*A hundred and sixty pounds?* How could I forget being given that much money? I want to admit everything but instead I carry on the pretense, no longer sure of myself. "I thought I'd pay by card."

She smiles reassuringly at me. "Well, now that that little drama's over, drink your coffee before it gets cold."

"It probably already is—shall I get us a fresh cup?"

"I'll go, you sit here and relax."

I watch her as she joins the queue at the counter, trying to ignore the sinking feeling in my stomach.

Although I managed not to tell her about seeing the woman in the car, I wish I hadn't had to admit that I'd forgotten about the luggage. Rachel isn't stupid. She'd witnessed Mum's deterioration on a weekly basis and I don't want her to worry, or to start thinking that I'm heading down the same road. The worst thing is, I have no memory of suggesting that we buy luggage, or of where I put the hundred and sixty pounds, unless it's in the little drawer in my old writing desk. I'm not worried about the money itself; if I can't find it, it doesn't really matter. But it's frightening to think I've forgotten everything to do with Susie's present.

Rachel comes back with the coffees.

"Do you mind if I ask you something?" she says, sitting down.

"Go on."

"It's just that it's not like you to get so upset over something as mundane as forgetting what present you're meant to have bought. Is there something else troubling you? Is everything all right with Matthew?"

For the hundredth time, I find myself wishing that Rachel and Matthew liked each other more. They try not to show it but there's always an undercurrent of mistrust between them. To be fair to Matthew, he doesn't like Rachel simply because he knows she disapproves of him. With Rachel, it's more complicated. She has no reason to dislike Matthew so sometimes a little voice in my head wonders if she's jealous that I now have someone in my life. But then I hate myself for the thought, because I know she's happy for me.

"Yes, everything's fine," I reassure her, trying to

push last night from my mind. "It really was just the present." Even those words seem like a betrayal of the woman in the car.

"Well, you were a little worse for wear that night," she says, smiling at the memory. "You didn't have to worry about driving home as Matthew was picking you up, so you had quite a few glasses of wine. Maybe that's why you forgot."

"You're probably right."

"Well, drink up and we'll go and choose something."

We finish our coffees and go down to the fourth floor. It doesn't take us long to choose a couple of powder-blue suitcases, and as we make our way out of the shop, I sense Rachel's eyes on me.

"Are you sure you want to go for lunch? If you don't, it doesn't matter."

The thought of lunch, of having to talk about anything and everything to avoid speaking about the woman in the car, suddenly seems too much. "Actually, I've got a splitting headache—a bit too much celebrating last night, I think. Can I take you to lunch next week instead? I can come into town any day now that I'm not working."

"Sure. You'll be all right to come to Susie's party tonight, won't you?"

"Of course. But could you take the cases, just in case?"

"No problem. Where are you parked?"

"At the bottom of the High Street."

She nods. "I'm in the multi-story, so I'll say goodbye to you here."

I point to the two suitcases. "Can you manage?"

"They're lightweight, remember? And if I can't, I'm sure I'll be able to find a nice young man to help me!"

I give her a quick hug and make my way to the car. As I turn on the ignition, the time comes up and I see that it's a minute past one. A part of me—quite a large part—doesn't want to listen to the local news, but I find myself turning on the radio anyway.

"*Last night, the body of a woman was found in a car in Blackwater Lane, between Browbury and Castle Wells. She had been brutally murdered. If you traveled that road between eleven-twenty last night and one-fifteen this morning, or know anyone who did, please contact us as soon as possible.*"

I reach out and turn the radio off, my hand shaking with stress. *Brutally murdered*. The words hang in the air, and I feel so sick, so hot, that I have to open the window, just to be able to breathe. Why couldn't they just have said "murdered"? Wasn't "murdered" already bad enough? A car pulls up alongside me and the driver makes signs, wanting to know if I'm leaving. I shake my head and he drives off, then a minute or so later another car comes along, wanting to know the same thing, and then another. But I don't want to leave, all I want is to stay where I am until the murder is no longer news, until everybody has moved on and forgotten about the woman who was brutally murdered.

I know it's stupid but I feel as if it's my fault she's dead. Tears prick my eyes. I can't imagine the guilt ever going away and the thought of carrying it around with me for the rest of my life seems too high a price to pay for a moment's selfishness. But the truth is, if I'd bothered to get out of my car, she might still be alive.

I drive home slowly, prolonging the moment when I have to leave the protective bubble of my car. Once I get home, the murder will be everywhere, on the television, in the newspapers, on everyone's lips, a constant reminder of my failure to help the woman in the woods.

As I get out of the car, the smell of a bonfire burning in the garden transports me instantly back to my childhood. I close my eyes and, for a few blissful seconds, it's no longer a hot, sunny day in July, it's a crisp, cold November evening and Mum and I are eating sausages speared onto forks, while Dad sets off fireworks at the bottom of the garden. I open my eyes to find that the sun has disappeared behind a cloud, mirroring my mood. Normally, I would go and find Matthew but, instead, I head straight for the house, glad to have a little more time to myself.

"I thought I heard the car," he says, coming into the kitchen a few minutes later. "I didn't expect you back so soon. Weren't you meant to be having lunch out?"

"We were, but we decided to leave it for today."

He comes over and drops a kiss on my head. "Good. Now you can have lunch with me."

"You smell of bonfire," I say, breathing it in from his T-shirt.

"I thought I'd get rid of all those branches I cut down the other week. Luckily, they were under the tarpaulin so the rain didn't get to them but they would have smoked the house out if we'd used them on the fire." He wraps his arms around me. "You do know that you're the one for me, don't you?" he says softly, echoing what he used to say when we first met.

I'd been working at the school for about six months when a group of us went to a wine bar to celebrate my birthday. Connie noticed Matthew the moment we arrived. He was sitting at a table by himself, clearly waiting for someone, and she'd joked that if his date didn't turn up she would offer to replace her. When it became obvious that his date wasn't going to materialize, she went over, already a little drunk, and asked him if he wanted to join us.

"I was hoping nobody would notice I'd been stood up," he said ruefully as Connie sat him down between her and John. It meant that I was opposite him and I couldn't help noticing the way his hair fell over his forehead, or the blue of his eyes whenever he looked over at me, which he did, quite a lot. I tried not to make too much of it, which was just as well, as by the time we stood up to leave, several bottles of wine later, he had Connie's number firmly in his phone.

A few days later she came up to me in the staff room, a huge grin on her face, to tell me that Matthew had called her—to ask for my number. So I let her give it to him and when he phoned, he nervously admitted, as he so sweetly put it, "As soon as I saw you I knew you were the one for me."

Once we began seeing each other regularly, he confessed that he couldn't father children. He told me he'd understand if I didn't want to see him again but, by then, I was already in love and although it was a major blow, I didn't feel it was the end of the world. By the time he asked me to marry him, we'd already talked about other ways to have a child and had decided that we would look into it seriously once we'd been married a year. Which is about now. Usually, it's a constant thought in my mind but now it seems so far away I can't reach it.

Matthew's arms are still around me. "Did you get what you wanted?" he asks.

"Yes, we bought Susie some luggage."

"Are you all right? You seem a bit down."

Suddenly, the need to be on my own is overwhelming. "I've got a bit of a headache," I say, pulling away from him. "I think I'll get an aspirin."

I go upstairs, get a couple of aspirins from the bathroom and swallow them down with water from the tap. As I lift my head I catch sight of my face in the mirror and search it anxiously, looking for something that could give me away; something which would tell people that everything isn't as it should be. But there's nothing to show I'm any different to the person I was when I married Matthew a year ago, just the same chestnut hair and the same blue eyes staring back at me.

I turn my back on my reflection and go into the bedroom. My pile of clothes has been moved from the chair to the now-made bed, a gentle hint from Matthew to tidy them away. On a normal day I would be amused but today I feel irritated. My eyes fall on my great-grandmother's writing desk and I remember the money Rachel spoke about, the hundred and sixty pounds that everybody gave me for Susie's gift. If I took the money, it would be in there, it's where I always put things I want to keep safe. Taking a deep breath, I unlock the little drawer on the left-hand side of the writing desk and pull it out. Lying inside is a scruffy pile of notes. I count them; there's a hundred and sixty pounds exactly.

In the warm peace of my bedroom the hard facts of what I forgot suddenly loom over me. To forget a name or a face is normal but to forget suggesting a gift and taking money for it isn't.

"Did you take some aspirin?" Matthew says from the doorway, making me jump.

I quickly push the drawer shut. "Yes, and I feel much better."

"Good." He smiles. "I'm going to have a sandwich. Do you want one? I thought I'd have mine with a beer."

The thought of food still makes my stomach churn. "No, go ahead. I'll get something later. I'll just have a cup of tea."

I follow him downstairs and sit down at the kitchen table. He puts a mug of tea in front of me and I watch him as he takes bread from the cupboard, a slab of cheddar from the fridge and makes himself a quick sandwich, pushing the two together and eating it without a plate.

"That murder has been on the radio all morning," he says, crumbs dropping to the floor. "The road's been closed and the police are all over it, looking for evidence. It's insane to think it's all happening five minutes from here!"

I try not to flinch and look absent-mindedly at the tiny white crumbs on our terracotta stone floor. They look as if they're stranded at sea with no help in sight. "Do they know anything about her yet?" I ask.

"The police must because they've advised her next of kin but they haven't released any details. It's awful to think what someone must be going through right now. Do you know what I can't get out of my mind? That it could have been you if you'd been stupid enough to take that road last night."

I stand, my mug in my hand. "I think I'll go and lie down for a bit."

He looks at me, concerned. "Are you sure you're OK? You don't look great. Perhaps we shouldn't go to the party tonight?"

I smile sympathetically because he's not a party person, he'd much rather have friends over for a casual dinner. "We have to, it's Susie's fortieth."

"Even if you still have a headache?" I hear the "but" in his voice and sigh.

"Yes," I say firmly. "Don't worry, you won't have to talk to Rachel."

"I don't mind talking to her, it's just those disapproving looks she always gives me. She makes me feel as if I've done something wrong. Did you remember to get my jacket from the cleaner's, by the way?"

My heart sinks. "No, sorry, I forgot."

"Oh. Well, never mind, I guess I can wear something else."

"Sorry," I say again, thinking of the present and all the other things I've forgotten lately. A few weeks ago, he had to come and rescue me and my trolley-load of food at the supermarket when I left my purse on the kitchen table. Since then, he's found milk where the detergent should be and detergent in the fridge, and has had to deal with an angry call from my dentist over an appointment I forgotten I'd made. So far he's laughed it off, telling me I'm in overload because of the end of the school year. But like with Susie's present, there have been other times when my memory has failed me, times he doesn't know about. I've driven to school without my books, forgotten both a hair appointment and a lunch with Rachel, and last month I drove twenty-five miles to Castle Wells, unaware I'd left my bag at home. The thing is, although he knows that Mum died when she was fifty-five and that toward the end she was forgetful, I've never actually come out and told him that for the three years before she died, I had to wash, dress and feed her. Neither does he know that she was diagnosed with dementia when she was 44, just ten years older than I am now. Back then, I couldn't believe he would still marry me if he thought there was a possibility that a dozen or so years down the line, I'd be diagnosed with the same thing.

I know now he would do anything for me but too much time has passed. How can I admit that I held things back from him? He'd been so open about not being able to have children and I'd repaid his honesty with dishonesty; I'd allowed my own selfish fears to get in the way of the truth. *How I'm paying for that now*, I think as I lie down on the bed.

I try to relax but images of last night flash through my mind, one after the other, like stills in a film. I see the car ahead of me on the road, I see myself swerving out around it, I see myself turning my head to look at the driver. And then I see the blur of a woman's face, looking back at me through the window.

In the middle of the afternoon, Matthew comes to find me. "I think I'll go to the gym for a couple of hours. Unless you want to go for a walk or something?"

"No, it's fine," I say, grateful to have some time on my own. "I need to sort through the stuff I brought back from school. If I don't do it now, I never will."

He nods. "Then we can both have a well-deserved glass of wine when I get back."

"Deal," I say, accepting his kiss. "Have fun."

I hear the front door slam but, instead of going into the study to sort out my work things, I stay at the kitchen table and let my mind clamber over the thoughts in my head. The house phone rings—it's Rachel.

"You'll never guess what?" she says breathlessly. "You know that young woman who was murdered? Well, it turns out she worked in my company."

"Oh, God," I mutter.

"I know, it's awful, isn't it? Susie's in bits. She feels terrible and is canceling the party—she just can't bring herself to celebrate when the murder was of someone we knew."

I feel a slight relief at not having to go out, but also slightly sick that the murdered woman is becoming ever more real.

"Although I didn't really know her because she worked in a different division to me . . ." Rachel continues, before hesitating a moment. "Actually, I feel really bad because when I went into the office from the airport yesterday, I had an argument with someone over a parking space and I think it was her. I was quite verbal—it was the jet-lag talking—and now I wish I'd let it go."

"You weren't to know," I say automatically.

"Susie said the people who worked with her are devastated. Some of them know her husband and, apparently, he's absolutely distraught—well, he would be, of course. And now he's been left to bring up two-year-old twins by himself."

"Twins?" The word echoes through my head.

"Yes, twin girls. It's such a tragedy."

I go ice cold. "What was her name?"

"Jane Walters, Susie said."

The name hits me with the force of a sledgehammer. "What? Did you say Jane Walters?"

"Yes."

My mind spins. "No, it can't be. It's not possible."

"That's what Susie said," Rachel insists.

"But . . . but I had lunch with her." I'm so stunned I can hardly speak. "I had lunch with her and she was fine. It must be a mistake."

"You had lunch with her?" Rachel sounds puzzled. "When? I mean, how did you know her?"

"I met her at that leaving party you took me to, for that man who worked in your company—Colin. You know, the one you said it was all right for me to tag along to because there'd be so many people nobody would notice that I didn't work for Finchlakers. I got talking to her at the bar and we swapped phone numbers, and then a few days later, she called me. I told you when you phoned from New York: I said I was going to lunch with her the next day—at least I thought I did."

"No, I don't think so," Rachel says gently, understanding how distressed I am. "And even if you did, even if you'd told me her name, I wouldn't have known who she was. I'm so sorry, Cass, you must feel dreadful."

"I was meant to be going round to hers next week," I say, realizing. "To meet her little daughters." Tears spring to my eyes.

"It's horrible, isn't it? And awful to think of her killer being out there somewhere. I don't want to worry you, Cass, but your house must only be a couple of miles from where she was killed and, well, it is a bit isolated, stuck down the end of the road by itself."

"Oh," I manage, feeling sick. Because in all the turmoil and worry, I hadn't thought about the killer still being out there. And that we can only get a mobile signal if we're upstairs, by a window.

"You don't have an alarm, do you?"

"No."

"Then promise you'll lock the door when you're home by yourself?"

"Yes—yes, of course I will," I tell her, desperate to get away, to stop talking about the woman who was murdered.

"Sorry, Rachel, I have to go," I add hurriedly. "Matthew's calling me."

I slam the phone down and burst into tears. I don't

want to believe what Rachel just told me, I don't want to believe that the young woman who was murdered in her car was Jane, my new friend, who would, I felt, have become a great friend. We had met by chance, at the party I had gone to by chance, as if we'd been destined to meet. Still sobbing, as clear as if it's happening before my eyes, I see her edging toward the bar at Bedales.

*"Excuse me, are you waiting to be served?" she asked, smiling at me.*

*"No, don't worry, I'm waiting for my husband to pick me up." I moved aside a little to make room for her. "You can squeeze in here, if you like."*

*"Thanks. It's a good job I'm not desperate for a drink," she joked, referring to the number of people waiting to be served. "I didn't realize Colin had invited so many people." She looked quizzically at me and I noticed how blue her eyes were. "I haven't seen you around before. Are you new to Finchlakers?"*

*"I don't actually work for Finchlakers," I admitted guiltily. "I came with a friend. I know it's a private function but she said there'd be so many people, nobody would notice if there was an extra person. My husband's watching the match with friends tonight and she felt sorry for me being on my own."*

*"She sounds like a good friend."*

*"Yes, Rachel's great."*

*"Rachel Baretto?"*

*"Do you know her?"*

*"No, not really."* She smiled brightly at me. *"My husband's watching the match tonight too. And baby-sitting our two-year-old twins."*

*"How lovely to have twins! What are their names?"*

*"Charlotte and Louise, better known as Lottie and Loulou."* She took her mobile from her pocket and thumbed through photos. *"Alex—my husband—keeps telling me not to do this, at least not to total strangers, but I can't help it."* She held the phone for me to see. *"Here they are."*

*"They're beautiful,"* I told her truthfully. *"They look like two little angels in those white dresses. Which is which?"*

*"This one is Lottie and that's Loulou."*

*"Are they identical? They seem it to me."*

*"Not exactly but it's quite difficult for most people to tell them apart."*

*"I bet."* I saw the barman waiting to take her order. *"Oh, I think it's your turn."*

*"Oh, good. A glass of South African red, please."* She turned to me. *"Can I get you something?"*

*"Matthew will be here soon but . . ."* I hesitated a moment *". . . I'm not driving, so why not? Thank you. I'll have a glass of dry white."*

*"My name's Jane, by the way."*

*"I'm Cass. But please don't feel you have to stay here now that you've been served. Your friends are probably waiting for you."*

*"I don't think they'll miss me for a few more minutes."* She raised her glass. *"Here's to chance meet-*

ings. It's such a treat to be able to drink tonight. I haven't been out much since the twins were born and when I do, I don't drink because I have to drive home. But a friend is dropping me home tonight."

"Where do you live?"

"Heston, on the other side of Browbury. Do you know it?"

"I've been to the pub there a couple of times. There's that lovely little park just across the road from it."

"With a wonderful play area for children," she agreed, smiling, "where I seem to spend quite a lot of my time now. Do you live in Castle Wells?"

"No, I live in a little hamlet this side of Browbury. Nook's Corner."

"I drive through it sometimes on my way back from Castle Wells, if I take that shortcut that goes through the woods. You're lucky to live there, it's beautiful."

"It is, but our house is a bit more isolated than I'd like. It's great to be only a few minutes from the motorway though. I teach at the high school in Castle Wells."

She smiled. "You must know John Logan then."

"John?" I laughed in surprise. "Yes, I do. Is he a friend of yours?"

"I used to play tennis with him until a few months ago. Is he still telling jokes?"

"Never stops." My phone, which I'd been holding in my hand, buzzed suddenly, telling me I had a text message. "Matthew," I told Jane, reading it. "The car park's full so he's double-parked in the road."

"You'd better go then," she said.

I quickly finished my wine, then said, truthfully, "Well, it was lovely talking to you, and thank you for the wine."

"You're welcome." She paused, then went on, her words coming out in a rush. "I don't suppose you'd like to have a coffee, or lunch even, some time, would you?"

"I'd love to!" I said, genuinely touched. "Shall we swap numbers?"

So we took each other's mobile numbers and I gave her my home one, too, explaining about the terrible network reception, and she promised to give me a call.

And less than a week later, she did, suggesting lunch the following Saturday, as her husband would be home to look after the twins. I remember being surprised, but pleased, that she'd phoned so soon, and had wondered if she perhaps needed someone to talk to.

We met in a restaurant in Browbury and, as we chatted easily together, it felt as if she was already an old friend. She told me how she had met Alex and I told her about Matthew, and how we were hoping to start a family soon. When I saw him standing outside the restaurant, because he'd arranged to meet me there, I couldn't believe it was already three o'clock.

"There's Matthew," I said, nodding toward the window. "He must have gotten here early." I looked at my watch and laughed in surprise. "No, he's bang on time. Have we really been here two hours?"

"We must have been." She sounded distracted and when I raised my head I saw that she was staring at

*Matthew through the window and I couldn't help feeling a little burst of pride. He'd been told on more than one occasion that he looked like a young Robert Redford and people, especially women, often gave him a second look when they passed him in the street.*

*"Shall I go and get him?" I asked, standing up. "I'd like him to meet you."*

*"No, don't worry, he looks busy." I glanced at Matthew; he had his phone out and was tapping away at it, engrossed in writing a text. "Some other time. I need to phone Alex, anyway."*

*So, I left and, as I walked off hand in hand with Matthew, I turned and waved at Jane through the restaurant window.*

The memory fades but my tears increase and somewhere inside me I'm aware that I hadn't shed as many tears when Mum died, because I'd been expecting it. But this news about Jane has shocked me to the core, shocked me so much that it's a while before everything comes together in my brain and I'm hit by the terrible realization that it was Jane I saw in the car last night, Jane who had looked back at me through the window as I'd driven past, Jane who I'd left there to be murdered. The horror I feel is matched only by the guilt that presses down on me, suffocating me. I try to calm down, telling myself that if it hadn't been raining so hard, if I'd been able to make out her features, if I'd known it was her, I would have gotten out of my car and run back to her through the rain without a second's hesitation. But what if she had recognized me and was waiting for me to go and help her? The thought is horrendous, but if she had, surely she would have flashed her lights, or gotten out of her car and come to me? Then another thought hits me, more horrendous than the last: what if the killer had already been there, and she had let me drive away because she wanted to protect me?

"What's the matter, Cass?" Matthew asks when he arrives back from the gym and finds me white-faced.

The tears that I can't manage to still, spill from my eyes. "You know that young woman who was murdered? It was Jane."

"Jane?"

"Yes, the girl I met a couple of weeks ago for lunch in Browbury, the one that I met at the party Rachel took me to."

"*What?*" Matthew looks shocked. "Are you sure?"

"Yes, Rachel phoned to tell me it was someone who worked for her company. I asked what her name was and she said Jane Walters. Susie's canceling her party because she knew her too."

"I'm so sorry, Cass," he says, putting his arms around me and holding me tight. "I can't imagine how you must be feeling."

"I just can't believe it's her. It doesn't seem possible. Maybe there's been a mistake, maybe it's another Jane Walters."

I sense him hesitate. "They've released a picture of

her," he says. "I saw it on my phone. I don't know if . . ." His voice trails off.

I shake my head because I don't want to look, I don't want to have to face the truth if it is Jane in the photo. But at least I would know.

"Show me," I say, my voice trembling.

Matthew moves his arms from around me and we go upstairs so he can get on the Internet on his phone. While he searches for the latest news update, I close my eyes and pray: *Please, God, please, God, don't let it be Jane.*

"Here." Matthew's voice is low. My heart thumps with dread but I open my eyes and find myself looking at a photo of the murdered woman. Her blonde hair is shorter than when we met for lunch and her eyes seem less blue. But it is definitely Jane.

"It's her," I whisper. "It's her. Who would do such a thing? Who would do such a terrible thing?"

"A madman," Matthew says grimly.

I turn and bury my face in his chest, trying not to cry again because he'll wonder why I'm so upset when in his eyes I barely knew Jane.

"He's still out there somewhere," I say, suddenly scared. "We need an alarm."

"Why don't you phone a couple of firms tomorrow and get them to come round and give us a quote? But don't commit to anything before we've gone through everything with a fine-tooth comb. You know what these people are like—they'll get you to sign up for things you don't even need."

"All right," I say. But for the rest of the afternoon

and evening, I'm desolate. All I can think of is Jane, sitting in her car, waiting for me to rescue her. "I'm sorry, Jane," I whisper. "I'm so sorry."

# FRIDAY, JULY 24TH

Jane haunts me. It's a week since her murder and I can't imagine there ever being a day when she isn't foremost in my mind. The guilt I feel hasn't lessened with time. If anything, it has increased. It doesn't help that her murder is still very much in the news, with non-stop speculation by the media as to why she chose to stop on such an isolated road in the middle of a storm. Tests show that nothing was wrong with her car but because it was a fairly old model with wipers that barely functioned, the theory put forward is that she was having trouble seeing through her windscreen and was waiting for the storm to pass before continuing her journey.

Gradually, a picture begins to emerge. Just before

eleven she left a voicemail message on her husband's mobile, saying she was leaving one of the bars in Castle Wells, where she'd been at a friend's hen night, and would be home soon. According to the staff at the restaurant, Jane had left the restaurant with her friends but had returned five minutes later to use the phone there because she'd realized she'd left her mobile at home. Her husband had fallen asleep on the sofa and hadn't heard the call come in, so he had no idea that she hadn't turned up until the police knocked on his door and told him the terrible news. Three people have come forward to say that although they drove down Blackwater Lane on Friday night, none of them saw her car, parked or otherwise. This allows the police to narrow the time of the murder down to somewhere between eleven-twenty—as it would have taken her around fifteen minutes to reach the lay-by from Castle Wells—and five to one, when the passing motorist found her.

There's a voice in my head urging me to contact the police, to tell them she was still alive when I passed her car at around eleven-thirty, but the other voice, the one telling me that they'll be disgusted that I didn't do anything to help her, is louder. And surely, narrowing the time down by such a small margin won't make any real difference to the murder inquiry. At least, that's what I tell myself.

In the afternoon, a man from Superior Security Systems arrives to give a quote for an alarm system. He immediately gets my back up by arriving twenty minutes early and asking if my husband is in.

"No, he's not," I tell him, trying not to get distracted

by the flakes of dandruff on the shoulders of his dark suit. "But if you run through the sort of system you think this house needs to make it secure, I'm sure I'll be able to understand. As long as you speak slowly."

The sarcasm is lost on him. Without waiting to be invited in, he comes into the hall. "Are you often in the house on your own?" he asks.

"No, not really." His question makes me uneasy. "My husband will be home soon, actually," I add.

"Well, looking at your house from the outside, I'd say it's a prime target for burglars, being stuck as it is at the end of the road. You need sensor alarms on your windows, on your doors, in the garage, in the garden." He looks around the hall. "On the stairs too—you don't want anyone creeping up on you in the middle of the night, do you? I'll just take a look over the house, shall I?"

Turning on his heels, he heads for the stairs, taking them two at a time. I follow him up and see him making a quick check of the window at the end of the landing. He disappears into our bedroom and I hover outside the door, uneasy about him being in there on his own. It suddenly occurs to me that I never asked him for proof of identity and I'm appalled that, in the light of Jane's murder, I wasn't more careful about letting him in. When I think about it, he hadn't said he was from the alarm company, I had just assumed he was, even though he was early. He could be anybody.

The thought lodges itself so firmly in my brain that the unease I'm already feeling at him being in the house grows into something akin to panic. My heart misses a beat and then speeds up furiously, playing catch-up, leaving me shaky. Keeping one eye fixed firmly on the bedroom door, I creep into the spare room and call Matthew from my mobile, glad that I can at least get a signal from here. He doesn't pick up but, a moment later, I get a text from him:

**Sorry, in meeting. Everything OK?**

I text back, my fingers clumsy on the keys:

*Don't like look of alarm man*

**Then get rid of him.**

I leave the bedroom and collide with the alarm man. Jumping back with a cry of alarm, I open my mouth, about to tell him that I've changed my mind about having an alarm, but he gets there first.

"I just need to check this room and the bathroom and then I'll take a look downstairs," he says, squashing past me.

Instead of waiting for him, I hurry down to the hall and stand near the front door, telling myself that I'm being stupid, that I'm panicking for nothing. But when he comes down, I stay where I am, leaving him to walk around the rest of the house by himself. It's a long ten minutes before he appears in the hall again.

"Right, shall we go and sit down?" he asks.

"I don't think that's necessary," I say. "I'm not sure we need an alarm after all."

"I don't like to bring it up but after the murder of that young woman not far from here, I'd say you're making a mistake. Don't forget that the murderer is still out there somewhere."

This virtual stranger mentioning Jane's death unbalances me and I desperately want him out of the house. "Have you got contact details? From your firm?"

"Sure." He reaches inside his jacket and I take a step back, half expecting him to draw out a knife. But all he brandishes is a card. I take it from him and study it for a moment. It says his name is Edward Garvey. Does he look like an Edward? My suspicion is addictive.

"Thank you," I say. "But it might be an idea if you come back when my husband is here."

"I could, I suppose. Not sure when it'll be, though. I know I shouldn't say it but murder is good for business, if you know what I mean? So, if you just give me ten more minutes of your time, I'll run through everything quickly and you can tell your husband all about it when he gets home."

He walks toward the kitchen and stands in the doorway, his hand outstretched, inviting me in. I want to remind him that it's my house but I find myself walking into the kitchen anyway. Is this how it works . . . ? Is this how people let themselves be led into potentially dangerous situations, like lambs to the slaughter? My anxiety increases when, instead of sitting down opposite me at the table, he sits down next to me, cornering me in. He opens the brochure but I'm so on edge that I can't concentrate on anything he's saying. I nod my head at appropriate moments and try to look interested in the figures he's totting up but sweat is trickling down my back and the only thing that stops me leaping to my feet and ordering him out of the house is my middle-class upbringing. Was it manners that prevented Jane from closing her window hurriedly and driving off when she realized she didn't want to give her killer a lift after all?

"Right, that's that then," he concludes, and I stare at him, bemused, as he stuffs the papers into his brief-case and pushes a brochure toward me. "You show that to your husband tonight. He'll be impressed, take my word for it."

I only relax once I've closed the door behind him but the realization that, once again, I did something stupid by not asking for proof of identity before letting him in, especially when a woman has just been mur-dered nearby, makes me question my lack of judgment. Feeling suddenly cold, I run upstairs to fetch a jumper and, as I go into the bedroom, I see that the window is open. I stare at it for a moment, wondering what it means, wondering if it means anything at all. *You're being neurotic,* I tell myself sternly, taking a cardigan from the back of a chair and shrugging it on. *Even if the man from Superior Security Systems did open it—which he probably did, to see where the sensors could be fitted—it doesn't mean that he left it open so that he could come back and murder you.*

I close the window and as I'm on my way back downstairs, the phone starts ringing. I expect it to be Matthew but it's Rachel.

"I don't suppose you want to meet for a drink, do you?" she asks.

"Yes!" I say, glad of an excuse to get out of the house. "Are you OK?" I add, detecting that she isn't her usually bubbly self.

"Yes, I just feel like a glass of wine. Is six all right for you? I can come to Browbury."

"Great. In the Sour Grapes?"

"Perfect. See you there."

Back in the kitchen, the Superior Security Systems brochure is still lying on the table, so I put it on the side for Matthew to look at once we've had dinner. It's already five-thirty—the whole thing with the alarm man must have lasted longer than I realized—so I grab my car keys and head off immediately.

The town is busy and as I hurry toward the wine bar, I hear someone call my name and look up to see my lovely friend Hannah making her way through the crowd. She's the wife of Matthew's tennis partner, Andy, and a relatively new friend but such fun I wish I'd met her earlier. "I haven't seen you for ages," she says.

"I know, it's been too long. I'm actually on my way to meet Rachel, otherwise I'd suggest going for a drink, but you must come over for a barbecue this summer."

"That would be lovely." Hannah smiles. "Andy was saying the other day that he hasn't seen Matthew at the club recently." She pauses. "Isn't it awful about that young woman who was murdered last week?"

The dark cloud that is Jane descends on me. "Yes, dreadful," I say.

She gives a little shiver. "The police still haven't found the person responsible. Do you think it was someone she knew? They say most murders are committed by someone known to the murderer."

"Do they?" I say. I know I should tell Hannah that I knew Jane, that I'd had lunch with her a couple of weeks before, but I can't because I don't want her to start asking me about her, about what she was like. And the fact that I can't seems like another betrayal.

"It could be just an opportunist murder," she goes on. "But Andy thinks it was someone local, someone who knows the geography of the area. He reckons they're holed up somewhere nearby. He thinks it won't be the last murder around here. It's worrying, isn't it?"

The thought of the murderer hiding nearby makes me go cold. Her words vibrate in my head and I feel so sick that I can't concentrate on what she's saying. I let her talk for a few more minutes, not really listening, murmuring responses at what I hope are appropriate places.

"I'm sorry, Hannah," I say, looking at my watch, "but I've just seen the time! I really have to go."

"Oh, of course. Tell Matthew that Andy is looking forward to seeing him."

"I will," I promise.


The Sour Grapes is packed and Rachel is already there, a bottle of wine in front of her.

"You're early," I say, giving her a hug.

"No, you're late, but it doesn't matter." She pours wine into a glass and hands it to me.

"Sorry. I bumped into my friend Hannah and we ended up chatting. I better not drink the whole glass, I'm driving." I nod toward the bottle. "You're obviously not."

"A couple of colleagues are meeting me for a bite to eat later so we'll finish it between us."

I take a sip of wine, savoring its crispness. "So, how are you?"

"Not great, actually. The police have been in the office for the last few days, questioning everybody about Jane. It was my turn today."

"No wonder you feel like a drink," I say sympathetically. "What did they want to know?"

"Just if I knew her. So I said that I didn't, because it's true." She fiddles with the stem of her glass. "The thing is, I didn't tell them about the run-in I had with her over the parking space and now I'm wondering if I should have."

"Why didn't you tell them?"

"I don't know. Actually, I do. I suppose I thought it might make me look as if I had a motive."

"A motive?" She shrugs. "What, to murder her? Rachel, people don't commit murder over a parking space!"

"I'm sure people have been murdered for less," she says dryly. "But what I'm worried about now is if somebody else—one of her friends in the office, because she's bound to have mentioned it—tells the police about the row."

"I doubt they will," I say. "But if you're that worried, why don't you call the police and tell them yourself?"

"Because they might start wondering why I didn't tell them in the first place. It makes me look guilty."

I shake my head. "You're reading too much into it." I try to smile at her. "I think that's the effect this murder is having on everybody. I had a man over this afternoon to give me a quote for an alarm and I felt really vulnerable being in the house on my own with him."

"I can imagine. I wish they'd hurry up and find whoever did it. It must be awful for Jane's husband to know that his wife's murderer is out there somewhere. Apparently, he's taken leave of absence to look after the children." She picks up the wine bottle and tops up her glass. "What about you? How are you doing?"

"Oh, you know." I shrug, not wanting to think about Jane's motherless children. "It's a bit difficult with Jane always on my mind." I give a nervous laugh. "I almost wish I hadn't had that lunch with her."

"That's understandable," she says sympathetically. "Did you book in to get an alarm fitttted?"

My shoulders tighten. "I want to but I'm not sure Matthew's very keen on having one, though. He's always said it's like being a prisoner in your own home."

"Better than being murdered in your own home," she says darkly.

"Don't."

"Well, it's true."

"Let's change the subject," I suggest. "Have you got any business trips coming up?"

"No, not until after my holiday. Only two more weeks, then I'll be in Siena. I can't wait!"

"I can't believe you've chosen Siena over the Ile de

Ré," I tease, because she's always said she'd never go on holiday to anywhere other than Ile de Ré.

"I'm only going to Siena because my friend Angela has invited me to her villa, remember. Even if it is because she wants to set me up with her brother-in-law, Alfie," she adds, rolling her eyes. She takes another sip of wine. "Speaking of the Ile de Ré, I'm thinking of going there for my fortieth, women only. You'll come, won't you?"

"I'd love to!" Thinking of getting away makes me feel so much better, and it'll be the perfect place to give her the present I've bought her. For a moment I forget about Jane, and soon Rachel is telling me about the places she plans to visit in Siena. For the next hour, we manage to keep the conversation away from anything to do with murder and alarms but, by the time I get home, I feel mentally exhausted.

"Did you have a good time with Rachel?" Matthew asks, reaching up and giving me a kiss from his seat at the kitchen table.

"Yes," I say, slipping off my shoes. The tiles are beautifully cool beneath my feet. "And I bumped into Hannah on my way to meet her, so that was nice."

"We haven't seen her and Andy for ages," he muses. "How are they?"

"Fine. I said they must come round for a barbecue."

"Good idea. How did it go with the alarm man? Did you manage to get rid of him?"

I take two mugs from the cupboard and switch the kettle on. "Eventually, yes. He left his brochure for you to look at. How about you? Did you have a good day?"

He pushes his chair back and stands, stretching his back, easing the muscles in his shoulders. "Busy. I could do without going away next week." He comes over and nuzzles my neck. "I'm going to miss you."

Shocked, I twist away from him. "Wait a minute! What do you mean, you're going away?"

"Well, you know, to the rig."

"No, I don't know. You never said anything about going to the rig."

He looks at me in surprise. "Of course I did."

"When?"

"I don't know, it must have been a couple of weeks ago, as soon as I found out."

I shake my head stubbornly. "You didn't. If you'd told me, I would have remembered."

"Look, you even said you'd use the time I was away to work on your lesson plans for September, so that we'd both be able to relax when I got back."

Doubt fingers its way into my mind. "I couldn't have."

"Well, you did."

"I didn't, all right," I say, my voice tight. "Don't keep insisting that you told me you were going away when you didn't."

I feel his eyes on me and busy myself making the tea so that he can't see how upset I am. And not just because he's going away.

# SATURDAY, JULY 25TH

My body clock still hasn't adjusted to being on holiday so, despite it being the weekend, I'm in the garden early, pulling up weeds and tidying beds, only stopping when Matthew arrives back from the shops with fresh bread and cheese for lunch. We picnic on the lawn and, once we've finished, I mow the grass, sweep the terrace, wipe down the table and chairs and dead-head the plants in the hanging baskets. I'm not usually so obsessive about the garden but I feel a pressing need to have everything looking perfect.

Toward the end of the afternoon, Matthew comes to find me.

"Would you mind if I go to the gym for an hour or

so? If I go now, instead of in the morning, I'll be able to have a lie-in."

I smile. "And breakfast in bed."

"Exactly," he says, kissing me. "I'll be back by seven."

After he's gone, I begin to make a curry, leaving the door to the garden open for air. I slice onions and dice chicken, singing along to the radio as I cook. In the fridge, I discover the bottle of wine we started a couple of evenings ago and pounce on it. I pour what's left into a glass and carry on with the curry, sipping the wine as I go along. By the time I've finished in the kitchen, it's almost six o'clock, so I decide to have a long, bubble-filled bath. I feel so relaxed that it's hard to remember the relentless anxiety that had burdened me last week. This is the first day that I've managed to push all thought of Jane to the back of my mind. It's not that I don't want to think about her, it's just that I can't stand the constant guilt. No matter how much I want to I can't turn the clock back, I can't not live my life because I didn't realize it was Jane in the car that night.

A news bulletin comes on but I turn the radio off quickly. Without the noise from the radio, the house is eerily quiet—and maybe because I've just been thinking about Jane, I'm suddenly conscious of being home alone. Going into the sitting room, I close the windows which have been left open all day, then the one in the study, and lock the front and back doors. I stand for a moment, listening to the house. But the only sound I hear is the soft *ca coo* of a wood pigeon outside.

Upstairs, I run the bath but before getting in I find myself hesitating over whether or not to bolt the bathroom door. I hate that the visit from the alarm man has played with my head, so in defiance to myself I leave it ajar, as I normally do, but undress facing the gap. I climb in and sink down under the water. The bubbles rise up around my neck and I lie back against their foamy cushion, my eyes closed, enjoying the stillness of the afternoon. We're rarely disturbed by neighbor noise—last summer the teenagers who live in the house nearest to us came to apologize in advance for a party they were throwing that night and we didn't hear a thing. It's why Matthew and I chose this house over the much larger, more impressive—and consequently more expensive—property that we also looked at, although I think price was also a consideration for Matthew. We'd agreed to buy it jointly and he was adamant that I wouldn't put in more than him, even though I could well afford to, despite having bought a house on the Ile de Ré six months previously. A house nobody knows about, not even Matthew. And certainly not Rachel. Not yet.

Under the bubbles, I let my arms bob to the surface and think about Rachel's birthday—the day I'll finally be able to give her the keys to the house of her dreams. It's been a hard secret to keep. It's perfect that she wants to go to the Ile de Ré for her birthday. She took me there a couple of months after Mum died and we stumbled upon the little fisherman's cottage on our second-to-last day there, an À VENDRE sign hanging from an upstairs window.

"It's beautiful!" Rachel had breathed. "I need to see inside." And without waiting to consult the estate agent, she marched up the little path and knocked on the door.

As the owner showed us round, I could tell that
Rachel had fallen in love with it even though she
couldn't afford it. To her it was just a pipe dream, but I
knew I could make it happen so I arranged it all in secret. I close my eyes, imagining her face when she realizes that the cottage is hers. I knew it was exactly what
Mum and Dad would have wanted me to do. If Dad
had lived to make a will, he would definitely have
bequeathed something to Rachel. And if Mum had
been of sound-enough mind, she would have done the
same.

A sound, like a *crack*, interrupts my thoughts. My
eyes snap open and my whole body tenses. Instinctively,
I know that something is wrong. I lie as still as I can,
straining my ears, listening through the open door for the
sound that told me I wasn't alone in the house. Hannah's
words about Jane's murderer being holed up nearby come
back to me. I hold my breath, and my lungs, deprived of
air, tighten painfully. I wait; but there's nothing.

Keeping my movements steady so as not to disturb
the water any more than necessary, I raise my arm carefully; it breaks through the suds and I stretch my hand
toward my mobile, perched precariously on the edge of
the bath near the taps. But it remains out of reach and,
as I slide farther down the bath toward it, the water lap-
ping against the side of the bath sounds as loud as waves
crashing onto the shore. Terrified that I've drawn attention to myself and horribly conscious that I'm naked,
I leap suddenly from the bath, taking half the water
with me, and lunge for the door, slamming it shut. The
sound reverberates around the house and, as I shoot the

bolt, my fingers shaking, I hear another creak. I can't work out where from, and my fear increases.

With my eyes fixed on the door, I take a couple of steps backward and grope along the edge of the bath for my mobile. It slips from my grasp and clatters to the floor. I freeze, my arm outstretched. But still there is nothing. Bending my knees slowly, I retrieve my mobile. The time appears on the screen, six-fifty, and the breath that I forgot I was holding comes whooshing out in relief, because Matthew will soon be home.

I dial his number, praying that I'll be able to get a signal, because with the bathroom at the back of the house, it's never a sure thing. When his mobile starts ringing, I'm dizzy with gratitude.

"On my way," he says cheerfully, thinking I want to know how long he's going to be. "Do you want me to stop off for anything?"

"I think there's someone in the house," I whisper shakily.

"What?" His voice is sharp with worry. "Where are you?"

"In the bathroom. I've locked the door."

"Good. Stay there. I'll phone the police."

"Wait!" I find myself hesitating. "I'm not sure. I mean, what if there's no one there? I only heard something twice."

"What did you hear? Someone breaking in, voices?"

"No, nothing like that . . . a crack and then some sort of creaking noise."

"Look, stay where you are. I'll be with you in two minutes."

"All right," I say, "but hurry!"

Feeling less anxious now that Matthew is coming, I sit down on the edge of the bath. The feel of it against my bare skin reminds me that I'm still naked, so I drag my dressing gown from the back of the door and shrug it on. I can't help wondering if I should have let Matthew phone the police after all. If there *is* someone in the house, he could be in danger when he arrives.

My mobile rings. "I'm here," Matthew says. "You OK?"

"Yes, I'm fine."

"I've parked in the road," he goes on. "I'm going to take a look around."

"Be careful," I say. "Stay on the phone."

"All right."

I listen nervously as I hear his footsteps crunch on the gravel and then round the side of the house.

"Can you see anything?" I ask.

"Everything seems fine. I'll just check the garden." A minute or so passes. "All good, I'm coming in."

"Be careful!" I warn again, before the signal goes.

"Don't worry, I grabbed a spade from the shed."

The call cuts off and from the bathroom, I hear him checking out the rooms downstairs. When I hear him on the stairs, I start unlocking the door.

"Let me check the bedrooms first!" he calls. It isn't long before he's back. "You can come out now."

I open the door and when I see him standing there with the spade in his hand, I feel suddenly foolish.

"Sorry," I say awkwardly. "I really did think someone was there."

He puts the spade down and wraps his arms around me. "Hey, better to be safe than sorry."

"I don't suppose you want to make me one of your gin and tonics, do you? I could do with a stiff drink. I'll just throw some clothes on."

"It'll be waiting for you in the garden," he promises, taking his arms from around me and heading for the stairs.

I pull on jeans and a T-shirt and follow him down. He's standing in the kitchen slicing some limes.

"That was quick," he says. But I'm too busy staring at the window.

"Did you open the window?" I ask.

"What?" He turns to look. "No, it was like that when I came in."

"But I shut it," I say, frowning. "Before I went up for my bath I shut all the windows."

"Are you sure?"

"Yes." I search my memory. I can remember closing the windows in the sitting room and the one in the study but I can't remember closing this one. "At least, I thought I had."

"Maybe you didn't close it properly and it came open," he says. "Maybe that was the noise you heard."

"You're probably right," I say, relieved. "Come on, let's have that drink."

Later, after dinner, we carry the rest of the bottle of wine through to the sitting room to finish in front of a film. It's hard to find one we haven't already seen.

"What about *Juno*?" he asks as we flick through the list. "Do you know what it's about?"

"A teenager who finds herself pregnant and looks for the perfect couple to adopt her baby. I don't really think it's for you."

"Oh, I don't know." He takes the remote from me and puts it to one side. "We haven't talked about having a baby for a while now," he says, gathering me in his arms. "You do still want to, don't you?"

I lay my head on his shoulder, loving how safe he makes me feel. "Yes, of course."

"Then perhaps we should start putting the wheels in motion. It can be quite a long process, apparently."

"We said when we'd been married a year," I say and, despite my joy, I realize that I'm stalling, because how can I think about having a child when, before it's even a teenager, I could be diagnosed with dementia, like Mum? I know I'm probably worrying about nothing, but to ignore the problems I've been having with my memory would be stupid.

"It's lucky it's our anniversary soon, then," he says softly. "Why don't we watch an action film instead?"

"All right. Let's have a look at what there is."

We watch a film until it's time for the news. As always, Jane's murder features prominently and I only carry on watching because I'm desperate to know if they're any nearer to catching her killer. But they've made little progress. Then a police officer comes on:

*"If you, or anyone you know, were in the vicinity of Blackwater Lane last Friday night, or in the early hours of Saturday morning, and saw Jane Walter's*

*car, a dark red Renault Clio, parked or otherwise, please call the following number.*"

He seems to be looking directly at me as he speaks, and when he adds that people can call the number anonymously, I realize it's the answer to my dilemma.

The news finishes and Matthew, ready for bed, tries to pull me to my feet.

"You go ahead, there's something I want to watch on another channel," I say, reaching for the remote.

"OK," he says cheerfully, "I'll see you later."

I wait until he's upstairs, then rewind the news until I find the number and jot it down on a piece of paper. I don't want the police to be able to trace the call back to me so I'll have to use a pay phone, which means I won't be able to phone until Monday, when Matthew's back at work. And once I have, hopefully some of my guilt will disappear.

# SUNDAY, JULY 26TH

The house phone rings while Matthew is in the kitchen, making breakfast to bring back to bed.

"Can you get it?" I call from the bedroom, shifting further down under the covers. "If it's for me, tell whoever it is that I'll call them back!"

A moment later, I hear him asking Andy how he is, so I guess bumping into Hannah has prompted his call. Remembering how I had suddenly run off to meet Rachel, I can't help feeling a little guilty.

"Let me guess—Andy wants you to play tennis this morning," I say when Matthew comes back upstairs.

"No, he wanted to know what time we're expecting them." He looks quizzically at me. "I didn't realize you'd invited them today."

"What do you mean?"

"Just that you didn't mention it was today they were coming for a barbecue."

"It isn't." Sitting up, I take one of the pillows from his side of the bed and put it behind my back. "I said they must come round but I didn't say when."

"Well, Andy seems to think it's today."

I smile. "He's having a joke with you."

"No, he was deadly serious." He pauses. "Are you sure you didn't invite them today?"

"Of course I am!"

"It's just that you did the garden yesterday."

"What's that got to do with it?"

"Just that Andy asked me if you'd managed to get the place tidied up. Apparently, you told Hannah that if they came for a barbecue, it would be a good excuse to get the garden into shape."

"Then why didn't they know the time? If I'd arranged something with Hannah, I would have said the time. She's got it wrong, not me."

Matthew gently shakes his head. The movement is so subtle, I nearly miss it. "I managed to hide the fact that I didn't have a clue what he was talking about and said twelve-thirty."

I look at him, appalled. "What, so they're all coming? The children too?"

"I'm afraid so."

"But I didn't invite them! Could you phone Andy back and tell him there's been a mistake?"

"I could, I suppose." Another pause. "As long as you're sure you didn't tell them to come today."

I stare at him, trying not to let him see how unsure I suddenly feel. Even though I can't actually remember inviting Hannah and Andy today, what I do remember is Hannah saying, just as we parted, something about Andy looking forward to seeing Matthew. My heart sinks.

"Look, don't worry," Matthew says, watching me. "It's no big deal. I can always pop out and buy a few steaks to throw on the barbecue. And some sausages for the children."

"We'll need to make a couple of salads as well," I say, feeling near to tears because I really don't feel up to having them round, not with my mind full of Jane. "And what about dessert?"

"I'll buy some ice cream from the farm shop when I go for the meat. And Andy said that Hannah's bringing a birthday cake—apparently, it's his birthday tomorrow—so there'll be plenty."

"What time is it now?"

"Just gone ten. Why don't you have your shower while I make some breakfast? We won't be able to have it in bed though."

"It doesn't matter," I say, trying to hide how depressed I feel.

"And then I'll do the shopping while you make the salads."

"Thank you," I mumble gratefully. "I'm sorry."

His arms come around me. "Hey, you've got nothing to apologize for. I know how tired you are at the moment."

I'm glad to be able to hide behind the excuse but how long is it going to be before he says something to me, because coming on top of having forgotten he was going away on Monday, this fiasco over the barbecue is one thing too many. I go through to the bathroom, trying to ignore the voice in my head: *You're going mad, you're going mad, you're going mad.* It would be so much easier to pretend that Hannah, wanting to come round for a barbecue, had decided to manipulate an invitation. But that's not something she'd ever do and I'd be mad to even think it. Anyway, what about my obsession to get the garden looking perfect? I'd been so sure that it was just a way of distracting myself, of keeping myself busy but, maybe, somewhere in my brain, I knew that I'd invited them.

Thinking back, I can guess what happened. I'd been so distracted by the talk of Jane, I'd only been half listening to what Hannah was saying by the end of our chat. Maybe it was then, during those lost minutes, that I'd invited Hannah and Andy to come today.

It used to happen to Mum all the time. She'd be there, nodding away at things I was saying, offering her opinion, even making suggestions, but a few minutes later she couldn't remember anything that we'd said at all. "I must have been away with the fairies," she'd say. "Periodic amnesia" the nurse who came to check on her called it. Was that where I'd been, away with the fairies? For the first time in my life, fairies seem like evil creatures.

\* \* \*

Hannah and Andy arrive a little after twelve-thirty, and it's not long before the conversation inevitably turns to Jane's murder.

"Did you see that the police are appealing for people to come forward in relation to that young woman's death?" Hannah says as she passes a plate to Matthew. "Don't you think it strange that nobody has?"

"Maybe, but I don't suppose many people take that road late at night," Matthew says. "Especially when there's a storm going on."

"If I'm coming back from Castle Wells, I take it all the time," says Andy cheerfully. "Day or night, storm or no storm."

"So where were you last Friday night?" Matthew asks and, when they all start laughing, I want to scream at them to stop.

Matthew catches sight of my face. "Sorry," he says quietly. He turns to Hannah and Andy. "Did Cass tell you she knew her?"

They stare at me.

"Not very well," I say quickly, cursing Matthew for mentioning it. "We had lunch together once, that's all." I close my mind to the image of Jane shaking her head reproachfully at my quick dismissal of our friendship.

"I'm so sorry, Cass, you must feel terrible," Hannah says.

"Yes, I do." There's a short silence where nobody seems to know quite what to say.

"Well, I'm sure they'll catch whoever's responsible soon," Andy says. "Somebody somewhere must know something."

I manage to get through the rest of the afternoon but as soon as they've gone I wish they'd come back. Their constant stream of chatter may have been exhausting but it's preferable to the silence that leaves me too much time to think about the things tumbling around in my mind.

I clear the table and carry the plates into the kitchen and, as I walk in through the door, I stop in my tracks, staring at the window I hadn't remembered closing yesterday, before I'd gone up for my bath. Because now, when I think about it, when I'd been making the curry, the back door had been open—but not the window.

# MONDAY,
# JULY 27TH

After Matthew leaves for the rig, I'm unnerved by the sense of abandonment I feel, but I can finally make the phone call I've been dreading. I find the piece of paper where I jotted the number down and, as I'm looking for my bag, the phone starts ringing.

"Hello?"

There's no reply so I presume whoever it is has lost their signal. I hold on for another ten seconds, then hang up. If it's Matthew, I know he'll phone again if he needs to.

I run upstairs to fetch my purse, push my feet into some shoes and leave the house. I had thought about driving into Browbury or Castle Wells and using one of the pay phones there but it seems a bit extreme when there's one five minutes up the road, near the bus shelter.

As I approach the pay phone, I feel as if someone is watching me. I look to the right and left, then turn and look surreptitiously behind me. But there's no one around, just a cat sunning itself on a low stone wall. A car drives past; lost in her own thoughts, the woman driver doesn't even look my way.

In front of the phone, I read the instructions—because it's years since I used one—fish for a coin in my purse and with shaking fingers push a pound into the slot. I take out the piece of paper where I jotted down the number to call and punch it into the phone, my heart racing, wondering if I'm doing the right thing. But before I can change my mind, my call is answered.

"It's about Jane Walters," I say breathlessly. "I passed her car in Blackwater Lane at eleven-thirty and she was still alive."

"Thank you for coming forward." The woman's voice is calm. "Could I—" But I've already put the phone down.

I leave quickly, hurrying down the road toward the house, the same uneasy feeling that I'm being watched following me as I go. Once inside, I make myself calm down. There wasn't anybody watching me, it was only my guilty conscience at doing something secretive that made me think that there was. And because I've done what I should have done at the beginning, I begin to feel better about everything.

After all my hard work on Saturday, there's nothing left to do in the garden but there's plenty of housework waiting. With the radio on for company, I drag the hoover upstairs and, armed with polish and cleaning materials, I make a start on the bedrooms. I work methodically, focusing on the task in hand, steering my mind away from Jane. And it works—until the news bulletin comes on at midday:

*"Police are appealing to the person who contacted them earlier today with information relating to the murder of Jane Walters to get back in contact with them. Jane Walters was found murdered in her car in the early hours of the eighteenth of July and . . ."*

I don't hear any more over the hammering of my heart. It reverberates in my eardrums, making me deaf. I sit down on the bed and take deep, shaky breaths. Why do the police want to speak to me again? I had told them everything I know. I try to squash down the panic rising inside me but it just keeps on coming. Even though nobody knows it was me who made that phone call, the fact the police have made it public means I no longer feel anonymous. Instead, I feel horribly exposed. The police had said something about the person who called them having information in relation to Jane's murder. It makes it sound as if I told them something important, something vital. If Jane's killer was listening to the news, he's bound to feel threatened by my existence. What if he thinks I saw him lurking around Jane's car that night?

Horribly agitated, I get to my feet and pace the bedroom, wondering what I should do. As I pass in front of the window, I glance distractedly outside and find myself freezing. There's a man, a man I haven't seen before, walking away from our house. Nothing to worry about, except that he must have come from the woods. Nothing to worry about, except that it's rare to see anybody walking past our house. Driving, yes, walking, no. To go for a walk in the woods, no one would go down Blackwater Lane on foot, not unless they wanted to get run over. The path that leads to the woods starts in the field opposite our house and is well signposted. I watch him until he's out of sight. He doesn't hurry, he doesn't turn around but it does nothing to calm my heart's furious racing.

"Is Rachel staying with you tonight?" Matthew asks when he phones me later from the rig. Before leaving this morning, he had suggested I invite her over. I haven't told him about the man I saw earlier because there's nothing really to say. Besides, he might call the police, and what would I tell them?

*"I saw a man walking away from our house."*

*"What did he look like?"*

*"Average height, average build. I only saw him from behind."*

*"Where were you?"*

*"In the bedroom."*

*"What did he do?"*

*"Nothing."*

*"So you didn't see him do anything suspicious?"*

*"No. But I think he might have been looking up at the house."*

*"You think?"*

"*Yes.*"

"*So you didn't actually see him looking at the house.*"

"*No.*"

"No," I tell Matthew. "I decided not to bother her."

"That's a pity."

"Why?"

"It's just that I don't like the thought of you being on your own."

His worry increases mine. "I wish you'd told me that before."

"You'll be fine. Just make sure that the doors are locked before you go to bed."

"They're already locked. I wish we had an alarm."

"I'll have a look at the brochure when I get back," he promises.

I hang up and phone Rachel.

"Are you doing anything tonight?"

"Sleeping," she replies. "I'm already in bed."

"At nine in the evening?"

"If you'd had the weekend I had, you'd have been in bed long ago. So if you're phoning to ask me to go out, I'm afraid it's a no."

"I was going to ask you to come round and share a bottle of wine with me."

I hear a yawn on the other end of the phone. "Why, are you on your own?"

"Yes, Matthew's got an inspection at one of the rigs. He's away all week."

"How about if I come and keep you company on Wednesday?"

My heart sinks. "What about tomorrow?"

"I can't, sorry, I already have something on."

"Wednesday it is, then." I can't keep the disappointment from my voice.

"Is everything OK?" she asks, picking up on it.

"Yes, everything's fine. Go on, go to sleep."

"See you Wednesday," she promises.

I wander into the sitting room. If I'd told her that I'm nervous about being on my own, she'd have come straight round. I turn on the television and watch an episode of a series I've never seen before. Then, feeling tired, I go up to bed, hoping I'll sleep straight through until the morning.

But I can't relax. The house is too dark, the night too silent. I reach out and turn the light on, but sleep eludes me. I put my headphones on to listen to music but take them off again when I realize they'd mask the sound of someone creeping up the stairs. The two windows I found open, the one in the bedroom after the alarm man left on Friday and the one in the kitchen on Saturday play on my mind, as does the man I saw outside the house this morning. When the sun begins to rise and I find myself falling asleep, I don't bother fighting it, telling myself that I'm less likely to be murdered in daylight than at night.

# WEDNESDAY, JULY 29TH

I'm woken by the phone ringing in the hall. I open my eyes and stare at the ceiling, hoping the caller will give up. Yesterday morning the phone had rung insistently at half-past eight but when I'd answered it there'd been no one there. I look at the clock: it's nearly nine so it's probably Matthew, phoning before he starts work for the day. Leaping out of bed, I run downstairs and snatch it up before the answering machine kicks in.

"Hello?" I say breathlessly. There's no answering hello, so I wait, because the connection is often bad from the rig.

"Matthew?" I try. There's still no answer so I hang up and dial his number.

"Did you just call?" I ask when he picks up.

"Good morning, darling," he says pointedly, but with laughter in his voice. "How are you today?"

"Sorry," I say hastily. "I'll start again. Hello, darling, how are you?"

"That's better. I'm fine, it's cold up here, though."

"Did you call me a moment ago?"

"No."

I frown. "Oh."

"Why?"

"The phone rang but there was no one there so I thought it was a bad connection from the rig."

"No, I was going to call you at lunchtime. I'm afraid I have to go, sweetheart, let's speak later."

I hang up, annoyed at having been gotten out of bed. There should be a rule against cold callers calling so early. The day stretches in front of me and I realize I don't want to spend another night on my own. During the night, when I'd got up to go to the loo, I'd looked out of the window and, for a second, I thought there was someone there. There wasn't, of course, but after that I couldn't get back to sleep until the early hours.

"Then go away for a couple of days," Matthew says when he phones and I tell him I've hardly slept for the last two nights.

"I could, I suppose," I say. "Maybe the hotel I went to a couple of years ago, after Mum died. It has a pool and spa. I'm not sure they'll have any room though."

"Why don't you phone them and find out? If they do, you could go today and I'll join you on Friday."

My spirits lift immediately. "That's a great idea! You really are the best husband in the world," I say gratefully.

I phone the hotel and while I wait for them to pick up, I take the calendar from the wall, just to make sure of the dates I need to book. I'm just calculating that I'll need to book it for four nights if we're to stay until Sunday when the words "Matthew to rig" jump accusingly out at me from Monday's square. I close my eyes, hoping they won't be there when I open them again. But they are, as are the words "Matthew back," written on the square for the 31st—Friday—followed by a smiley face. My heart drops and worry begins its familiar gnawing in my stomach, so that when the hotel finally answers and the receptionist tells me they're fully booked apart from a suite, I don't even ask him how much it costs, I just go ahead and reserve it.

I hang the calendar back on the wall, turning the page over to August, ready for when we come back from the hotel—and so that Matthew won't see he was right when he said he'd told me he was going to the rig.

It's only once I'm at the hotel, waiting to check in, that I begin to feel better. The suite is fabulous, with the biggest bed I've ever seen and once I've unpacked, I text Matthew to let him know where I am, then change into a swimsuit and make my way down to the pool. I'm just pushing my belongings into a locker when a text arrives, but from Rachel:

*Hi, just to let you know I've arranged to leave early to-
night so will be with you around 6. Are you cooking or
shall we go out?*

My heart plummets so fast I feel as if I've stepped
off a cliff. How could I have forgotten that Rachel was
coming to stay tonight when we'd only arranged it on
Monday? I think of Mum and a hot-sick fear claws my
stomach. I can't believe I forgot. Jane's murder and the
guilt I feel have distracted me, yes, but to forget about
Rachel coming to stay? I fumble with my phone and
press the Call button, desperate to confide my growing
fears in someone.

Despite Rachel only just sending the message, she
doesn't pick up. The changing room is empty so I sit
down on a damp wooden bench. Now that I've made
the decision to tell Rachel I'm worried about my short-
term memory, I'm desperate to act on it in case I dis-
suade myself later. I call Rachel again and this time she
answers.

"I don't suppose you'd like to spend the night in a
luxury hotel instead of at the house," I say.

There's a pause. "Depends where it is."

"Westbrook Park."

"The one with the fantastic spa?" She's whispering,
so I guess she's in the middle of a meeting or something.

"That's the one. Actually, I'm already there. I felt
like having a bit of a break."

"It's all right for some," she sighs.

"So will you join me?"

"It's a bit far to come for one night—I have to work tomorrow, remember. How about I join you on Friday?"

"You could," I say, "Matthew's coming here straight from the rig, so it'd be the three of us."

She gives a quiet laugh. "Awkward."

"Sorry for standing you up tonight."

"Don't worry about it. See you next week?"

"Hang on, Rachel, there's something else . . ."

But she's already gone.

# FRIDAY,
# JULY 31ST

By the time the afternoon comes, I'm desperate to see Matthew. The weather isn't brilliant so I hang around in our room, waiting for his call to tell me what time he'll be arriving. I watch a bit of television, relieved that there's nothing on the news about Jane's murder, yet strangely annoyed that two weeks on from her violent death, she's already been forgotten.

The phone rings and I snatch it up.

"I'm at the house," Matthew says.

"Good," I say happily. "You'll be here in time for dinner."

"The thing is, when I arrived, there was a man here from that alarm company, practically sitting on the doorstep." He pauses. "I didn't realize you'd actually gone ahead with it."

"Gone ahead with what?"

"Well, the alarm."

"I don't understand."

"The guy said he agreed with you that someone would fit the alarm this morning but when the technician turned up there was nobody in. They've been phoning every half an hour, apparently."

"I didn't agree to anything at all," I say, annoyed. "All I said was that we'd get back to him."

"But you signed a contract," Matthew says, sounding puzzled.

"I did no such thing! Be careful, Matthew, he's trying it on, pretending I agreed to something when I didn't. It's a scam, that's all."

"That's what I thought. But when I said that as far as I was concerned we hadn't decided anything yet, he showed me a copy of the contract with your signature on it."

"Then he must have forged it." There's a silence. "You think I went ahead and ordered it, don't you?" I say, realizing.

"No, of course not! It's just that the signature looked a lot like yours." I sense him hesitate. "After I got rid of him I had a look at the brochure you left in the kitchen and, inside, there's a client copy of the contract. Shall I bring it to the hotel so that you can see it? Then if it's not aboveboard, we can do something about it."

"Sue the pants off him, you mean," I say, trying to

lighten things, trying not to let any doubt cloud my mind. "What time will you be here?"

"By the time I've showered and changed—about six-thirty?"

"I'll wait in the bar for you."

I hang up, momentarily annoyed that he could think I'd order an alarm without telling him. But a little voice is mocking me: *Are you sure, Cass, are you really sure?* Yes, I tell it firmly, I am sure. Besides, the man from the alarm company had seemed like the type of person who would do anything to get a contract, even if it meant lying and cheating. I'm so confident I'm right that when I go down to the bar, I order a bottle of champagne.

It's waiting in an ice bucket when Matthew arrives.

"Tough week?" I ask, because he looks horribly tired.

"You could say that," he says, kissing me. He eyes the champagne. "That looks good."

The waiter comes to open the bottle and serves us.

"To us," Matthew says, raising his glass and smiling over at me.

"To us. And our suite."

"You booked a suite?"

"It was all they had left."

"What a shame," he says, grinning.

"The bed is huge," I go on.

"Not so big that I'll lose you in it, I hope?"

"No chance." I put my glass down on the table. "Have you got the copy of the contract I'm meant to have signed?" I ask, wanting to get it out of the way so that nothing can ruin our weekend away.

He takes a while taking it from his pocket and I know he doesn't really want to show it to me.

"You have to admit it looks like your signature," he says, apologetically, handing it across the table, and I find myself staring, not at the signature at the bottom of the page, but at the contract itself. Filled out in what is unmistakably my handwriting, it's even more damning than my signature, at least from my point of view. Anybody could have forged my signature, but not the line after line of neatly completed spaces, each capital letter formed exactly as I would form it. I scan the page, looking for something to tell me that it wasn't me who filled it in but the longer I look, the more convinced I am that it was, to the point where I can almost see myself doing it, I can almost feel the pen in my hand and my other hand resting lightly on the paper, anchoring it down. I open my mouth, prepared to lie, ready to tell Matthew that it definitely isn't my handwriting but, to my horror, I burst into tears.

He's beside me in a minute, holding me close. "You must have been tricked into signing it," he says and I can't work out if he really believes it or if he's giving me a way out, just as he had only days before when he said he must have forgotten to tell me he was going to the rig. Either way, I'm grateful. "I'll contact the firm first thing tomorrow and tell them there's no way we're going through with it."

"But it'll be their salesman's word against mine," I say shakily. "Let's just leave it. He'll only deny everything and it'll only delay things. The fact is, we need an alarm."

"All the same, I think we should try and get the contract canceled. What did he say, that it was just a quote or something?"

"I'm not sure what he actually said but, yes, I suppose I thought I was only agreeing to a quote," I answer, grabbing at the excuse. "I feel so stupid."

"It's not your fault. They shouldn't be allowed to get away with using those sort of tactics." He hesitates. "I'm not sure what to do now, to be honest."

"Could we just let them install it, especially as I'm partly to blame?"

"I'd still like to have it out with him." Matthew's voice is grim. "Although the chances are, I won't even see him tomorrow because they'll send one of their technicians. He's just the salesman."

"I really am sorry."

"I suppose in the great scheme of things it's not such a disaster." He drains his glass and looks at the bottle longingly. "Shame I can't have another."

"Why not? It's not as if you have to drive anywhere."

"Well, yes, I do. Because I thought everything was above-board, I agreed they could come and install it tomorrow morning. So if we're not going to try and get it canceled, I have to be there for when they arrive."

"Can't you stay the night anyway and leave early?"

"What, at six-thirty in the morning?"

"You wouldn't need to leave that early."

"Well, I will if they're going to be there at eight."

I can't help wondering if his refusal to stay the night

is his way of punishing me because he won't let himself be angry with me for ordering the alarm in the first
place.

"But you will come back tomorrow evening, once
they've finished?" I say.

"Yes, of course," he says, taking my hand in his.

He leaves shortly after and I go up to my room and
watch a film, until my eyes droop with tiredness. But
I can't sleep. The knowledge that I managed to fill in
a whole contract without any recollection of doing so
has shaken me to the core. I try to tell myself that I'm
not doing anything as bad as Mum was when I first
realized there was a real problem. It was in the spring
of 2002—she'd gone to the local shops and had gotten lost on her way back home, only turning up three
hours later. Before the alarm, it was only little things
that slipped from my memory. Forgetting what I was
meant to have bought for Susie, forgetting Matthew
was going away, forgetting I'd invited Hannah and
Andy for a barbecue, forgetting Rachel was coming
to stay—all those things are bad enough. But ordering
an alarm without realizing what I was doing is huge. I
want to believe more than anything that the salesman
tricked me into it. But when I think back to when we
were in the kitchen together, I realize that I don't remember very much at all—except at the end when he
handed me the brochure and assured me that my husband would be impressed.

# SUNDAY, AUGUST 2ND

We don't talk very much as we check out from the hotel. I'd suggested going on somewhere for lunch but Matthew said he preferred to get home. I know we're both disappointed that the weekend didn't live up to our expectations. Even though Matthew's explanation of why he didn't want to stay at the hotel on Friday night held up, I couldn't help worrying that he was getting fed up of all the hassle my forgetfulness has been creating. So, yesterday, while he was at the house waiting for the alarm system to be fitted, I plucked up my courage and googled "periodic amnesia," which directed me to "transient global amnesia." Although the term was familiar to me in relation to Mum, my heart still dropped a little farther with each line I read and I closed off the page quickly, trying to squash the panic mounting inside me. I don't know if it's what I've got and, more important, I don't want to know. For now, ignorance is bliss.

When Matthew finally turned up at seven last night, in time for a drink in the bar before dinner, I was aware that he was watching me more closely than usual and I kept expecting him to tell me that he was worried about me. But he didn't say anything, which made it somehow worse. I thought that maybe he was waiting until we were in the privacy of our room. But when we eventually went up, instead of saying that he wanted to talk to me, he turned on the television and I wished that he hadn't because there was a special report about Jane's murder following her funeral earlier in the day. They showed footage of her flower-covered coffin being carried into the little church in Heston with her distraught parents following behind, and tears had seeped from my eyes.

Then a photo of Jane appeared on the screen, a different one from the one they'd been using before.

"She was so pretty," Matthew said. "It's such a terrible shame."

"So it would be less of a shame if she hadn't been pretty?" I retorted, suddenly angry.

He looked at me in surprise. "That's not what I meant and you know it. It's terrible when anyone gets murdered but especially so in her case as she has two young children, who are bound to find out one day that their mother was violently killed." He turned back to the television, where the report showed police stopping and searching cars in Blackwater Lane, which was once again open to the public. "They're hardly going to find the murder weapon in someone's boot," he went on. "They'd be better off looking for the murderer. Someone must know who he is. He must have been covered in blood that night."

"Can you just stop talking about it?" I muttered.

"You're the one who started."

"I wasn't the one who turned on the television."

I felt him looking at me. "Is it because the murderer's still at large, is that what's bothering you? Because if it is, you'll be perfectly safe now that we have an alarm. Anyway, whoever's responsible is probably miles away by now."

"I know," I said.

"So stop worrying."

I realized that it was the opening I'd been waiting for, the perfect time to confide in him, to tell him that I was worried about what was happening to me, to my mind, to explain about Mum and her dementia. But I let the moment slip away.

I hoped a bath would calm me but I couldn't stop thinking about Jane's husband. I wished there was something I could do to make his pain easier to bear; I wished I could tell him how much I'd enjoyed meeting Jane, how lovely she was. The need to do something was overwhelming and I decided to ask Rachel if she knew his address so that I could write to him. I lay in the bath, composing the letter in my head, aware that I was writing it as much for my sake as for his. By the time I got out of the bath, the water was cold and later, as Matthew and I lay side by side in bed without touching, the distance between us had never seemed greater.

I glance over at him now, standing beside me at the reception desk, and wish he would bring my memory lapses into the open instead of pretending that everything is all right when it's so obviously not.

"Sure you don't want to go somewhere for lunch?" I ask.

He shakes his head, smiles. "I'm fine."

We drive off, each in our own car, and when we arrive at the house I watch while he turns off the new alarm.

"Will you show me how it works?" I ask.

He insists on letting me choose the code and I choose our birthdays, backward, so that I'll remember it easily. He makes me practice a couple of times, showing me how to isolate certain rooms if I'm alone in the house, and I suddenly remember telling the salesman that I'd like to be able to do that, which means I must have had more of an in-depth conversation with him than I realized.

"Right, I've got it," I say.

"Good. Shall we see what's on television?"

We go into the sitting room but it's time for the news so I escape into the kitchen.

"Stabbing someone is one thing but actually slitting their throat with a massive kitchen knife, that's just sick." Matthew stands in the doorway, looking shocked. "That's how she died, apparently—she had her throat cut."

Something inside me snaps.

"*Shut up!*" I cry, thumping the kettle down on the side. "Just shut up!"

He looks at me in astonishment. "For God's sake, Cass, calm down!"

"How can I calm down when you're always going on about the bloody murder? I'm sick of hearing about it!"

"I just thought you'd be interested, that's all."

"Well, I'm not, all right? I'm not the least bit interested!" I start to leave the room, angry tears pricking my eyelids.

"Cass, wait!" He takes hold of my arm, pulling me back, into his. "Don't go. I'm sorry—that was really insensitive of me. I keep forgetting that you met her."

The fight goes out of me and I slump against him. "No, it's my fault," I say tiredly. "I shouldn't have shouted at you."

He kisses the top of my head. "Come on, let's watch a film."

"As long as it's not about a murder."

"I'll find a comedy," he promises.

So we watch a film, or rather Matthew does and I laugh when he laughs so he won't know how desperate I feel. It's hard to believe that my split-second decision to take a shortcut through the woods that fateful Friday night has had such a devastating impact on my life. Jane may have been in the wrong place at the wrong time but so was I. So was I.

# TUESDAY, AUGUST 4TH

The call comes while I'm stacking the dishwasher and I think that it must be Rachel phoning to ask about my few days at the hotel. But when I answer, there's no one there—or rather, no one speaks because I'm sure that there *is* someone there. I suddenly remember a call I received yesterday, and the ones I'd received the previous week, before I left for the hotel. The silence. I hold my breath, listening for the slightest sound that will tell me there's someone there but there's nothing—no static, no breathing, no sound at all—as if he, like me, is holding his breath. *He.* Unease worms its way through my body and I hang up abruptly. I check the answering machine, wanting to know if any had come in while I was away but there was only a call from the alarm company on Thursday, confirming that they were coming to install the alarm the next day, and three on Friday, two from the alarm company, asking me to call them urgently, and one from Connie.

I'd planned to start working on lesson plans for September but I can't focus. The phone rings again and my heart immediately starts pounding. *It's all right,* I tell myself, *it'll be Matthew, or Rachel, or another friend phoning for a chat.* But when I check the number, it's withheld.

I don't know why I take the call. Maybe it's because I've already understood what is expected of me. I want to say something, to ask him who he is, but the chilling silence freezes the words in my mouth so that I can only listen. But again there is nothing and I slam the phone down, my hands shaking. Suddenly, my house seems like a prison. Hurrying upstairs, I fetch my mobile and my bag from the bedroom, jump in the car and drive to Castle Wells. On the way to a café, I stop to buy a card to send to Jane's husband, but at the till it's impossible to ignore the piles of newspapers stacked near the counter, or their headlines screaming that there have been new developments in the murder case. I don't particularly want to read about it but, with the chance that the police are closer to catching the murderer, I buy one anyway. In the café next door, I find a table in the corner, open the paper and start to read:

Until now, the police have believed Jane's murder to be a random attack but someone has now come forward to say that he passed what he believes was her car, parked in roughly the same place the Friday before she was killed, at around eleven-thirty. It changes the whole direction of the investigation as it suggests that Jane might have known her killer and that on the night she died she had gone to the lay-by to meet him and had done so the previous week as well. The press are all over her private life, suggesting that she had a secret lover, that her marriage was in trouble, and my heart goes out to her husband—although there's also speculation that he's responsible for his wife's death. As the newspaper points out, his alibis—the two little daughters he said he was looking after at home—could easily have been left by themselves during the time it would have taken for him to commit the crime.

Next to the article there's a photo of a knife similar to the one the police believe was used by the killer and, as I stare at the black-handled kitchen knife with its finely serrated blade, I feel sick to my stomach with fear.

Like a racing car leaving the starting line, my heart accelerates so quickly that I feel dizzy. I close my eyes but when I open them again the fear is still there, gathering momentum. Maybe the murderer was already lurking in the woods, about to commit his terrible crime, when I pulled into the lay-by. If he saw me, he might think that I saw him. Maybe he memorized my license plate in case I became a threat to him. And, now, in his eyes, I may have. He knows that someone went to the police, because they've made my call to them public, and maybe he's guessed it was me. He doesn't know that I didn't tell them anything, that I had nothing to tell them. What matters is that he knows I exist. Has he found out who I am and is making silent calls as a threat?

I look around desperately for something to ground me; my eyes fall on the café menu and I start counting the letters in the first item on there: one, two, three, four, five, six. It works: the even pacing of the numbers slows my heartbeat and soon I'm breathing normally again. But I still feel shaky, and horribly alone.

I take out my mobile and phone Rachel, glad that her offices aren't too far away from the town center.

"I'm in Castle Wells. I don't suppose you can take a long lunch hour, can you?" I ask.

"Let me check my diary." Her voice is brisk, which tells me she's heard the desperation in mine. "Let's see—I have a meeting at three, so I'd have to be back for that, and if I juggle things around a bit I could be with you around one. Will that do?"

"That would be great."

"Shall we meet in the Spotted Cow?" she says.

"Perfect."

"Is the town busy? Where did you park?"

"I found a place in the little car park in Grainger Street but you might have to go to the multi-story."

"All right. See you at one."

"What's the matter, Cass?" Rachel asks, concerned.

I take a sip of wine, not quite sure what to tell her. "I just don't feel safe in the house anymore."

"Why not?"

"It's since the murder. It said in the paper that Jane was probably killed by someone she knew, which means he must live locally."

She reaches out and gives my hand a squeeze. "Her death has really affected you, hasn't it?"

I nod miserably. "I know I only had lunch with her once but I know we would have become good friends," I say. "And I hate that they're saying she had a lover. I don't believe it for a minute. She couldn't stop talking about her husband, about how wonderful he was and how lucky she was to have him. I bought a card to send to him—would you be able to find his address for me?"

"Yes, of course, I'll ask around at work." She nods at the newspaper I bought earlier. "Did you see the picture of the knife? It's horrible."

"Don't," I say shakily. "I can't bear to think about it."

"You'll feel better once you have an alarm installed," she says, shrugging off her red cardigan and putting it on the back of her chair.

"We have one. It was put in on Friday"

She reaches for her glass and her silver bangles, released from the constraints of sleeves, jangle together. "Can you put it on when you're in the house?"

"Yes, I can alarm the windows and any of the rooms I want."

"And you still don't feel safe?"

"No."

"Why not?"

"Because I keep getting weird calls." My words come out in a rush.

She frowns. "What sort of weird?"

"Silent. From a withheld number."

"You mean there's no one there?"

"No, there is someone there, they just don't say anything. It's really creeping me out."

She thinks for a moment. "These calls—how many have you had?"

"I'm not sure . . . five or six? There were two this morning."

She does a sort of double-take. "And that's what's upset you? A few calls from a withheld number? Cass, I get loads of those! Usually, it's someone trying to sell me something or wanting feedback on something I've bought." She thinks for a moment. "I take it these calls are on your house phone?"

"Yes." I fiddle with the stem of my glass. "I can't help wondering if it's personal."

"Personal?" Rachel looks uncomprehendingly at me.

"Yes."

"Come on, Cass, it's just a few calls. I don't get why they've upset you so much."

I shrug, trying to make light of it. "I guess it's Jane's murder . . . you know? Happening so close to home."

"What does Matthew think?"

"I haven't told him."

"Why not?" The concern in her eyes makes me decide to confide in her.

"Because I've done a few stupid things lately and I don't want him to think I really am crazy," I admit.

She takes a sip of wine but her eyes don't leave mine. "What sort of things?"

"Well . . . first, I forgot I'd invited Hannah and

Andy round for a barbecue. I bumped into Hannah in Browbury the day I met you for a drink in the Sour Grapes . . ."

"I know," she says. "I remember you saying that's why you were late."

"I already told you?"

"Yes. You told me that you'd invited them for a barbecue because you hadn't seen them for a while."

"Did I say when I'd invited them for?"

"Yes, you said you'd asked them for the Sunday, so that weekend."

I close my eyes, take a breath. "Well, I forgot," I say, looking at her again.

"Forgot?"

"Yes. I forgot I'd invited them. Or didn't realize I had . . . I'm not quite sure which. Andy phoned in the morning to ask what time we were expecting them, so we managed to avoid the embarrassment of them turning up and there being nothing to eat. But that's not all . . . I also managed to order the alarm system without remembering anything about it. I filled in the form, signed it, everything—yet, I wasn't aware that I had." I look at her across the table. "I'm scared, Rachel, really scared. I don't know what's happening to me. And because Mum—"

"I don't understand about the alarm," she interrupts. "What happened, exactly?"

"Do you remember, when we met in the Sour Grapes, I told you that I'd had a man from an alarm company round to give a quote?"

"Yes, you said he spooked you or something."

"That's right. Well, when Matthew got back from the rig last Friday, he found the man waiting on the doorstep. So Matthew told him we'd never agreed to have an alarm fitted, but the man pulled out a form signed by me."

"That doesn't mean anything," Rachel interrupts. "He could have forged your signature. There are a lot of cowboys out there."

"That's what I thought at first. But it wasn't just the signature, Rachel, it was all the rest. The whole form had been filled in, and it was definitely my handwriting. Matthew said I must have been tricked into signing it and I went along with it because it got me off the hook. But I think we both knew I wasn't."

She churns it over in her mind. "You know what I think? I think you were probably coerced into it in some way. You said you didn't like the man, that he made you feel uncomfortable, so maybe you agreed to the alarm to get rid of him and, after, you blocked the whole episode from your subconscious because you were ashamed you'd let yourself be taken advantage of."

"I never thought of that."

"I'm sure that's what happened," she says firmly. "So stop worrying."

"But that doesn't explain the rest. What about the present I was supposed to buy for Susie? What about inviting Hannah and Andy for lunch?" I don't mention forgetting that she was meant to be spending the night with me the time I went and booked into a hotel.

"How long ago did your mother die, Cass?"

"Just over two years ago."

"And in that time you've gone back to work, got married and moved house. Basically, you've reinvented yourself. For someone who spent the previous three years caring day and night for someone with full-blown dementia, I'd say you've done too much too quickly and have reached burnout."

I nod slowly, thinking about it—and the more I think about it, the more I begin to believe that she's right.

"It has been a bit of a whirlwind," I admit.

"There you are then."

"But what if it's more than that?"

"What do you mean?"

It's hard to voice my worst fear. "What if I'm becoming like Mum? What if I start forgetting every little thing, like she did?"

"Is that what you're worried about?"

"Be honest, Rachel: have you noticed anything?"

"No, nothing. Sometimes you're a little distracted—"

"Am I?"

"You know? When you start thinking about something else and don't hear a word I'm saying."

"Do I?"

"Don't look so worried—we all do it!"

"So you don't think I'm heading in that direction?"

Rachel shakes her head vigorously. "No, I don't."

"What about the phone calls?"

"They're just random calls. There's nothing sinister about them," she says earnestly. "What you need is a rest. You should get Matthew to take you somewhere you can relax."

"I've just had five days away. Anyway, it's difficult

for him to have time off in August. You're off soon, aren't you?"

"On Saturday," she says happily. "I can't wait! Oh, good, here's lunch."

By the time Rachel leaves, fifteen minutes later than she should have, I feel so much better. She's right about my life since Mum died. Basically, I've gone from one with very little excitement and a lot of routine to one full of new experiences. It's normal that everything I've been through has suddenly caught up with me and thrown me off-balance. It's a minor blip, not a major disaster. All I need is to put Jane's murder from my mind, stop thinking that there's something sinister in the phone calls I've been getting and concentrate on what's important to me, which is Matthew. It gives me an idea and, instead of continuing toward the car park, I turn back the way I came.

I stand for a while in front of the window of the Baby Boutique, looking at the gorgeous baby clothes on display. Then, pushing the door open, I go inside. There's a young couple, the woman heavily pregnant, looking at prams for their soon-to-be-born baby, and the thought that one day it'll be Matthew and me standing there choosing a pram for our child fills me with a longing that takes my breath away. I begin to look through the rails of clothes and find a tiny sleep-suit decorated with pastel-colored balloons. The shop assistant, a petite young woman with the longest hair I've ever seen, comes over to see if she can help.

"Yes, I'd like to buy this," I say, handing her the sleep-suit.

"It's gorgeous, isn't it? Would you like it gift-wrapped?"

"No, it's fine, thank you, it's for me."

"How lovely! When's your baby due?"

Her question throws me and I feel embarrassed that I'm buying a sleep-suit for a baby that doesn't exist.

"Oh, I'm only just pregnant," I hear myself say.

She laughs delightedly and pats her stomach. "Me too!"

"Congratulations!" I turn and see the young couple coming toward us. "Do you know yet if it's a boy or a girl?" the young woman asks, looking at me.

I shake my head quickly. "Early days."

"Mine's a boy," she says proudly. "Due next month."

"Lovely."

"We can't make up our minds which buggy to buy," she goes on.

"Maybe we can help," says the shop assistant and, before I know it, we're inspecting the row of prams and buggies, discussing the pros and cons of each one.

"I'd choose that one," I say, pointing to a beautiful navy-and-white pram.

"Why don't you try it?" the shop assistant suggests, so the young couple and I take turns wheeling it up and down the shop, agreeing that it really is the perfect option as, not only does it look classy, it's easy to handle.

We move to the counter and the shop assistant insists on putting the sleep-suit in a pretty box, even though I've told her that it's for me, and as we chat about possible names for our babies, I feel more positive than ever about becoming a mother. Rachel's assertion that all I'm suffering from is burnout has given me back my confidence and I can't wait to tell Matthew this evening that we can start IVF. Maybe I'll present him with the tiny sleep-suit first, as a hint.

"We have a loyalty scheme you might find interesting." The smiling assistant holds out a form to me. "You just need to fill in your name and address. Once you've built up a certain number of points, you get a discount on your future purchases."

I take the form and start filling it in. "That sounds great."

"You can use it to buy maternity wear too," she goes on. "We have some lovely jeans with a waistband that expands along with your pregnancy. I've got my eye on a pair already."

Suddenly brought back to reality, because I am not pregnant, I hand the form back to her and say a hurried goodbye. I'm almost at the door when she calls me back.

"You haven't paid!" she reminds me, laughing.

Flustered, I go back to the counter and hand her my card. By the time I actually make it out of the door, I feel so fraught by the lies I've told that my newfound confidence has all but deserted me. I don't feel like going home but I don't want to stay in town in case I bump into the young couple from the shop, and they start talking about my pregnancy, so I head back to the car park anyway.

I haven't gotten very far when I hear someone calling

my name. Turning around, I see John, my colleague from school, hurrying toward me.

"I saw you come out of the shop back there and I've been trying to catch up with you ever since," he explains, giving me one of his huge smiles. He gives me a spontaneous hug and his dark hair flops onto his forehead. "How are you, Cass?"

"I'm fine," I lie. I see his eyes drift toward the bag I'm carrying and I'm immediately embarrassed.

"I don't mean to pry, but I need to buy a present for a friend's new baby and I have no idea what to get. I was about to go into the shop when I saw you coming out, so I'm hoping you can help."

"I bought a sleep-suit for a friend's baby. Maybe you could buy something like that."

"Great, I'll get one of those then. So, are you enjoying the holidays?"

"Yes and no," I admit, grateful to be changing the subject. "It's lovely to have some time off but since the murder, I'm finding it hard to relax."

His face clouds over. "I used to play tennis with her. We belonged to the same club. I couldn't believe it when I heard the news. I felt terrible. I still do."

"I forgot that you knew her too," I say.

He looks surprised. "Why, did you?"

"Only a little. I met her at a party Rachel took me to. We got chatting and when I told her that I worked at the high school, she said that she knew you. Then, a couple of weeks ago, we had lunch together." I cast around for something else to talk about. "You're off to Greece soon, aren't you?"

"No, not anymore." I look at him questioningly. "Let's just say, my girlfriend is no longer on the scene."

"Ah . . ."

John shrugs. "These things happen." He looks at his watch. "I don't suppose you have time for a drink, do you?"

"A coffee would be lovely," I say, glad to fill in a bit more time.

Over coffee, we talk about school and about the Inset day scheduled for the end of the month, ahead of the new school year in September. Half an hour later, we leave the café and, after we've said goodbye, I watch, my stress levels rising, as he crosses over the road and walks back toward the Baby Boutique. What if he tells the assistant that he wants to buy a sleep-suit like the one a friend of his bought half an hour ago? She'll know he's talking about me and she might say something about me being pregnant and, when we see each other at school, he might congratulate me in front of everyone. And what would I do then? Pretend it was a false alarm? He might even phone me later on today and I'll have no choice but to admit I lied to the assistant or tell him that she must have misunderstood. My head begins pounding and I wish I'd never bumped into him.

I get home and, as I let myself into the house, the flashing red light on the keypad reminds me that I need to turn the alarm off, so I close the front door and type in the code. But instead of the green light coming on, the red light begins flashing furiously. Thinking I've made a mistake, I type the code in again, pressing

firmly on each number—9-0-9-1—but the light flashes
even faster. Horribly aware of the time counting down,
because I only have thirty seconds before the alarm
goes off, I try to work out what I've done wrong. I'm so
sure I've got the code right that I try the same numbers
again—and fumble it.

Within seconds all hell is let loose. A siren pierces
the air, then another joins in, shrieking intermittently.
As I stand dithering in front of the keypad, trying to
work out if there's some other way of turning the alarm
off, I hear the phone ringing behind me and my heart,
already racing with the stress of having messed up
the code, speeds up even more because all I can think
is that whoever's been plaguing me with silent calls
knows that I've just arrived home. Abandoning the
alarm, I run to the gate and look up and down the road
for someone to help me. But despite the noise from the
alarm, no one comes to investigate, and the irony of it
makes me feel a bit hysterical.

At that moment, Matthew's car comes into sight,
sobering me up. Realizing I'm holding the carrier bag
from the Baby Boutique, I quickly open my car and
fling it under the seat before he's near enough to see.
The puzzlement on his face as he drives through the
gate tells me the noise from the alarm has already
reached him.

He brings the car to an abrupt stop and jumps out.

"Cass, what's happened? Are you all right?"

"I can't turn off the alarm!" I shout over the noise.
"The code doesn't work!"

The relief on his face, that we haven't been burgled, is quickly replaced by one of surprise.

"What do you mean, it doesn't work? It did yesterday."

"I know, but it doesn't anymore!"

"Let me have a look."

I follow him into the house and he punches the code into the keypad. The noise stops immediately.

"I don't believe it," I say, bewildered. "Why didn't it work for me?"

"Are you sure you put the code in correctly?"

"Yes, I put in 9091, exactly as I did yesterday, exactly as you just did. I even put it in twice but it still wouldn't work."

"Wait a minute—what number did you say?"

"9091, our birthdays backward."

He shakes his head in despair. "It's 9190, Cass, not 9091. Your birthday, then mine. You got them round the wrong way, that's all. You put mine in first instead of yours."

"Oh, God," I groan. "How could I be so stupid?"

"Well, it's easily done, I suppose. But didn't it occur to you to try the numbers the other way round when they wouldn't work the first time?"

"No," I say, feeling even more stupid. Over his shoulder, I see a police car draw up in front of the house. "What are the police doing here?"

Matthew turns to look. "I don't know. Maybe the alarm company called them out—you know, because of the murder happening so close to here."

A policewoman gets out of the car. "Is everything all right?" she calls over the fence.

"Yes, everything's fine," Matthew assures her.

She comes down the drive anyway. "You haven't had a break-in then? We were notified that your alarm had gone off and that you weren't responding to the follow-up call so we thought we'd come out to check."

"I'm sorry—you've had a wasted journey, I'm afraid," Matthew says. "It's a new alarm and we had a bit of a mix-up with the code."

"Would you like me to check the house, just to make sure? The alarm wasn't going off when you arrived home, was it?"

"No, it wasn't," I say apologetically. "I'm sorry, it's my fault, I put the wrong code in."

The policewoman smiles reassuringly at me. "No harm done."

I find her presence strangely comforting and I know it's because I'm dreading being on my own with Matthew. He might have decided to overlook, or find excuses, for all the other stupid stuff I've done recently but he's not going to be able to ignore what's just happened with the alarm.

The policewoman gets back in her car and I follow Matthew into the kitchen.

As he makes us both tea, the silence is so uncomfortable that I long for him to say something, even if it's not what I want to hear.

"Cass, can we talk?" he asks, handing me a mug.

"What about?"

"It's just that you've been a bit distracted lately—you know, forgetting things . . ."

"Ordering alarms, setting them off," I say, nodding.

"I just wondered if you're stressed about something."

"I've been getting silent phone calls," I say, because admitting my fear around these is preferable to telling him that I'm losing my mind. I know Rachel didn't think the calls were anything to worry about but I'd like to have Matthew's take on them.

"What? When?"

"Always in the morning."

"On your mobile or the house phone?"

"The house phone."

"Did you check the number?"

"Yes, it was withheld."

"Then they're probably coming from a call center somewhere over the other side of the world. Seriously, is that's what's bothering you? A few calls from a withheld number?"

"Yes."

"Why? It can't be the first time you've received those sort of calls, everybody gets them."

"I know, but these seem personal."

"Personal?" He frowns. "In what way?"

I hesitate, unsure about going on. But I've started now. "It's as if they know who I am," I say.

"Why, do they say your name?"

"No. They don't say anything, that's the problem."

"So it's a heavy breather?"

"Except that they don't breathe."

"So what do they do?"

"Nothing. But I know there's someone there."

"How?"

"I can sense him."

Now he looks confused. "They don't know who you are, Cass. You're just a number on a very long list of numbers. All he wants is to ask questions for a survey or sell you a kitchen. Anyway, how do you know it's a man?"

Startled, I look at him. "What?"

"You said you could sense him. So how do you know it's a man? It could be a woman."

"No, it's definitely a man."

"But if they don't say anything, how do you know?"

"I just do. Would we be able to trace where a call is coming from, even if the number is withheld?"

"Possibly. But you don't really think it's personal, do you? I mean, why would it be?"

It's hard to voice my fear. "There's a murderer somewhere out there."

"What's that got to do with it?"

"I don't know."

He furrows his brow, trying to work it out. "Do you mean that you think the murderer is behind the calls?" he asks, trying not to sound incredulous.

"No, not really," I say half-heartedly.

"Sweetheart, I can understand why you're frightened, anybody would be, especially when the murder happened so close to here and the murderer is still at large. But if the calls are coming in on the house phone, then they're not targeting you specifically, are they?" He thinks for a bit. "How about if I work from home Thursday and Friday? Would it help if I was here for a few days?"

Relief floods through me. "Yes, it really would."

"It'll be nice to have a few days off for my birthday," he goes on, and I nod, wondering how I could have forgotten it was coming up.

"Anyway," Matthew says, "from what I heard on the radio earlier, the police are beginning to think that Jane knew her killer."

"Maybe she did but I don't believe he was her lover," I say. "She just wasn't the type."

"Yes, but how well did you really know her? You only met her twice."

"I could see that she loved her husband," I say stubbornly. "She wouldn't have cheated on him."

"Well, if she did know the person who killed her— and the police think that she did—he's hardly likely to come after anyone else. Even less phone them up."

Put like that, I can only agree. "You're right."

"Promise you won't worry anymore?"

"I promise," I say. And I wish it could be that simple.

# WEDNESDAY, AUGUST 5TH

It's while I'm sitting on the bench under the damson tree the next day, looking down toward the end of the garden, that I come up with the perfect birthday present for Matthew: a shed. I've lost count of the number of times he's said he'd love one. If I order it today, I can probably get it delivered by the end of the week and he'll be able to put it up over the weekend.

The call comes as I'm on my way back into the house to look for a shed on the computer. It doesn't matter that I've been half expecting it, it stops me in my tracks and glues me to the spot, poised halfway between <u>house</u> and garden, halfway between flight and fight. Anger wins and, running into the hall, I snatch up the phone.

"Leave me alone!" I cry. "If you ever phone me again, I'll go to the police!"

I regret the words as soon as they're out. Shocked, I draw in my breath, hardly able to believe I've just threatened him with the very thing he must fear the most, because now he'll think that I really did see him that night. I want to tell him that it isn't what I meant, that there's nothing I could possibly tell the police, that all I want is for him to stop phoning me. But fear has robbed me of my voice.

"Cass?" The confirmation that he knows who I am paralyzes me. "Cass, is everything all right?" The voice comes down the line again. "It's John."

My legs go weak. "John." I give a shaky laugh. "Sorry, I thought you were someone else."

"Are you OK?"

"I am now." I fight for control. "It's just that I've had one of those call companies pestering me and I thought they were calling me again."

He laughs softly. "They're a real nuisance, aren't they? But don't worry, if you shout at them like you just did, there's no way they'll call you back! Although, if you don't mind me saying so," he goes on, amused, "threatening them with the police does seem a little harsh."

"Sorry," I say again, "I just lost it, I'm afraid."

"I don't blame you. But look, I won't keep you. I'm just phoning to see if you want to come for a drink

on Friday evening with a few of us from school. I'm
phoning round to see who's free."

"Friday?" My mind races ahead. "The thing is, Matthew's taking the next two days off and we might decide
to go away somewhere. I don't suppose I could let you
know, could I?"

"Sure."

"I'll give you a call."

"Great. Well, bye, Cass, hope to see you there. And
if that company does phone back, make sure you give
them another piece of your mind."

"I will," I promise. "Bye, John, thanks for calling."

He rings off and I stand there feeling drained, and
stupid, wondering what he must think of me. At that
moment, the phone, which is still in my hand, starts
ringing again and, this time, a terrible shaking takes
hold of me. I desperately want to believe that it's John
phoning back to tell me something he forgot to tell
me the first time round, so I take the call. The silence
screams down the line and I hate that, once again, I'm
doing exactly as he wants.

Or perhaps not. Maybe my silence frustrates him,
maybe he wants me to yell down the phone like I just
did to John, maybe he wants me to threaten to go to
the police so that he'll have an excuse to kill me, like
he killed Jane. I hang on to the thought, glad that I was
able to vent my frustration on John, and as I hang up, I
feel the tiniest of victories. And relief that now that the
call has come, I'll be able to get on with my life.

Except that I can't. The house feels so oppressive that

I choose a shed for Matthew hurriedly, more concerned by the promise of delivery by Saturday than by its dimensions. Back downstairs, I take a book and a bottle of water and go into the garden. It takes me a while to choose where to sit because I don't want anyone to be able to creep up on me, which I know is unlikely as they'd have to climb over a six-foot hedge. Unless they come in through the gate. I pick a spot at the side of the house with a view of the drive, annoyed that my home is no longer the haven it used to be. But until the police catch the killer, there's not a lot I can do.

Just as I'm about to make myself some lunch, I get a text from Rachel with the address that I asked for, so I take the card from my bag and sit down to write to Jane's husband. It's easier than I thought it would be, simply because I write from the heart and, when I've finished, I read it over just to make sure I'm happy with it.

*Dear Mr. Walters,*

*I hope I'm not intruding in sending you this letter. I just wanted to say how terribly sorry I was to hear the sad news about Jane. I only knew her briefly but in that short time she made such an impression on me. We first met a month ago, at a party for someone who was leaving Finchlakers, and then we had lunch together a couple of weeks ago, in Browbury. I hope you will understand when I say that I have lost a friend, because that is how it feels.*

*My thoughts are with you and your family,*
                                                    *Cass Anderson*

Glad to have an excuse to get out of the house for a few minutes, I find a stamp and walk the five hundred yards to the postbox at the top of the road. There's no one around but, as I slip my letter through the slot, I sense someone watching me, just as I had the day I'd used the pay phone to call the police. The hairs on the back of my neck stand on end and I whip round, my heart thudding, but there's no one there, only the branches of a tree some twenty feet away from me stirring in the wind. Except that, today, there isn't any wind.

It isn't fear that I feel, but terror. It drains the blood from my face and robs me of my breath, knots my insides and turns my limbs to jelly. And then it makes me lose all sense of reason and hurtles me down the road, away from the houses at the top, toward my house at the end, close to the woods. My feet pound on the tarmac, loud in the silence of the afternoon and as I take a sharp turn into the drive, my chest heaving, my breath rasping, I skid on loose gravel. The ground rushes up to meet me and whacks the air from my lungs. And as I lie there, fighting for breath, my hands and knees already stinging, the voice in my head mocks me: *There's no one there!*

I get slowly to my feet and hobble to the front door, pulling the keys gingerly from my pocket with my finger and thumb, protecting the scraped skin on the palms of my hands. In the hall I head for the stairs, glad I hadn't turned on the alarm when I left as I'm in such a state I'd have probably set it off again. I climb the stairs, my eyes smarting with unshed tears. I only let them fall when I'm cleaning myself up because I can pretend that I'm crying over the damage I've done to my hands and knees. But the truth is, I don't know how much more of myself I can take. I'm ashamed of how pathetically feeble I've become since Jane's murder. If I hadn't already been having problems with my memory, I know I would have coped better. But with the possibility of dementia hanging over me, I've lost all confidence in myself.

# FRIDAY, AUGUST 7TH

We're lazing in bed when I hear a lorry pulling up in front of the house.

"It's not the day for the bin lorry, is it?" I say innocently, knowing Matthew's present should arrive today.

Matthew gets out of bed and goes to the window. "It's a delivery of some kind. Probably for that man who's just moved in up the road," he says, pulling on jeans and a T-shirt. "He's had quite a lot of furniture delivered recently."

"What man who's just moved in up the road?"

"Into that house that was for sale."

My heart thuds. "I thought it had been sold to a couple who were moving in at the end of September?"

"No, I don't think so."

The sound of someone crunching up the drive followed by the ring of the doorbell sends him hurrying downstairs. I lie back against the pillows, thinking about what Matthew just said. Maybe the man I saw outside the house is no more than our new neighbor. I should feel reassured, but I don't, because somewhere in the dark recess of my mind I'm already wondering if he's my silent caller. There might not have been anybody chasing me when I ran down the road yesterday but there was definitely someone watching me as I stood at the postbox. I wish I could tell Matthew but I can't, not today, not without some sort of proof. He's already bewildered enough by the way my mind has begun to work.

Suddenly impatient, because he hasn't come back, I throw off the covers to go and find him and hear his footsteps on the stairs.

"Surprise!" I say as he comes into the room.

He looks at me in puzzlement. "So it's not some kind of joke then?"

"No, of course it isn't," I say, taken aback by his lack of enthusiasm. "Why would it be?"

He sits down on the edge of the bed. "I just don't understand why you've bought one now."

"Because I thought it would be a nice gesture?"

"I still don't understand."

He looks so bewildered that my good humor evaporates fast.

"It's your birthday present!"

He nods slowly. "Right. But why is it for me? Surely it should be for both of us?"

"Why? I'm hardly going to use it, am I?"

"Why not?"

"Because you're the one that's been banging on about having one! But it doesn't matter. If you don't want it, I'll send it back."

"I've never said I wanted one, not specifically, and anyway, it's not a question of not wanting it, I just don't see the point, that's all. We haven't even started looking into having a baby yet so it might be years before we have a child."

I stare at him. "What's having children got to do with it?"

"I give up," he says, getting to his feet. "I don't understand anything. I'm going downstairs."

"I thought you'd be happy!" I shout after him. "I thought you'd be happy to have a garden shed! I'm sorry if I got that wrong too!"

He comes back into the room. "A garden shed?"

"Yes. I thought you wanted one," I say accusingly.

"Well, of course I want one."

"So what's the problem? Is it the size, because if it is, we can always change it."

A frown furrows his brow. "Let me get this straight—you've bought me a garden shed?"

"Yes—why, isn't that what was delivered?"

"No," he says, starting to laugh. "No wonder I didn't understand anything! They've made a mistake, sweetheart. They didn't deliver a garden shed, they delivered a pram! God, I was seriously worried for a moment back there. I thought you'd completely lost it."

"A pram?" I look at him incredulously. "How did they make that mistake?"

"God knows. It's a very nice one, I admit, navy and white, just the sort I can see us buying one day. Well, I'd better go and phone the delivery company and see if they can come back and collect it. They can't have gone very far."

"Wait a minute." I push the covers back and get out of bed. "Where is it?"

"In the hall. But even if you fall in love with it, I'm afraid you can't keep it," he jokes. "It's obviously destined for someone else."

I run downstairs, a horrible feeling in the pit of my stomach. Standing by the front door, the packaging lying on the floor around it, is the pram I saw in the shop in Castle Wells, the one I'd picked out as being the most practical.

Matthew's arms come round me. "Now can you see why I was so surprised?" He nuzzles my neck. "I can't believe you've ordered me a garden shed for my birthday."

"I know you've always wanted one," I say distractedly.

"I love you," he murmurs in my ear. "Thank you, thank you so much. I can't wait to see it, although you have to feel sorry for the poor guy who realizes the shed he's just received isn't for him after all."

"I don't understand," I mutter, looking at the pram.

"Did you order the shed online?"

"Yes."

"Then they've got two orders mixed up. We've got someone's pram and they've got our shed. I'll phone the delivery company and, with a bit of luck, I'll have the shed by this afternoon."

"But I saw this pram in a shop in Castle Wells on Tuesday. There were some other people there, a young couple, and they asked me what I thought of all the different prams, so I looked at them for a bit and said that I thought this one was the best."

"So did they order it?"

"They must have."

"Well, that explains it then. It's got sent here by mistake."

"But how did the shop get my address?"

"I don't know. What sort of a shop was it? If it was a department store and you bought something there, maybe you gave them your address."

"It wasn't a department store, it was a shop that sold baby clothes."

"Baby clothes?"

"Yes. I bought a sleep-suit for our future baby. I meant to give it to you but with all the fuss over the alarm I forgot about it. It must still be in the car. I wanted to tell you that we could start looking into having a baby. It seemed like a good idea at the time but I suppose it seems stupid to you now."

He tightens his arms around me. "No, it doesn't. It's a lovely thought and you can still give it to me."

"It's spoiled now," I say miserably. "Everything's gone wrong."

"It hasn't," he insists. "Look, when you bought the

baby clothes, are you sure you didn't give the shop our address?"

"I filled in a form for a loyalty card," I say, remembering now. "I had to give my name and address."

"There we are then, problem solved! Which shop was it?"

"The Baby Boutique. There must be an invoice or something." I peer into the pram. "Look, here."

He reaches for the phone. "Give me their number and I'll call them. And while I'm doing that, you can make a start on breakfast."

I read the number out to him and go into the kitchen to make some coffee. As I switch on the machine, I hear him explaining that a pram has been delivered to us by mistake and when he goes on to joke that if it's destined for the young couple who were in the shop at the same time as his wife on Tuesday, I should get a commission for encouraging them to buy it, I can't help feeling pleased that they took my advice.

"Let me guess—they said we can keep it anyway, for our future baby," I smile, when he comes into the kitchen.

"So it's true, then." He shakes his head in wonderment. "I didn't believe it at first, I thought she must be mistaken." He comes over and puts his arms around me. "Are you really pregnant, Cass? I mean, it's wonderful if you are but I don't see how." He looks uncertainly at me. "Unless the doctors got it wrong. They told me I couldn't father children but maybe they were wrong, maybe I can, maybe the problem isn't with me after all."

The look on his face makes me hate myself more than I've ever hated myself.

"I'm not pregnant," I say quietly.

"What?"

"I'm not pregnant."

"But the woman I spoke to congratulated me, she remembered you, she remembered you ordering the pram for our baby."

His disappointment is hard to take. "She must have got me mixed up with someone else. I told you, there was a young couple there . . ."

"She said you told her you were pregnant." He moves away from me. "What's going on, Cass?"

I sit down at the table. "I told her the sleep-suit was for me, because it was, and she presumed I was pregnant," I say dully. "And I went along with it because, at the time, it seemed easier."

"And the pram?"

"I don't know."

He can't hide his frustration. "What do you mean, you don't know?"

"I don't remember!"

"Well, did you let yourself be persuaded into buying it?"

"I don't know," I say again.

He sits down opposite me and takes my hands in his. "Look, sweetheart, would it help if you talked to someone?"

"What do you mean?"

"You haven't been yourself recently, and it's, well, it's

just that this murder seems to have affected you more than it should have. And then there's the phone calls."

"What about them?"

"You seem to be reading more into them than you should. It's difficult for me to judge when I haven't heard any of them, but . . ."

"It's not my fault they stop the minute you're around!" I snap, because I was strangely annoyed that a call hadn't come in the last two mornings. He looks at me in surprise. "Sorry." I sigh. "I'm just frustrated that as soon as you're with me, he doesn't call." The word "he" hangs in the air.

"Well, it won't do any harm for you to see Dr. Deakin, just for a check-up."

"Why?" I say, back on the defensive. "I'm tired, that's all. Rachel thinks I'm suffering from burnout because so much has happened since Mum died."

He frowns. "Since when did she become an expert?"

"Well, I think she's right."

"Maybe she is. But it wouldn't do you any harm to see a doctor."

"I'm fine, Matthew, honestly. I just need a rest." I see the doubt in his eyes.

"Please, will you let me make an appointment? If you can't do it for yourself, maybe you could do it for me. I can't go on like this, I really can't."

I get a grip on myself. "What if they find there's something wrong with me?" I say, wanting to prepare him.

"Like what?"

"I don't know." I can hardly get the word out. "Dementia or something."

"Dementia? You're far too young to have dementia, it's more likely to be stress, just like you say." He gives my hands a little shake. "I just want you to have the help you need. So, can I make an appointment?"

"If it'll make you happy."

"I'm hoping it will make you happy. Because I don't think you're very happy at the moment, are you?"

The tears that never seem to be far away fill my eyes. "No," I say, "not really."

# SATURDAY,
# AUGUST 8TH

Matthew somehow managed to get a cancelation appointment with Dr. Deakin for this morning and I'm nervous. Matthew and I registered with him soon after moving into the house and I haven't seen him yet because I haven't been ill. I thought it was the same for Matthew, so when we're called in it's a surprise to find our doctor seems to know him—and even more of a surprise to find that Dr. Deakin already knows all about my memory lapses.

"I didn't realize my husband had already spoken to you," I say, flustered.

"He was concerned about you," Dr. Deakin explains.

"Can you tell me when you first noticed that you were having trouble remembering things?"

Matthew gives my hand a reassuring squeeze and I resist the urge to snatch it away. I try to ignore the sense of betrayal I feel but the fact that they've been discussing me without my knowledge makes me feel at a disadvantage.

"I'm not sure," I say, because I don't want to admit to things that Matthew hadn't noticed at the time because I'd managed to cover them up. "A few weeks ago, I suppose. Matthew had to come and rescue me in the supermarket because I'd left my purse at home."

"But before that you went all the way to Castle Wells without your bag—and what about that time you left half the shopping in the supermarket," Matthew says quietly.

"Oh, yes, I forgot about those," I say, realizing too late that I'd just admitted to two more memory lapses.

"Those sort of things can happen to anybody," Dr. Deakin says reassuringly, and I'm glad he's a grandfatherly kind of doctor who's been around a bit and knows how life works and not someone straight out of medical school who does everything by the textbook. "I don't think it's anything to worry about. However, I would like to ask you about your family history," he goes on, dashing my hopes that our session is over. "I know you no longer have your parents but can I ask what they died of?"

"My father was killed in a car accident—he was run over while crossing the road outside our house. And my mother died of pneumonia."

"And did either of them show any signs of other illnesses before they died?" he asks.

"My mother had dementia." Beside me, Matthew gives a start of surprise, only a small one but I sense it nonetheless.

"And can you tell me when it was diagnosed?"

My skin has flushed so hot I'm certain Dr. Deakin has noticed. I look down, flicking my hair over my face. "In 2002."

"And she would have been how old?"

"Forty-four," I say, quietly. I can't look at Matthew.

From then on, things go from bad to worse. My face burns even more when I realize that Matthew hasn't been fooled by any of my efforts at subterfuge and that he's always been far more aware of what's been going on than I gave him credit for. As the number of incidents Dr. Deakin adds to his list increases, all I want is to leave before any more damage is done.

But he and Matthew haven't finished yet. There's still the murder to talk about and, although both of them agree that it's normal it has upset me, seeing as I'd met Jane, and that I'm right to be worried, given that it happened close to where we live, when Matthew explains that I think the murderer might have been phoning me, I fully expect Dr. Deakin to call for the men in white coats.

"Can you tell me about the calls?" Dr. Deakin looks at me encouragingly, so I have no choice but to tell him even though I know he'll diagnose me with paranoia, especially as I can't tell him why I thought they were coming from the murderer.

By the time we leave the surgery an hour later, I feel so wretched that I refuse to take Matthew's hand as we walk to the car park. In the car, I turn my head away from him and stare out of the window, trying not to give in to tears of hurt and humiliation. Maybe he senses that I'm at breaking point because he doesn't say anything and, when he stops outside the chemist to get the medication Dr. Deakin prescribed for me, I stay in the car, leaving him to deal with it. We travel the rest of the way home in silence, and when we arrive I get out of the car before he's even had a chance to turn the engine off.

"Sweetheart, don't be like this," he pleads, following me into the kitchen.

"What do you expect?" I turn angrily to him. "I can't believe you talked to Dr. Deakin about me behind my back. Where's your sense of loyalty?"

He flinches. "It's where it's always been, where it always will be, right by your side."

"Then why did you have to mention every little thing I've ever forgotten?"

"Dr. Deakin asked for examples of what's been happening and I wasn't going to lie to him. I've been worried about you, Cass."

"So why didn't you tell me instead of making excuses for me and pretending everything was all right? And why did you have to mention that I told the woman in the baby shop that I was pregnant? What has that got to do with the problems I've been having with my memory? Nothing, nothing at all. Now you've made me seem like a fantasist on top of everything else! I explained it to you, I explained that the assistant misunderstood when I told her the sleep-suit was for me and that by the time I realized she thought I was pregnant it was easier to go along with it. Why you chose to tell Dr. Deakin about it is beyond me."

He sits down at the kitchen table and puts his head in his hands. "You ordered a pram, Cass."

"I didn't order a pram!"

"You didn't order an alarm either."

I grab the kettle angrily, banging it against the tap as I fill it. "Weren't you the one who said I must have been tricked into ordering it?"

"Look, all I want is for you to get the help you need." There's a pause. "I didn't realize your mum was diagnosed with dementia when she was forty-four."

"Dementia isn't usually hereditary," I say sharply. "Dr. Deakin said so."

"I know, but it would be stupid to carry on pretending that you don't have a problem of some sort."

"What, that I'm not amnesic, deluded and paranoid?"

"Don't."

"Well, I'm not going to take whatever it is that he prescribed for me."

He raises his head and looks at me. "It's only something for stress. But don't take it if you think you can cope without it." He gives a hollow laugh. "Maybe I'll take it instead."

Something in his voice brings me up short and when I see how strained he looks, I feel terrible for never having put myself in his place, for never having thought what it must be like for him to see me going to pieces. I go over and crouch next to his chair, putting my arms around him.

"I'm sorry."

He kisses the top of my head. "It's not your fault."

"I can't believe I've been so selfish; I can't believe that I've never thought what it must be like for you to have to put up with me."

"Whatever it is, we'll get through it together. Maybe you just need to take things easy for a while." Taking my arms from around him, he looks at his watch. "Let's start now. While I'm here, I'm not going to let you do a thing, so why don't you sit down while I rustle up some lunch."

"All right," I say gratefully.

I sit down at the table and watch him take the makings of a salad from the fridge. I feel so tired, I could sleep here, right now. Although it had been humiliating to have my catalog of errors spread out before me, I'm retrospectively glad that I've seen Dr. Deakin, especially as all he thinks I'm suffering from is stress.


I look over at the boxes of pills Dr. Deakin prescribed, lying near the kettle. It's a road I don't really want to go down but it's comforting to know that they're there if I ever feel I can't cope, especially now that Matthew is going back to work and Rachel is flying out to Siena today. But with all the lesson preparation I have to do in the next couple of weeks, I'll be too busy to worry.

As I sit there, I remember the day I found Mum

standing in the kitchen, staring at the kettle and, when I asked her what she was doing, she said that she couldn't remember how to switch it on. Suddenly, I miss her more than I ever have. The pain is acute, almost physical, and leaves me breathless. I want more than anything to be able to take her hand in mine and tell her that I love her, for her to put her arms around me and tell me that everything will be all right. Because sometimes I'm not sure that it will be.

# SUNDAY, AUGUST 9TH

I never thought I was a DIY kind of girl but I enjoy helping Matthew with his garden shed. It's nice to be able to focus on something different and to feel at the end of the day that I've achieved something. It's also a nice way to spend his birthday.

"Gin-and-tonic time," he says, as we stand admiring our handiwork. "In the shed. I'll get the drinks, you get the chairs."

So I drag two chairs into the shed and we christen it with another of Matthew's special G&Ts, which he makes with fresh lime juice and a splash of ginger ale. We take our time over dinner outside and, when dusk begins to fall, we go back inside to watch a travel documentary, leaving our dishes to deal with later. It's not long before Matthew starts yawning, so I tell him to go on up to bed while I clear up.

I go into the kitchen and head for the dishes stacked by the dishwasher. I'm almost there when, out of the corner of my eye, I see it lying on the side at the far end of the kitchen, near the door that leads to the garden, and I freeze in mid-step, one arm half-outstretched in front of me, not daring to move. Danger permeates the air, settling on my skin, telling me to run, to get out of the kitchen, out of the house, but my limbs are too heavy, my mind too chaotic for flight. I want to call Matthew but my voice, like my body, is paralyzed by fear. Seconds pass, and the thought that he could burst through the back door at any moment brings my legs to life and I stumble into the hall.

"Matthew!" I cry, collapsing onto the stairs. "Matthew!"

Galvanized by the fear in my voice, he comes tearing back out of the bedroom.

"Cass!" he shouts, running down the stairs, reaching me in seconds. "What is it? What's the matter?" he says, holding me close.

"In the kitchen!" My teeth are chattering so badly I can hardly get the words out. "It's in the kitchen, lying on the side!"

"What is?"

"The knife!" I gabble. "It's there, in the kitchen, on the side, near the door!" I clutch his arm. "He's out there, Matthew! You have to call the police!"

Taking his arms from around me, he puts his hands on my shoulders.

"Calm down, Cass." His voice is steady, soothing, and I take a gulp of air. "Now, start again—what's the matter?"

"The knife, it's on the side in the kitchen!"

"What knife?"

"The one he used to kill Jane with! We have to call the police, he might still be in the garden!"

"Who?"

"The murderer!"

"You're not making any sense, sweetheart."

"Just call the police," I plead, wringing my hands. "It's there, the knife, in the kitchen!"

"All right. But, first, I'll need to take a look."

"No! Just phone the police, they'll know what to do!"

"Let me go and check first."

"But . . ."

"I will call them, I promise." He pauses, giving me time. "But before I do, I need to see the knife because they'll ask me to describe it and they'll want to know exactly where it is." He frees himself gently and eases past me.

"What if he's in there?" I ask fearfully.

"I'll just look from the door."

"All right. But don't go in!"

"I won't." He moves toward the kitchen door. "Where did you say it was?" he asks, craning his neck around the doorway.

My heart thumps painfully. "On the side, near the back door. He must have come in from the garden."

"I can see the knife I used earlier to cut the limes," he says calmly, "but that's all."

"It's there, I saw it!"

"Can you come and show me?"

I lift myself from the stairs and, holding on to him, look fearfully into the kitchen. Over by the door, lying on the side, I see one of our small black-handled kitchen knives.

"Is that what you saw, Cass?" Matthew asks, watching my face. "Is that the knife you saw?"

I shake my head. "No, it wasn't that one, it was much bigger, like the one in the photo."

"Well, it seems to have gone," he says reasonably. "Unless it's somewhere else. Shall we go and look?"

I follow him into the kitchen, still hanging on to him. He makes a show of looking around, humoring me, and I know he doesn't believe there ever was another knife. And I start weeping pathetically, from despair that I'm going mad.

"It's all right, sweetheart." Matthew's voice is kind but he doesn't put his arms around me, he stays as he is as if he can't bring himself to comfort me.

"I saw the knife," I sob. "I know I did. This isn't the same one."

"So what are you saying? That someone came into the kitchen, replaced the knife I used earlier with a larger knife and swapped them back again?"

"He must have."

"If that's what you really think, you'd better call the police because there's definitely a maniac on the loose."

I look up at him through my tears. "That's what I've

been trying to tell you! He's trying to frighten me; he wants me to be scared!"

He walks over to the table and sits down, as if he's considering what I've just said. I wait for him to say something but he sits staring into space and I realize he's beyond speaking, because there are no words to describe how my insistence that there's a murderer after me makes him feel.

"If there was a reason, however small, why the murderer is targeting you, maybe I could understand," he says quietly. "But there's no damn reason at all. I'm sorry, Cass, but I don't know how much more of this I can take."

The desperation in his voice brings me to my senses. It's a struggle to get a grip on myself but the fear of Matthew leaving me is greater than the fear of the murderer getting me.

"I must have made a mistake," I say shakily.

"So you don't want to call the police?"

I fight the urge to tell him that, yes, I want the police to come and search the garden. "No, it's fine."

He gets up. "Can I give you a piece of advice, Cass? Take the pills the doctor prescribed for you. Then we might both get some peace of mind."

He leaves, not quite slamming the door behind him but almost. In the silence that follows I look at the little knife lying innocently on the side. Even from the corner of an eye it would be impossible to mistake it for something much more menacing. Unless you were mad, delusional, neurotic. It decides me. I walk over to the kettle and reach for the packet of pills. Dr. Deakin had said to start with one, three times a day, but that I could up the dose to two if I felt really anxious. Really anxious doesn't come anywhere near to describing how I feel but two is better than nothing so I pop them out and swallow them down with a glass of water.

# MONDAY,
# AUGUST 10TH

A figure looms over me, dragging me from sleep. I open my mouth to scream but nothing comes out.

"You didn't have to sleep down here, you know." Matthew's voice comes from a long way off. It takes me a while to work out that I'm lying on the sofa in the sitting room. At first, I'm not sure why. Then I remember.

"I took two of the pills," I mumble, struggling to sit up. "And then I came to sit in here. They must have knocked me out."

"Maybe you should only take one next time, as you're not used to them. I just came to tell you that I'm off to work."

"All right." I sink back onto the cushions. I sense

he's still angry but sleep is dragging me back. "I'll see you later."

When I next open my eyes I think at first that he's come back, or that he didn't leave at all, because I can hear him speaking. But he's leaving me a message on the answering machine.

I get to my feet, feeling strangely disorientated. I must have been in a really deep sleep not to have heard the phone ringing. I look at the clock; it's nine-fifteen. Going into the hall, I activate the answerphone.

"Cass, it's me. You're obviously still asleep or in the shower. I'll phone back later."

As messages go, it's pretty unsatisfactory. I take a couple of seconds to clear my head then call him back.

"Sorry, I was in the shower."

"I was just phoning to see how you are."

"I'm fine."

"Did you go back to sleep?"

"For a while."

He pauses, and I hear a small sigh. "I'm sorry about last night."

"Me too."

"I'll come home as early as I can."

"You don't have to."

"I'll call you before I leave."

"All right."

I put the phone down, aware that it's one of the most stilted conversations we've ever had. The reality suddenly hits me of how all this has affected our relationship, and I wish I hadn't sounded ungracious when he offered to come home early. Desperate to put things right between us, I reach for the phone to call him back and when it starts ringing before I've even dialed his number, I know he feels as wretched as I do.

"I was about to call you," I say. "I'm sorry if I sounded ungrateful. I was still feeling drowsy from the pills."

He doesn't say anything and, thinking he's not impressed with my apology, I decide to try a bit harder. Until I realize it isn't Matthew at the end of the line.

My mouth goes dry. "Who's there?" I ask sharply. "Hello?" The menacing silence confirms my greatest fear, not that he's back, but that he never went away. The only reason he didn't phone on Thursday or Friday was because Matthew was home. If he's phoned today, it's because he knows I'm home alone again. Which means he's watching the house. Which means he's close by.

Fear crawls over my body, prickling my skin. If I needed proof that the knife I saw in the kitchen last night was real and not my mind playing tricks on me, I have it. Dropping the phone, I run to the front door and shoot the bolt with trembling fingers. I turn to the alarm, trying to remember how to isolate certain rooms, my mind racing, trying to get air into my lungs to calm my breathing, trying to work out where I'll be safest. Not the kitchen, because he managed to get in through the back door last night, not in one of the bedrooms, because if he gets in I'll be trapped upstairs. So the sitting room. The alarm set, I run into the sitting room and slam the door shut. I still don't feel safe, because there's no key to lock it, so I look for something to push against the door. The nearest thing is an armchair and as I maneuver it into place, the phone starts ringing again.

Fear squeezes the rest of the air from my lungs. All I can think about is the knife I saw last night. Was there blood on it? I can't remember. I scan the room, looking for a weapon to protect myself with and my eyes fall on a pair of iron tongs lying in the fireplace. I run over and snatch them up then cross to the windows and pull the curtains shut, first the window that looks onto the back garden, then the one that looks onto the front, terrified that he's watching, that he's outside looking in. The sudden darkness increases my terror so I flick the light switches quickly. I can barely think straight. I want to call Matthew but the police will get here faster. I look around for the phone and when I realize that I don't have one, because I left it in the hall, and my mobile, even if I had it on me, wouldn't work down here, all the fight goes out of me. There's nothing I can do. I can't fetch the phone from the hall in case he's already out there. All I can do is wait until he comes and finds me.

Stumbling over to the sofa, I crouch down behind it, clutching the tongs, my whole body shaking. And the phone, which had stopped ringing, starts up again, mocking me. Tears of fright fall from my eyes—until I realize it's stopped. I hold my breath—and it starts ringing again. The tears come back, and then the ringing stops and I hold my breath again in case this time he really has gone away. But then it starts up again, dashing my hopes. Caught up in his vicious circle of fear, hope, fear, hope, I lose all sense of time. And then, tired of playing with my emotions, he eventually stops calling.

At first the silence is welcome. But then it becomes as threatening as the incessant ringing. It could mean anything. Maybe he hasn't tired of tormenting me, maybe he's stopped phoning because he's here, in the house.

There's a noise in the hall—the click of the front door opening, then closing. Soft footsteps approaching. I stare at the sitting room door in terror and, as the handle begins to turn, dread descends on me, shrouding me like a blanket, wrapping me in its menace, suffocating me so that I can't breathe. Sobbing openly now, I leap to my feet and run to the window, desperately pushing aside the curtains, and the pots of orchids that are on the sill. As I fling the window open, I become aware of the door pushing against the armchair and am just about to climb into the garden when a siren pierces the air. And above its frantic shrieking, I hear Matthew calling my name from the other side of the door.

It's hard to describe how I feel once I've pushed the armchair out of the way and am clinging on to him, gabbling hysterically about the murderer being outside.

"Hold on—let me turn the alarm off!"

He tries to take my arms from around him but, before he can, the phone starts ringing again.

"It's him!" I cry. "It's him! He's been phoning me all morning!"

"Let me turn the alarm off!" Matthew says again. Shaking himself free, he goes over to the keypad and silences the alarm in mid-shriek. Only the shrill of the telephone remains.

Matthew picks it up. "Hello? Yes, it's Mr. Anderson." I stare at him wild-eyed, wondering why he's telling the murderer his name. "I'm sorry, Officer, I'm afraid it's another false alarm. I came home to check on my wife because she wasn't answering the phone and I didn't realize she'd set the alarm so I triggered it when I came in. I'm sorry you've been troubled. No, really, everything's fine."

The pennies drop with agonizing slowness, one after the other. Waves of shame flood my body, turning my skin hot. I sink onto the stairs, painfully aware that somehow, once again, I've got it wrong. I try to pull myself together, for Matthew's sake as well as mine, but I can't stop shaking. My hands seem to have taken on a life of their own and, in an effort to hide them from him, I cross my arms over my body and tuck them out of sight.

Matthew finishes reassuring the police that they don't need to come out and makes another call, again reassuring the person at the other end that everything is fine and that there's nothing to worry about.

"Who was that?" I ask dully.

"The office." He stays with his back turned as if he can't bring himself to look at me. I don't blame him. If I were in his shoes, I'd walk straight out the front door and never come back. "Valerie asked me to let them know that you were all right." Now he turns and I wish he hadn't because of the bewildered look on his face. "What's going on, Cass? Why wouldn't you answer any of my calls? I've been worried sick about you. I've been phoning you on and off for the best part of an hour. I even tried your mobile in case you were upstairs. I thought something had happened to you."

I give a harsh laugh. "What, that I'd been murdered?"

Shock registers on his face. "Is that what you wanted me to think?"

I regret my words instantly. "No, of course not."

"Then why didn't you answer my calls?"

"I didn't know they were from you."

"You must have known; my number comes up!" He runs his hand through his hair, trying to understand. "Were you trying to teach me some kind of lesson, is that what this is about? Because if you were, I'm not sure I'll be able to forgive you. Have you any idea what I've just been through?"

"What about me?" I cry. "What about what I've gone through? Why did you have to keep phoning? You know about the calls I've been receiving."

"I kept phoning because when you hung up without saying goodbye, I knew you were upset and I wanted to make sure you were all right! And why did you presume it was one of those calls without even checking the number? Nothing you say adds up, nothing at all!"

"I didn't check who was calling because I got another silent call immediately after yours! After that, I was too scared to answer in case it was him again."

"So scared that you barricaded yourself inside the sitting room?"

"Well, at least you know how much those calls frighten me."

He shakes his head wearily. "This has got to stop, Cass."

"Don't you think I want it to?" He walks toward the door. "Where are you going?"

"Back to work."

I look at him in dismay. "Can't you stay?"

"No. When I couldn't get through to you, I had them reschedule a meeting."

"Then can you come back as soon as it's finished?"

"No, I'm afraid not. There are too many people away."

"But you told me earlier that you'd try and come home early!"

He sighs. "I've just taken an hour out of my working day to come and check up on you, so I'll be home at the usual time," he says patiently. He takes the car key from his pocket. "I need to go."

He leaves, closing the front door firmly behind him, and I wonder how much more he's going to be able to take before he snaps completely. I hate myself, I hate what I've become.

Desperate for a cup of tea, I go into the kitchen and switch on the kettle. If it hadn't been for the knife I'd seen lying on the side last night, I would have coped better this morning. The call would still have upset me but I wouldn't have been so traumatized that I couldn't check who the next call was coming from. If I had, I would have seen it was from Matthew, I would have answered it and everything would have been all right.

Now, it seems ridiculous I was so terrified that I barricaded myself into the sitting room. *You're going mad*, says a singsong voice in my head. *You are going mad.*

I carry my tea to the sitting room. The window I tried to climb out of is still open and, as I go to close it, I realize that it could have been me that set off the alarm, not Matthew. The thought that it might have been a joint effort—me with the window, Matthew with the front door—makes me start laughing and it feels so good I don't try to control it. As I walk toward the other window, the one that looks onto the front of the house, I'm still laughing, a laugh that I recognize borders on hysteria. I pull the curtains back—and the laughter dies in my throat. Because standing in the road outside is the man, the man I saw before, walking past the house, the man that could be our new neighbor, the man that could be my silent caller, the man that could have murdered Jane. We stare at each other for a moment and then he walks away, not toward the houses at the top of the road but in the other direction, toward the woods.

The little strength I had left drains from my body and I walk into the kitchen, not to fetch my computer but to swallow down some of my pills. They make the rest of the day just about bearable. I spend it huddled on the sofa, only stirring an hour before Matthew gets home. And when he does, we have the most silent dinner ever.

# WEDNESDAY,
# AUGUST 12TH

The sound of relentless rain drags me from my sleep. My limbs feel heavy, as if I'm wading through water. I force my eyes open, wondering why everything is so difficult, and remember the pills I took in the middle of the night, like a child sneaking a midnight feast. It's amazing how quickly they've become my crutch. I'd already taken two yesterday, swallowed down hastily with my cup of tea as soon as Matthew left for work, because I knew I couldn't afford a repeat of the previous day, when I'd barricaded myself in the sitting room. They did the trick because when my silent call had come in, I hadn't gone into a blind panic, I had answered, listened and hung up. In short, I had done what he required of me. It hadn't stopped him from phoning back, but by then I'd been too drowsy to make it to the phone and after, I'd been in such a deep sleep that I wouldn't have heard it ring again anyway. When I eventually woke, just before Matthew got home, I was shocked at how easy it had been, once again, to sleep away the day, and I vowed not to take any more pills.

But then, last night, on the news, there'd been an update on Jane's murder. The police now think she picked up her killer before arriving at the lay-by—which means that he would have been in the car when I drove past.

"So she did have a lover," Matthew said.

"Why do you say that?" I demanded, trying to hide the agitation I felt. "Maybe she was just giving somebody a lift."

"Not unless she was out of her mind. I can't imagine any young woman being foolish enough to stop and pick up a total stranger. I mean, would you?"

"No, I wouldn't. But it was a terrible night and maybe he flagged her down."

"Maybe he did. But I think that once the police have delved a bit further into her background, they'll find that they were right the first time and that she had a lover. So whoever killed her wouldn't be after anyone else. As I said before, it was personal."

Even though I still didn't believe that Jane had had a lover, his words had calmed me. "I hope you're right," I said.

"I know I'm right. You can stop worrying, Cass.

Whoever's responsible will be behind bars before you know it."

But then Jane's husband had come on, hounded by a reporter who asked him if he could confirm that his wife had had a lover. In his refusal to answer he was quietly dignified, just as he was at his wife's funeral, and the terrible guilt I feel whenever I think of Jane was magnified a hundred-fold. It pressed down on me, crushing me with its intensity. We'd gone up to bed but the thought that, as I was driving past Jane's car, the killer was watching me through the window, made sleep impossible. I was so wound up that I'd had to go downstairs at three in the morning and pop a couple of pills just to be able to get through the rest of the night. Which is why I'm feeling so sluggish.

I look at Matthew lying beside me, his face relaxed in sleep. My eyes fall on the clock: it's eight-fifteen, which means it's Saturday, otherwise he'd already be up. Reaching out, I run a finger down his cheek, thinking how much I love him. I hate that he's seen a side of me that even I didn't know existed, I hate that he must be wondering what on earth he got himself into by marrying me. Would he still have married me if I'd been honest with him and told him that Mum had been diagnosed with dementia at the age of forty-four? It's a question that's plaguing me. It's also a question I'm not sure I want to know the answer to.

The need to show him how much I appreciate him focuses my mind. Planning to bring him breakfast in bed, I throw the covers off, swing my legs from the bed and sit for a moment, because it seems too much of an effort to actually stand. My eyes fall on Matthew's work clothes neatly laid out on the chair—a clean shirt, a different tie from the one he wore yesterday—and I realize it's not Saturday but . . . Wednesday; and that for just about the first time since I've known him, Matthew has slept through his alarm.

Knowing he'll be appalled, I reach over to shake him awake—then stop, my hand poised in midair. If I let him carry on sleeping, he might still be around when my caller checks in. And then he could hear the call for himself.

My heart pounding, because here I am, about to deceive him again, I lie back down and pull the covers over me quietly. I face the clock, hardly daring to breathe in case I wake him, watching the hands as they move painfully slowly toward eight-thirty, then eight-forty-five. I feel bad making him late for work but I tell myself that if he had taken the calls seriously, I wouldn't have had to resort to this. Yet how can I blame him for not taking them seriously when I've never told him that I saw Jane in her car that night? If I had, he would have understood why I think they're coming from the murderer.

He wakes of his own accord just before nine, leaping out of bed with a cry of alarm.

"Cass! Cass, have you seen the time? It's almost nine!"

I do a good impression of someone roused from a deep sleep.

"What? No, it can't be."

"It is! Look!"

Rubbing my eyes, I sit up. "What happened to your alarm? Did you forget to put it on?"

"No, I must have slept right through it. Didn't you hear it?"

"No, otherwise I would have woken you up." The lie slips easily out of my mouth and sounds so false that I'm sure he's going to realize I knew all along. But he's distracted, looking between the clock and his clothes, his hand in his hair, trying to understand how it could have happened.

"Even with the best will in the world, I'm not going to make it to the office much before ten," he groans.

"Does it really matter? You're never late and you often work longer hours than you should," I point out.

"No, I suppose not," he concedes.

"Then why don't you shower while I make breakfast?"

"All right." He reaches for his phone. "I'd better let Valerie know."

He calls Valerie to tell her he won't be in until ten and, leaving him to shave and shower, I go down to the kitchen, feeling as tense as I always do, despite Matthew's presence. I never thought I would actually want my silent caller to phone but the thought that he might not makes me sick with apprehension. Because if he doesn't, it means he knows Matthew is here.

"Not hungry?" Matthew asks over breakfast, looking at my empty plate.

"Not at the moment. If the phone rings," I go on hesitantly, "will you answer it? If it is one of those calls, I'd like you to hear it for yourself."

"As long as they phone within the next ten minutes."

"And if they don't?"

He frowns, then tries to look sympathetic, but the cracks are starting to show. "I can't hang around all day, sweetheart."

Less than ten minutes later, my prayers are answered. The phone starts ringing and we go to the hall together. He lifts the receiver and checks the number. It's withheld.

"Don't say anything," I mouth. "Just listen."

"OK."

He takes the call and, after listening for a few seconds, reaches out and puts on the loudspeaker so that I can hear the silence for myself. I can see that he's dying to say something, to ask who is there, so I put my finger on my lips and motion to him to hang up.

"Is that it?" he asks, unimpressed.

"Yes. It wasn't the same, though." The words spill out of my mouth before I can stop them.

"What do you mean, it wasn't the same?"

"I don't know, there was just something different about it."

"In what way?"

I shrug, my face flushing. "Usually, I can sense someone there. Today, I couldn't. The silence—it was different."

"Silence is silence, Cass." He checks his watch. "I'm going to have to get going." I stand there mutely and he gives my shoulder a squeeze. "Maybe it sounded different because it was on loudspeaker."

"Maybe."

"You're not convinced."

"It's just that the calls are usually more menacing."

"Menacing?"

"Yes."

"Well, maybe that's because you're usually on your own when they come through. There's nothing sinister in the calls, sweetheart, so stop thinking there is. It's just some call center trying to get through, that's all."

"You're probably right," I say.

"I am," he says firmly, and he sounds so certain that, suddenly, I decide to believe him, I decide to believe that all along the calls have been coming from a call center on the other side of the world. A huge weight lifts from my shoulders. "Why don't you relax in the garden today?" he suggests.

"I need to do some shopping first, there's hardly a thing to eat in the house."

"I don't suppose you want to make one of your curries for tonight, do you?"

"Good idea," I say, happy at the thought of spending the afternoon pottering in the kitchen.

He leaves me with a kiss and I run upstairs to fetch my bag, wanting to get to the farmer's market in Browbury before it gets too busy. As I pull the front door closed behind me, the phone starts ringing. I hover on the doorstep, undecided what to do. What if he knew it wasn't me who answered the phone and is phoning back? Immediately, I'm annoyed with myself. Hadn't I just decided that it was a call center phoning? *Go on*, a voice taunts, *go back and answer it, then you'll know.* But I don't want to put my newfound confidence to the test.

I drive to Browbury and mooch around the market for a while, buying vegetables and coriander for the curry and figs for dessert. At the flower stall, I buy a huge bunch of lilies and head to the wine shop to choose a bottle for the evening. Then I spend a happy afternoon cooking. At one point, above the sound of the radio, I think I hear the phone ringing but instead of panicking I turn the radio up a little louder, determined to stick to what I've decided to believe.

"Are we celebrating?" Matthew asks when he sees me taking a bottle of champagne from the fridge.

"Yes."

He smiles. "Can I ask what?"

"Me feeling a whole lot better," I say, thrilled that I've managed to get through the day without taking any pills.

Relieving me of the champagne, he takes me in his arms. "That's the best news I've had in a long while." He nuzzles my neck. "How much better did you say you felt?"

"Enough to start thinking about us having a baby."

He looks at me delightedly. "Really?"

"Yes," I say, kissing him.

"How about we take the champagne up to bed?" he murmurs.

"I've made your favorite curry."

"I know, I can smell it. We can have it later."

"I love you." I sigh.

"I love you more," he says, scooping me into his arms. And I feel happier than I've felt for a long time.

# THURSDAY, AUGUST 13TH

I sleep late the next day, so Matthew has already left by the time I wake. Remembering the night we spent together, I give a shiver of pleasure. I get out of bed, pad to the bathroom and shower, taking my time. The sun has come back with a vengeance so I pull on shorts and a T-shirt, push my feet into a pair of espadrilles and go downstairs, taking my laptop with me. Today, I'm going to do some work.

I have breakfast, fetch the papers that I need from my school bag and turn on my computer. But it's hard to focus because, annoyingly, I've got one ear out for the phone. The tick of the clock is also distracting me. It seems to be getting louder with each second that passes, drawing my eyes toward the hands as they inch slowly forward toward nine o'clock, then nine-thirty. They come and go without incident and I'm just beginning to believe that it really is all over when the phone starts ringing.

I stare into the hallway from the kitchen, my heart thudding. This is a new day, I remind myself firmly, a new me, one who is no longer afraid of a ringing phone. I push my chair back and go resolutely into the hall, but before I can answer it, the answering machine cuts in and Rachel's voice floods the room.

*"Hi, Cass, it's me, phoning from sunny Siena. I already tried your mobile, so I'll phone back. I have to tell you about Alfie. Oh, my God, he's soooo boring!"*

Laughing with relief, I go upstairs to call her from my mobile. I'm halfway up when the house phone starts ringing again so, guessing it's her, I run back down and snatch it up. But as soon as I put it to my ear, I know, I know that it's not her, just as I knew that the call I heard coming in as I was leaving the house yesterday was him, even though I chose to believe that it wasn't. And I feel such rage at having hope snatched away from me that I cut the call, effectively slamming the phone down. He calls straight back, as I knew he would, so I answer and cut the call, like before. After a minute or so—as if he can't quite believe what I've done—he calls again. So I answer and hang up, and he calls back, so I answer and hang up and he calls back and we go back and forth for a while because, for some reason, our little game amuses me. But then I realize it's one I'm not going to win, because he's not going to leave me alone until I've given him what he wants. So I stay on the phone and listen to his silent menace coming down the line. And then I phone Matthew.

The call goes straight through to his voicemail, so I phone the main number and ask to be put through to his assistant.

"Hello, Valerie, it's Cass, Matthew's wife."

"Hi, Cass. How are you?"

"I'm fine, thanks. I tried to call Matthew but it went straight through to his voicemail."

"That's because he's in a meeting."

"Has he been in there long?"

"Since nine o'clock."

"I suppose once he's in there, he won't come out until it's finished?"

"Well, only to get coffee or something. But if it's urgent, I can get him for you."

"No, it's fine, don't worry. I'll catch him later."

Well, at least I had one day's respite, I tell myself dully as I pop a couple of pills and swallow them down with water. At least I managed to believe for one day that Matthew was right when he said the calls were coming from a call center. And now that I can no longer fool myself, at least I have the pills to help get me through the day.

While I wait for them to take effect, I slump on the sofa in the sitting room, the remote in my hand. I've never watched daytime television before and as I flick through the channels I come across a shopping channel. I watch it for a while, marveling at all the different gadgets that I never knew I needed, and when I see a pair of long silver earrings, which I know Rachel would love, I quickly find a pen and jot down the details so that I can order them later.

An hour or so goes by, then the phone rings and because the pills have begun to work, I feel only apprehension, not dread. It's Matthew.

"Good morning, sweetheart, did you sleep well?" His voice is tender, a legacy of our lovemaking the previous night.

"Yes, I did." I pause, not wanting to spoil the intimacy of the moment by mentioning the call I received.

"Valerie said you called," he prompts.

"Yes. I got another call this morning."

"And?" He can't hide his disappointment and I kick myself for not having found something more loving to say before dragging him back into my nightmare.

"I just thought I'd tell you, that's all."

"So what do you want me to do?"

"I don't know. Maybe we should tell the police."

"We could, but I'm not sure they'd take a few silent calls seriously, not when they're busy looking for a murderer."

"They might if I tell them I think they're coming from the murderer." The words are out before I can stop them and, although I don't hear it, I can imagine Matthew stifling a sigh of impatience.

"Look, you're tired, run-down, it's easy to jump to conclusions when you're feeling a bit fragile. But it's not logical to suppose that the calls are coming from the murderer. Try and remember that."

"I will," I say dutifully.

"I'll see you later."

"All right." I put the phone down, hating that I've destroyed the sense of relief he must have felt yesterday when I told him I was feeling a whole lot better. Ignoring my laptop, I go back to watching the shopping channel until I sink into oblivion.

The phone wakes me. Outside, the sun has shifted toward the afternoon and as my mind clears I instinctively hold my breath. The answering machine picks up the call and my lungs collapse in relief. I expect it to be Rachel, calling me back, but it sounds suspiciously like Mary, our head teacher, saying something about the forthcoming Inset day. I don't want to feel under any more pressure than I already do so I block out the sound of her voice. But once the call is finished, feeling like a student who hasn't done her homework, I fetch my laptop and carry it through to the study to work at the table there.

I've barely made a start when a car accelerates hard in the road outside, making me jump. I listen as it travels up the road toward the other houses, the sound of its engine growing fainter by the second, wondering why I hadn't heard it approaching. Unless it had been sitting outside the house all along.

I try to push the thought away but I can't. Panic sets in and questions tumble feverishly through my mind. Had the car arrived earlier, while I'd been asleep? Who had been driving it? The murderer? Had he been watching me through the window as I slept on the sofa, like a puppet in a play? I know it sounds crazy, my mind tells me it is. But the fear I feel is horribly real.

I run into the hall, grab the car keys from the table and unlock the front door. The glare of the sun catches me unawares and, as I hurry to the car, I duck my head, shielding my eyes with my hand. I drive out of the gate, not really thinking about where I'm going, only intent on getting away, and find myself on the road to Castle Wells. When I arrive, I try two of the smaller car parks but they're both full so I park in the multi-story. I walk aimlessly around the shops, buy a few things, nurse a cup of tea in a café for a while, then walk around the shops a little more, trying to put off the moment when I'll have to go back to the house. At six o'clock, I head for the car park, hoping that Matthew will already be home because the thought of going back to an empty house makes me feel panicky.

Suddenly, my arm is grabbed from behind and with a cry of alarm I whip round. Connie is standing there, a huge smile on her face. The sight of her makes everything normal again and I hug her in relief.

"Don't do that!" I say, trying to gain control of my racing heart. "You're lucky I didn't have a heart attack!"

She hugs me back, her floral perfume familiar and reassuring. "Sorry, I didn't mean to scare you. How are you, Cass? Enjoying the holidays?"

I pull my hair off my face and nod, wondering if I look as crazy as I feel. She's still looking at me, waiting for an answer. "Yes, especially when the weather's as good as it is today," I say, smiling at her. "It's glorious, isn't it? How about you? You must be leaving soon."

"Yes, on Saturday. I can't wait."

"I hope you didn't mind me not coming back to yours after the end-of-year dinner," I go on, because I still feel guilty about pulling out at the last minute.

"No, of course not. Except that as you didn't come, John didn't either, so we had to make our own entertainment."

"Sorry," I say, grimacing.

"It was fine—we put a karaoke thing on the television and tried to drown out the sound of the thunder with our singing. I have an incriminating video somewhere."

"You'll have to show it to me."

"Don't worry, I will!" She takes out her phone and checks the time. "I'm meeting Dan for a drink. Why don't you join us?"

"I won't, thanks, I was just on my way back to the car park. Are you all packed?"

"Almost. I just need to get everything ready for the Inset day—I presume you got the call from Mary confirming Friday the twenty-eighth?—as I only get back on the Wednesday. I'm almost there, how about you?"

"Almost there too," I lie.

"I'll see you on the twenty-eighth then."

"Definitely." I give her a last hug. "Have a great time!"

"You too!"

I carry on to the car park, feeling much better for having seen Connie, despite having lied to her about the work I'd supposedly done. And now I'm going to have to listen to the call Mary left on the answering machine in case there's something she's expecting me to bring to the table at the meeting. Worry gnaws away at me because how can I get down to work when there's so much else going on? If only the murderer was behind bars. He might soon be, I tell myself. Now that the police think that he was somebody Jane knew, surely they'll be able to find him.

I arrive at the car park, take the lift to the fourth floor and head toward Row E, where I left my car. Or where I thought I'd left it, because it isn't there. Feeling stupid, I walk up and down the row and, when I still can't find it, turn and scan Row F. But my car isn't there either.

Baffled, I begin to walk up and down the other rows, even though I know I parked in Row E. And I know I parked on the fourth floor because, knowing I wouldn't find a space on the first two floors, I'd driven straight to the third. It had been full so I'd carried on up here. So why can't I find my car? Within a few minutes, I've covered the whole floor so I take the stairs to the fifth, because maybe I did make a mistake. Again, I walk up and down the rows, sidestepping the cars moving in and out of parking places, trying not to look as if I've lost mine. But there's no sign of my Mini there either.

I go back down to the fourth floor and stand for a moment, trying to get my bearings. There's only one lift so I walk over to it and retrace the steps I would have taken that morning, except in the other direction, until I come to where my car would be. But it isn't there. Tears of frustration prick my eyelids. The only thing I can do is go down to the booth on the ground floor and report it missing.

I head toward the lift but at the last minute I change my mind and make my way down on foot, stopping off at each level to check that my car isn't there. On the ground floor I find the booth, where a middle-aged man is sitting in front of a computer.

"Excuse me, I think my car has been stolen," I say, making an effort not to sound hysterical.

He carries on looking at the screen and, presuming he didn't hear me, I speak again, only louder.

"I heard you the first time," he says, raising his head and looking back at me through the glass.

"Oh. Well, in that case, can you tell me what I should do?"

"Yes, you should take another look."

"I have looked," I say indignantly.

"Where?"

"On the fourth floor, where I left it. I also checked on the second, third and fifth floors."

"So you're not sure where you left it."

"Yes, I'm perfectly sure!"

"If I had a pound for every person who told me their car's been stolen, I'd be a rich man. Do you have your ticket?"

"Yes," I say, taking my purse out of my bag and opening it. "Here." I push the ticket under the hatch, expecting him to take it.

"So how did whoever has taken your car manage to get it through the barrier without the ticket?"

"I presume they pretended they'd lost it and paid here, at the exit."

"What's the registration number?"

"R-V-zero-seven-B-W-W. It's a Mini, black."

He looks at his computer screen and shakes his head. "That car registration hasn't been logged as going through on a reissued ticket."

"What are you saying?"

"I'm saying that your car hasn't been stolen."

"So where is it then?"

"Probably where you left it."

He goes back to his screen and I stare at him, shocked at how much I suddenly hate him. I know it's because of what this might mean—more proof of my disintegrating memory—but I hate the way he's so dismissive and, anyway, I know where I parked my car. I slam my hand against the glass and he eyes me warily.

"If you come with me, I can prove that it's not," I say firmly.

He looks at me for a moment, then turns his head and calls over his shoulder. "Patsy, can you cover for me!" A woman comes out from the office behind. "This lady has had her car stolen," he explains.

She looks at me and grins. "Of course she has."

"I can assure you, I have!" I snap.

The man comes round from the booth. "Come on then."

We go toward the lift together and while we're waiting for it to arrive my mobile rings. I don't really want to answer it in case it's Mary but I know it'll look strange if I don't, so I take it from my bag. When I see that it's Matthew, relief washes over me.

"Hello?"

"You seem pleased to hear from me," he remarks. "Where are you? I've just got home."

"I'm in Castle Wells. I decided to come in and do some shopping but there's a bit of a problem. I think my car's been stolen."

"Stolen?" His voice rises sharply. "Are you sure?"

"Well, it looks that way."

"Are you sure it hasn't just been towed away? Did you forget to put a ticket on it, or stay longer than you should have?"

"No," I say, moving away from the parking attendant and the smirk on his face. "I parked in the multi-story."

"So it definitely hasn't been towed away?"

"No, it's been stolen."

"You haven't just forgotten where you parked it, have you?"

"No! And before you ask, yes, I've checked the whole car park."

"Have you called the police?"

"Not yet. I'm with someone from the car park and we're on our way up to check."

"So you're not sure it's been stolen?"

"Can I call you back in a minute?" I ask, my face now burning. "The lift is here."

"All right."

The lift doors open and people come flooding out. We get into the lift and the man watches as I press the button for the fourth floor. On the way up, we stop at the second, then at the third. At the fourth, I get out, the man following close behind.

"I parked it over there," I say, pointing to the other side of the car park. "Row E."

"Lead the way," he says.

I thread my way through the rows of cars.

"It should be somewhere around here."

"R-V-zero-seven-B-W-W?"

"Yes." I nod.

"It's right there."

"Where?"

"There," he says, pointing.

I follow his eyes and find myself staring at my car.

"It's not possible," I mutter. "It wasn't there before, I promise." I walk over to it, wanting it—perversely—to be the wrong car. "I don't understand. I checked the whole row, twice."

"It's easily done," he says, generous in victory.

"I don't know what to say."

"Well, you're not the first and you certainly won't be the last. Don't worry about it."

"But it wasn't here, it really wasn't."

"Maybe you weren't on the right floor."

"I was," I insist. "I came straight up here and when I couldn't find it I went up to the fifth and then checked the third. I even checked the second floor."

"Did you go up to the sixth?"

"No, because I knew I hadn't gone up to the very top of the car park."

"The seventh is the top."

"It doesn't matter. I parked it on the fourth."

"Yes, you did," he agrees. "Because it's here."

I look around. "Is there another lift?"

"No."

The fight goes out of me. "Well, I'm very sorry to have wasted your time," I say, desperate to be gone. "Thank you."

"You're welcome," he says, walking away with a wave of his hand.

In the safety of my car, I lean my head back against the seat and close my eyes, turning everything around in my mind, trying to work out how I managed to miss my car when I first came up to the fourth. The only conclusion I can come to is that I wasn't on the fourth floor but on the fifth. How could I have made such a stupid, stupid mistake? Even worse is the thought of telling Matthew. If only he hadn't phoned me earlier, if only I hadn't told him that my car had been stolen. I know I should phone him to tell him that I've found it but I can't bring myself to admit that I made a mistake.

I start the engine and head slowly for the exit, my mind heavy with exhaustion. At the barrier I realize that with everything that's happened, I forgot to pay at the machine before leaving the fourth floor. I check my rearview mirror; cars are already stacking up behind me, waiting impatiently for me to go through and, in a complete panic, I press the help button.

"I forgot to pay!" I shout, my voice shaking. A horn sounds behind me. "What do I do?"

Just as I'm wondering if the car-park attendant is going to punish me by making me get out of the car and go to the nearest machine, incurring the wrath of half a dozen drivers, the barrier swings up.

"Thank you," I mouth gratefully toward the box and before he can change his mind and bring the barrier down on top of me, I drive off with a crunch of gears.

As I head out of town I feel so agitated I know I should pull over and wait until I'm calmer before driving on. My mobile rings, giving me the perfect excuse for stopping but, guessing it's Matthew, I carry on. The thought of not going home, of staying in the car and driving until it runs out of petrol, is tempting but I love Matthew too much to want to worry him more than is reasonable.

My mobile continues to ring on and off for the rest of the journey and, as I turn into the drive, Matthew comes hurrying out of the house. His face is twisted with worry, and guilt tangles with my exhaustion.

"Are you all right?" he asks, opening my door before I've even got my seat belt off.

"I'm fine," I say, reaching into the well of the passenger seat for my bag so that I don't have to meet his eyes.

"You could have let me know," he reproaches. "I've been worried."

"Sorry."

"What happened?"

"False alarm. I was looking on the wrong floor."

"But you said you'd checked all the floors."

"Does it really matter? The car hasn't been stolen. Isn't that enough?"

There's a pause while he struggles not to ask me how I could have missed it. "You're right," he says, rallying.

I get out of the car and go into the house. "You look all done in. I'll get dinner, if you like."

"Thanks. I'll go and have a shower."

I stay a long time in the bathroom and an even longer time getting into my old jogging pants in the bedroom, putting off the moment when I'll have to face Matthew again. I feel so depressed that all I want is to fall into bed and sleep the rest of my horrible, horrible day away. I keep expecting Matthew to call up to see where I am but the only noise that comes from the kitchen is the sound of the dinner being prepared.

When I finally go down, I make myself chat away about anything and everything—school, the weather, bumping into Connie—determined not to let him get a word in edgeways, determined to make him think that mislaying the car hasn't fazed me at all. I even write the date of the Inset day on the calendar, telling him that I'm looking forward to seeing everybody again at the meeting and going back to work. But worry gnaws away inside me and I have to force myself to eat the risotto he's made. I want to tell him about the car I suspect was parked outside the house earlier, but how can I after what's happened? All it will sound like is more hysteria, more paranoia on my part.

# FRIDAY, AUGUST 14TH

It's four weeks to the day since Jane's murder and I can't believe how much my life has changed since in so short a space of time. Fear and guilt have become such constant companions that I can't remember what it was like to live without them. And misplacing my car yesterday has really shaken me. If I needed more proof that I'm on the road to dementia, that was it.

It's hard not to feel depressed. I sit lethargically in the sitting room, the television on for company, tuned to the same mind-numbing shopping channel as before. A call comes in at around ten o'clock and when I immediately go into panic mode, my breath trapped in my lungs, my heart accelerating to the point where I feel dizzy, I realize I've become conditioned to experiencing fear every time the phone rings. Even when the answering machine kicks in—so I know it isn't my silent caller—there's no relief, because he *will* be calling.

The letter box clatters, making me jump. How did it come to this, that any noise, not just the phone ringing, makes my heart race, my skin prickle with unease? When had I become so frightened? I'm ashamed—ashamed that I'm no longer the strong person I once was, ashamed that I let the slightest thing get to me. I hate the way I'm holding my breath, listening for the sound of the postman's feet scrunching back down the gravel path so that I'll know it really was him pushing something through the door and not the murderer. I hate the way my stomach jumps into my mouth when I retrieve the post and find a letter addressed to me, I hate the way, as I stare at the handwritten envelope, that my hands start shaking, because maybe it's from him. I don't want to open it but, propelled by something stronger than me—because knowing is better than not knowing—I rip it open and find a single sheet of paper. I unfold it slowly, hardly daring to read the words written there.

*Dear Cass,*
*Thank you for your letter. I can't tell you how much it means to me to know that you have such good memories of your lunch with Jane. I remember her coming home and telling me how well the two of you got on, so I'm glad that you felt the same way. I really appreciate you taking the time to write, let-*

*ters such as yours are incredibly important to me at what is a horrendous time.*

*Thank you also for asking about the girls. They miss their mother dreadfully but are thankfully too young to understand what has happened. All they know is that their mummy has gone to be an angel.*

*I know from your address that you live fairly locally so if you ever see me in the street (unfortunately, my face has become recognizable) please come and say hello. I understand that people don't know what to say but it is hard when I see people avoiding me.*

*Kind regards,*
*Alex*

My breath, which I didn't realize I'd been holding, comes out in a shudder and my eyes blur with tears, from relief that it's only an innocent letter and from desperate sadness for Jane's husband. His kind words of gratitude are like a balm to my soul—except he would never have written them if he knew I'd left Jane to her fate that night. As I reread his letter, each word is like an arrow, piercing my conscience, and suddenly all I want is to tell him the truth. Maybe he would condemn me. But maybe, just maybe, he would tell me that there was nothing I could have done, that Jane was doomed to die long before I drove past. And if it came from him, maybe I'd believe it.

The phone rings, bringing me back to the present where there is no comfort, no forgiveness, just relentless fear and hounding. I snatch it up, wanting to scream at him to leave me alone. But I don't want him to know how terrified I am, so we wait, each with our own agenda. The seconds tick by. And then I realize that if I can sense the menace coming down the line from his end, he can sense the fear coming from mine. I'm just about to hang up when I realize that there's something different about this call.

I strain my ears, trying to work out what it is. Somewhere in the background, I hear the faintest of sounds; a tiny whisper of wind maybe, or the slight rustling of a leaf. Whichever it is, it tells me that he's out in the open and, instantly, Fear, which had gone back to nestling in the pit of my stomach, rises up inside me, threatening to consume me. Adrenaline kicks in, driving me into the study, clearing the blind panic from my eyes so that I'm able to look out into the road and see that it's empty. Relief steps in but Fear, hating to be beaten, reminds me that it doesn't mean the murderer isn't there. Dread takes hold and peppers my skin with tiny beads of sweat. I want to phone the police but something— Reason, maybe—tells me that even if they were to come and search the garden, they wouldn't find him. He—my tormentor—is far too clever for that.

I can't stay in the house to await whatever he's decided for me, like a sitting duck. I run into the hall, throw on the first pair of shoes I find, take the car keys from the table and open the front door. I look around: the drive is clear but I don't want to take any chances so I unlock the car from where I'm standing and cover the few yards between it and the house in a couple of seconds. Inside the car I lock all the doors and drive quickly through the gate, breathing heavily. As I pass the house that was for sale, I see a man standing in the garden, and recognize him as the one I'd seen hanging around the house. I can't see if he has a mobile in his hand but it doesn't matter. He could be my silent caller, he could be Jane's killer, he could be her secret lover. He's also perfectly placed to see Matthew leave for work each morning, to know when I'm alone.

It's time to go to the police. But first, I need to speak to Matthew, I need to tell him what I suspect and I need him to tell me that I could be right because I don't want to get it wrong again. Making a fool of myself in front of him is preferable to making a fool out of myself in front of the police. How can I ask them to check out the man up the road without some sort of proof, or backup from Matthew? They already have me down as an idiot for setting the alarm off.

In my agitation I almost run a red light and, worried that I'll have an accident, I make myself calm down. I wish I could spend the day with someone but Rachel is still in Siena and everyone else is on holiday too, or leaving in the next day or so.

In the end I decide to drive to Browbury, my eyes constantly checking my rearview mirror, making sure no one is following me. I park in the High Street, planning to find somewhere to sit, waste time and pretend to have lunch. Relieved that I have a plan, I grope around for my bag and realize, appalled, that it's not there, that in my haste to leave the house I've left it behind. I need to be able to buy myself at least a drink so I rummage around in the glove compartment for coins. A sharp knock on the window frightens the life out of me and, straightening up, I see John smiling in at me.

Unable to smile back because of the shock he gave me, I turn back to the glove compartment and close it, giving myself time. Back in control, I turn the key back in the ignition and slide the window down.

"You gave me a fright," I say, trying to smile.

"I'm sorry," he says, contrite. "I didn't mean to scare you. Are you arriving or leaving?"

"Both." He looks at me quizzically. "I've just arrived but I seem to have left my bag at home, so now I'm going to have to drive back and fetch it," I explain.

"Can I help out at all?"

I hesitate, weighing up my options. I don't want to encourage him but he knows I'm with Matthew. And I definitely don't want to go back to the house but I can't wander aimlessly around Browbury for the rest of the day without the means to buy myself a coffee and newspaper.

"I don't suppose you'd like to buy me a coffee, would you?"

"I was hoping you'd say that." He puts his hand in his pocket and draws out two one-pound coins. "I'll even pay for your parking, unless you want to get a ticket?"

"I forgot about that," I say, pulling a face. "A pound will be enough though; I'll only need an hour."

"Not if you let me take you for lunch as well as coffee."

"Why not?" I say, my spirits lifting at the thought of two hours of my day now filled. "As long as you'll let me return the favor."

"Done."

He goes over to the parking meter, puts the coins in and hands the ticket through the window.

"Thanks."

I get out of the car and he nods at my feet. "Nice shoes."

I look down at my feet, clad in the old brown moccasins I use for gardening, which used to belong to Mum.

"I was doing some weeding and I forgot to change out of them," I say, laughing. "Are you sure you still want to be seen out with me?"

"Absolutely. Where would you like to go?"

"You choose."

"How about Costello's?"

"Do you have time?"

"Definitely. How about you? You're not in a rush, are you?"

"No, not at all."

I have such a lovely time over the next couple of hours that I don't want it to end. The thought of going home and only having my head for company makes me feel depressed again and I quickly take a sip of water.

"Thank you," I say gratefully, as John signals for the bill. "I really needed that."

"Me too."

"Why's that?" I ask.

"Just that I've been at a bit of a loose end since my girlfriend disappeared off the scene. What about you? Why did you need to get away for a couple of hours? You're not still being plagued by phone calls, are you?"

I look at him sharply. "What do you mean?"

"From the call center. It took my ears quite a long time to recover from the bashing they received."

"I still feel embarrassed about that." I groan.

"I hope that's not why you didn't come for a drink last Friday. We missed you."

"I completely forgot!" All my anxieties come tumbling back. "I'm sorry, John, I feel dreadful!"

"Don't worry about it. You did say that Matthew had a couple of days off and that you might go away somewhere," he reminds me.

I know I should say something, ask if they had a good evening, but I'm too devastated to speak.

"Are you OK?" he asks. "You seem a bit upset."

I nod and look away, out over the High Street at all the people living their lives. "It's just that it's been rather a strange summer."

"Do you want to talk about it?"

I shake my head slowly. "You'll think I'm mad."

"Never."

I look at him and try to smile. "Actually, there's a real possibility I am going mad. My mother had dementia for several years before she died and I'm worried that I might have the same condition."

He stretches his arm out and for a moment I think he's going to take my hand. But he reaches for his water glass. "Dementia and madness aren't the same thing," he says, taking a sip of water.

"No, they aren't," I agree.

"Have you been diagnosed with dementia?"

"No, not yet. I'm meant to be seeing a specialist but I'll probably forget to go." We both start laughing and

I find I can't stop. "God, it's so good to laugh again," I say, still giggling.

"Well, for what it's worth, you don't seem the least bit mad to me."

"That's because you're not living with me on a day-to-day basis. It's not much fun for Matthew when I keep doing stupid things—you know, forgetting to change my shoes when I go out, leaving my bag at home."

"That's the sign of someone who left her house in a hurry, not someone who's mad." He looks questioningly at me, his intense dark eyes refusing to leave mine. "Did you leave in a hurry?"

"I just don't like being in the house on my own anymore," I say, shrugging.

"Since Jane's murder?"

"It's just that everything spooks me. Our house is a little too isolated for my liking."

"But there are other houses nearby, aren't there?"

"Yes." I hesitate, wondering if I should confide in him the true nature of the phone calls I've been getting and tell him about the man up the road. But the waitress arrives with the bill and the moment is lost.

"It's just as well that school starts again soon," John says, taking out his wallet. "We'll have so much to do, we won't have time to dwell on things." He pulls a face. "Inset day on the twenty-eighth. Please don't tell me you've already done all your lesson plans for the coming term."

"I haven't even looked at the syllabus," I confess.

He stretches, his T-shirt rising to show his tanned skin. "Me neither," he confides, grinning.

"Really?"

"Yes, really."

I heave a sigh of relief. "You can't believe how much better that makes me feel. I bumped into Connie yesterday in Castle Wells and she said she'd almost finished."

"Ouch!" He grimaces.

I look at him curiously. "She said that you didn't go back to hers that night, you know, after our end-of-term dinner."

"No, I didn't really feel like it."

"Right," I nod.

"Anyway, what would be the point of going without you there?" he goes on lightly.

"No point at all," I agree. "I'm such the life and soul of the party."

He laughs. "Exactly." But we both know that's not what he meant.

We leave the restaurant and he walks me back to my car.

"Did you buy a sleep-suit, by the way?" I ask.

"I did. A blue one with an elephant on the front. My friend seemed a bit surprised—I chose it because I liked it but I forgot the baby was a girl."

"I'm glad I'm not the only one with a bad memory," I joke.

"There you are, proof that it happens to everyone. Are you doing anything nice this weekend?"

"Just chilling in the garden, I hope."

"Well, have a good rest." He nods at my car. "This is you, isn't it?"

"Yes." I give him a hug. "Thank you, John, for everything."

"My pleasure," he says gravely. "See you back at
school, Cass. Drive safely."

He waits on the pavement until I've pulled out of
the parking space and I set off down the High Street,
wondering what I can do to fill in the rest of the time
until Matthew gets home. As I arrive at the junction
where I would normally turn right, I see a signpost for
Heston and, the next thing I know, I'm driving toward
the village where Jane lived, the village she was driving back to the night she was murdered. I feel a moment of panic, wondering what I'm doing, what I hope
to achieve by going there. But for some reason I feel
compelled to go.

It only takes five minutes to get there. I park on a
road between the park and the pub and get out of the
car. The park is small but beautifully kept. I go through
the gate and walk slowly down the pathways, admiring the wonderful variety of flowers. The few benches
in the shade are taken, mostly by elderly couples having a rest from their afternoon stroll, so I find one in
the sun and sit for a while, glad I've found somewhere
to spend the next couple of hours. I think about Jane,
wondering how many times she sat on this bench, how
many times she walked this path. There's a play area
at the other end of the park where young children are
rocking back and forth on wooden animals and I imagine her helping her children on and off them, or hovering anxiously as they go up and down the slide, as
some of the adults are doing now. And, as always, the

guilt I feel whenever I think about Jane presses down on me.

As I watch, wondering wistfully if Matthew and I will ever be blessed with children, a little girl tries to get off her rocking animal and I can see that for all her determination, she's not going to make it because one of her feet is stuck. Instinctively, I open my mouth to shout out, to warn one of the adults that she's about to fall, but before I can she tumbles to the ground. Her cries of pain bring a man running over but another little girl stretches out her arms to him, wanting to get off her rocking animal, so he scoops her up quickly before stooping to tend to the other child. And as I watch him brush her down and kiss her blonde head, I realize I'm looking at Jane's husband.

Shock runs through me. I stare at him, wondering if I'm mistaken. But with his photo plastered over newspapers and television for the last few weeks, his is a familiar face. Besides, the little girls look like twins. My instinct is to flee, to leave the gardens as quickly as I can before he sees me. But then I calm down. He doesn't know I'm the person who could have saved his wife.

He begins to leave the play area, carrying the child who's been hurt and holding the other by the hand. Both of them are crying as they walk along the path toward the bench where I'm sitting and I can hear him trying to soothe them with promises of plasters and ice cream. But the one in his arms won't be comforted, upset by her grazed knees, one of which is bleeding quite heavily.

"Would you like a tissue for that?" I ask, before I can stop myself.

He comes to a stop in front of me. "It might be a good idea," he says, looking relieved. "It's still a bit of a way to the house."

I take one from my pocket and hand it to him. "It's clean."

"Thank you."

Sitting the injured child down next to me on the bench, he crouches in front of her and shows her the tissue.

"See what this nice lady has given me? Shall we see if it makes your knee better?"

He presses it gently on the graze, soaking up the blood, and her tears miraculously stop.

"Better, Lottie?" her sister asks, looking anxiously at her.

"Better," she says, nodding.

"Thank God for that." Jane's husband looks solemnly up at me. "Imagine what it would have been like if she'd fallen onto concrete, like we used to when we were kids." He removes the tissue. "All gone," he says.

His little daughter peers at her knee and, seemingly satisfied, scrambles down from the bench.

"Play," she says, running over to the grass.

"And now they don't want to go home," he groans, straightening up.

"They're lovely," I say, smiling. "Beautiful."

"Most of the time," he agrees. "But they can be a bit of a handful when they want to be."

"They must miss their mother." I stop, appalled at

what I've just said. "I'm . . . sorry," I stammer. "It's just that . . ."

"Please, don't apologize," he says. "At least you don't pretend not to know who I am. You can't believe the number of people who come to Heston, hoping to bump into me, as if I'm somebody famous. They strike up a conversation with me, usually using the girls as a starting point and then they ask me about their mother, asking if she's at home making the lunch, or if she has blonde hair like the girls. At first, before I got wise to it, I'd find myself having to tell them that she'd died, and then they'd probe further and I'd end up telling them that she'd been murdered. And they'd pretend surprise and say how sorry they were and how awful it must have been for me. It was only after one woman went a step too far and asked me how the police had broken the news to me that I caught on to them." He shakes his head in disbelief. "There must be a name for people like that but I don't know what it is. At least the village shop and the pub get a roaring trade out of it," he adds, giving a rueful smile.

"I'm sorry," I say again. I want to tell him who I am, that I received his letter this morning, but after what he's just said he might think that, like all the others, I came to the park hoping to bump into him, especially as I have no real reason for being in Heston. It's not as if he invited me to come and see him. I get to my feet. "I should go."

"I hope it's not because of what I said." In the bright sunlight I can see streaks of gray in his brown hair and I wonder if they were there before Jane died.

"No, not at all," I reassure him. "I have to get back."

"Well, thank you for coming to the rescue." He looks over to where the girls are playing. "It's all forgotten now, thank goodness."

"You're welcome." I try to smile but the irony of his words make it difficult. "Enjoy the rest of the afternoon."

"You too."

I walk away, my heart hammering in my chest, his words about me coming to his rescue ringing in my ears. They mock me all the way to the gate and out to the car and I wonder what on earth had possessed me to come here, unless it was my need for absolution. What would happen if I went back and told him who I am, and that I saw Jane in the lay-by that night? Would he smile that sad smile of his and tell me that it didn't matter, that it was just as well I hadn't stopped because I might have been murdered too? Or would he be appalled at my non-intervention and point his finger at me and tell everyone in the park that I had done nothing to help his wife. Because I have no way of knowing, I turn on the engine and drive home, but all I can think about is Jane's husband and the two little daughters she left behind.

Although I drive as slowly as I can, I'm home by five. As I go in through the gate my anxiety comes rushing back and I know I'm not going to be able to go into the house, not until Matthew comes back, so I stay in the car. Even in the shade it's hot so I open the windows to try to get a bit of a draft going. My phone beeps, telling me I've got a message, and when I see it's from Mary,

I switch my mobile off. I'm so busy worrying about the work I still haven't done that I don't notice the time passing, so when I see Matthew's car turning into the drive, I think at first that he's come home early. A quick check of my watch tells me it's already six-thirty. He pulls up alongside me and I take the keys from the ignition and get out of the car, making it look as if I've just arrived.

"Beat you," I say, smiling at him.

"You look hot," he remarks, giving me a kiss. "Didn't you have the air conditioning on?"

"I was only in Browbury, so I didn't bother putting it on for the short journey home."

"Did you go shopping?"

"Yes."

"Buy anything nice?"

"No."

We go toward the front door and he unlocks it with his keys. "Where's your bag?" he says, nodding at my empty hands.

"In the car." I walk quickly into the house. "I'll get it in a minute, I need a drink first."

"Hold on, let me turn the alarm off first! Oh, it's not on." Behind me, I sense him frowning. "Didn't you turn it on when you left?"

"No, I didn't think it was necessary as I didn't intend staying out for long."

"Well, I'd rather you turned it on in the future. Now that we have an alarm, we may as well use it."

Leaving him to go and change, I make some tea and carry it out to the garden.

"Don't tell me you went out with those on," he says, when he joins me a few minutes later.

I look down at my feet. Not wanting to give him more to worry about, I fake a laugh. "No, I just put them on."

He smiles and sits down next to me, stretching his long legs out. "So what did you do today, apart from shopping in Browbury?"

"I prepared a few more lessons," I say, wondering why I'm not mentioning that I bumped into John.

"That's good." He looks at his watch. "Ten past seven. When you've finished your tea, change your shoes and I'll take you out to dinner. We may as well get the weekend off to a flying start."

My heart sinks, because I'm still full after my lunch with John.

"Are you sure?" I ask, doubtfully. "Wouldn't you rather stay in?"

"Not unless there's some of your curry left from the other day."

"Sorry."

"So let's go out for one, then."

"All right," I say, relieved he hasn't suggested going to Costello's for pasta.


I go upstairs to change and take a small bag from the wardrobe, hide it under my cardigan and, while he's putting on the alarm, I go out to my car and make a show of taking it from behind the seat. We drive into Browbury and go to our favorite Indian restaurant.

"You know our new neighbor?" I say while we're looking at the menu. "Have you spoken to him at all?"

"Yes, yesterday, when I was scouring the road for you coming back from Castle Wells. He walked past the house and we got chatting. Apparently, his wife left him just before they were due to move in."

"Where was he going?"

"What do you mean?"

"You said he walked past the house."

"Yes, he was going up to his. He must have been for a walk. I said we'd have him round for dinner one evening."

My heart thumps. "What did he say?"

"That he'd love to. That's all right, isn't it?"

I look down at my menu, pretending to study it. "As long as he's not the murderer."

Matthew bursts out laughing. "You are joking, aren't you?"

"Of course." I force a smile. "So, what's he like?"

"He seemed nice enough."

"How old?"

"I don't know—early sixties, I suppose."

"He didn't seem that old when I saw him."

"He's a retired pilot. They probably have to keep themselves in good shape."

"Did you ask him why he's always standing outside our house?"

"No, because I didn't know he was. But he did tell me that he thought it was beautiful so maybe he's been admiring it." He looks at me, a frown on his face. "Is he always standing outside our house?"

"I've seen him there a couple of times."

"Not an arrestable offense," he says, as if he's guessed where I'm going with my questions and is warning me off.

"I didn't say it was."

He gives me an encouraging smile. "Let's choose what we're going to eat, shall we?"

I want to point out to him that a nice enough, retired pilot in his early sixties could still be a murderer but I know he won't go there, let alone tell the police.

# SATURDAY, AUGUST 15TH

The sharp *slam* of the post arriving vibrates through the house as we're having breakfast. Matthew stands, a piece of buttered toast hanging halfway out of his mouth, and walks into the hallway, coming back moments later with a couple of letters and a small package.

"Here," he says, handing it to me. "It's for you."

I eye it apprehensively. Yesterday, the letter had been from Alex but there's little chance the package is from him. "What is it?"

"I don't know." He studies the plain white packaging. "Something you ordered?"

"I didn't order anything." Nervously, I put it on the

kitchen table, almost scared to touch it. Could it have been sent by my silent caller?

"Are you sure?" Matthew puts his hand on my shoulder.

"Positive."

"Do you want me to open it?"

"No, it's all right," I say hastily. Even though I could easily rip it open, I pick it up and carry it to the study. Taking a pair of scissors from the drawer, I snip through the packaging. Inside, there's a small box. I take it out and ease open the lid, my heart pounding. A pair of exquisite silver earrings sit on a black velvet cushion and, recognizing them, relief washes over me.

"Very nice," Matthew says, peering over my shoulder.

I hadn't heard him follow me. "They're for Rachel," I tell him, closing the box. "I didn't expect them to come so quickly."

"For her birthday?"

I think of the cottage on the Ile de Ré. "Yes," I say.

Smiling approval, he leaves to mow the lawn. I slip the earrings into a drawer, and stand for a moment, looking out of the study window, looking across the road to the field opposite. I used to feel so safe here, as if nothing could ever touch us.

The house phone rings. I freeze, then remember it's the weekend. My silent caller has never called on a Saturday before. Even so, I let the answering machine pick up the call. It's Mary, wondering if I got the various messages she left me about the Inset day. My heart drops. The holidays are going to end soon and I still haven't done the work I was supposed to have done.

She carries on talking and jokingly adds that she hopes I haven't lost my mobile because she's also sent quite a few text messages.

After Mary ends her message, the telephone rings again almost immediately. I check the number, wondering if Mary is going to become as persistent as my silent caller. But it's Rachel, so I pick up.

"Hi," I say brightly.

"So, how are you?"

Going mad, I want to tell her. "Busy preparing lessons," I say instead.

"Any more calls?"

"No, not recently," I lie. "What about you? How's Siena?"

"Beautiful. I'm having great fun, despite Alfie." Her throaty laugh comes down the line. "I can't wait to tell you all about him but we're just about to go out."

"No wedding bells then?" I ask, amused.

"Definitely not. Anyway, you know me, I'm not the marrying kind. Why don't we meet for lunch the Tuesday after I get back—the Monday's a bank holiday. It'll be my first day back at work so it'll be nice to have something to look forward to. And you don't go back to school until the Wednesday, do you?"

"No, so lunch on the Tuesday will be lovely. At the Sour Grapes?"

"I'll see you there."

I hang up, realizing that there are only two weeks of the summer holidays left. A blessing and a curse. I can't wait to be away from the house, away from the calls. But all the work looming over me makes going back to school seem impossible.

"Ready?" I look up and see Matthew standing there. He's dressed smartly in khaki trousers and a polo shirt and is carrying a small sports bag.

"Ready?" I frown.

"For our afternoon at the spa."

I nod and force a smile but I'm not ready because I'd completely forgotten that at the restaurant yesterday, he'd surprised me with a couples booking for this afternoon at a spa near Chichester. We went there just after we got engaged, and his gesture last night had eased the tension that remained after the conversation about our new neighbor.

"I just need to put my shoes on," I say, smoothing down the cotton skirt I'd put on this morning instead of the shorts I would have normally worn. So maybe, this morning, I had remembered about the spa.

I run upstairs and stuff a bikini into a bag, thinking about what else I might need.

"We need to go, Cass!"

"Coming!" I pull off the vest top I'm wearing and open the wardrobe door, looking for something a little smarter. I take out a white cotton shirt with tiny buttons and shrug it on. In the bathroom I run a brush through my hair. I'm just about to put some makeup on when Matthew calls again from downstairs.

"Cass, did you hear me, the booking is for two o'clock!"

I glance at the clock and realize that we only have

forty-five minutes to get to Chichester. "Sorry," I say, running down the stairs. "I was looking for my bikini."

We get in the car and as we pull out of the drive, I lean my head back and close my eyes. I feel exhausted, but here in the car with Matthew, where no dangers can reach me, I also feel safe. We turn a sudden corner and, thrown against the door, I open my eyes and blink a couple of times, trying to work out where we are. And then I realize.

"Matthew!" I hear the fear in my voice. "We're heading the wrong way!"

He glances over at me and frowns. "We're going to Chichester."

"I know, but why are we going down Blackwater Lane!" The words feel thick on my tongue.

"Because this way will take ten minutes off our journey time. We'll be late otherwise."

My heart thumps. I don't want to go this way—I can't! Through the windscreen I see the lay-by coming up and my mind starts spiraling. Panic-stricken, I turn toward the door, my fingers reaching for the handle.

"Cass!" Matthew cries, alarm in his voice. "What are you doing? You can't just get out of the car! We're going at forty!" He slams his foot on the brake and the car jolts, throwing me forward. He brings it hurriedly to a stop, just opposite the lay-by where Jane was killed. Someone has laid flowers and the plastic wrapping flutters in the breeze. Horrified to be back where my nightmare began, I burst into tears.

"No!" I sob. "Please, Matthew, we can't stop here!"

"Oh, God," he says wearily. He slips the car into gear, about to move on, then stops. "This is crazy."

"I'm sorry," I sob.

"What do you want me to do? Shall I keep driving? Or do you want to go home?" He sounds at the end of his tether.

I'm crying so hard I can hardly breathe. He reaches over and tries to put his arms around me but I shrug him off. Sighing, he starts doing a three-point turn in the middle of the road, turning the car back the way we came.

"No," I tell him, still sobbing. "I can't go home, I just can't."

He stops in mid-maneuver, leaving the car dangerously at an angle. "What's that supposed to mean?"

"I don't want to go home, that's all."

"Why not?" His voice is calm but I can sense a tension underneath it, hiding something more serious.

"I just don't feel safe there anymore."

He takes a deep breath, steadying himself. "Is this about the murder again? Come on, Cass, the murderer isn't anywhere near our house and he doesn't know who you are. I know Jane's murder has upset you but you need to get over it."

I round on him furiously. "How can I get over it when her killer still hasn't been caught?"

"So what do you want me to do? I've alarmed the whole house for you. Do you want me to drop you off at a hotel somewhere? Is that what you want? Because if it is, just tell me and I'll do it!"

By the time we get home, I'm in such a state that Matthew calls Dr. Deakin, who offers to come out. Even for him I can't stop crying. He asks about my medication and, when Matthew tells him that I haven't been taking it regularly, Dr. Deakin frowns and says that if he prescribed it, it's because I need it. Under his watchful eye, I gratefully gulp down two of the pills and wait for them to take me to a place where nothing matters anymore. And while I wait, he asks me gentle questions, wanting to know what triggered my meltdown. I listen as Matthew explains about me barricading myself into the sitting room while he was at work and, when Dr. Deakin asks if there's been any other worrying behavior on my part, Matthew mentions that the week before I'd become hysterical because I thought I saw a huge knife lying on the side in the kitchen when in reality it was only a small kitchen knife. I sense them exchanging glances and they begin speaking about me as if I'm not there. I hear the word "breakdown" but I don't care because the pills have already begun to work their magic.

Dr. Deakin leaves, urging Matthew to make sure I rest and to call him if I deteriorate further. I spend the rest of the evening lying drowsily on the sofa while Matthew watches television next to me, my hand in his. When the program comes to an end, he turns off the television and asks me if there's anything else worrying me.

"Just all the work I'm meant to do before school starts up again," I say, tears welling in my eyes despite the pills.

"But you've already done quite a lot of it, haven't you?"

My lies have caught up with me. "Some, but there's still a lot to do and I'm not sure I'm going to get it done in time."

"Well, maybe you could ask someone to help you."

"I can't, they've got enough of their own work to do."

"Then can I help?"

"No, not really." I look at him hopelessly. "What am I going to do, Matthew?"

"If you can't get anyone to help and you can't do it on your own, I don't really know."

"I just feel so tired all the time."

He smooths my hair off my face. "If you feel you can't cope, why don't you ask to work part-time?"

"I can't."

"Why not?"

"Because it'll be too late for them to find someone to replace me."

"Nonsense! If something happened to you, they'd have to."

I stare at him. "What do you mean?"

"Just that no one is indispensable."

"But why did you say something might happen to me?"

He frowns. "I was making a point, that's all—as in, if you broke a leg, or got run over by a bus, they'd have to replace you."

"But you said it as if you knew something was going to happen to me," I insist.

"Don't be ridiculous, Cass!" His voice is sharp with

annoyance and I flinch, because he doesn't often raise his voice. He catches the flinch and sighs. "It's just a figure of speech, OK?"

"Sorry," I mumble. The pills are chasing the panic away, bringing sleep in its place.

He puts his arms around me and draws me to him but it feels awkward.

"Just think about speaking to Mary about going back part-time," he says.

"Or not going back at all," I hear myself say.

"Is that what you want, to stop working altogether?" He moves back and looks down at me in puzzlement. "On Thursday, you said you were looking forward to going back."

"It's just that I don't know if I'll manage to do everything that's expected of me, not when I'm feeling like this. Maybe I could ask for a couple more weeks off and go back in the middle of September, once I'm feeling better."

"I doubt whether they'd allow that, not unless Dr. Deakin says you're not fit to go back just yet."

"Do you think he would?" I say, even though there's a part of me telling me to stop, to remember the phone calls, to remember Jane, to remember that I'm not safe at home. But I can't hold on to those thoughts long enough to focus on them.

"He might. Let's just see how you get on with the pills you're taking. There's two weeks until school starts. Once you're taking them on a regular basis, you'll probably feel a lot better."

# FRIDAY,
# AUGUST 28TH

The front door closes behind Matthew. From the bedroom, I listen as he starts the car, drives to the gate and disappears down the road. Silence settles on the house. Struggling into a sitting position, I reach for the two little peach-colored pills lying on my breakfast tray and scoop them into my mouth, washing them down with orange juice. Ignoring the two slices of toasted brown bread, sliced down the middle and arranged artistically rather than just stacked, and the little bowl of Greek yogurt and granola, I lie back against the pillows and close my eyes.

Matthew was right. Now that I'm taking the pills on a regular basis, I feel so much better. My life has

improved dramatically in the last . . . week? Two
weeks? I open my eyes and squint at the clock, looking
for the date. Friday 28 August, so thirteen days. I might
not remember very much but 15 August is ingrained in
my brain as the date I had my breakdown. It was also
Mum's birthday. I only remembered once Dr. Deakin
had left that night and, when I realized I hadn't gone
to lay flowers on her grave, I became distraught all
over again and blamed Matthew for not reminding me.
Which was hardly fair, as I'd never told him her birth
date, something he refrained from pointing out, telling
me instead that I could go the next morning.

I still haven't been because, physically, I can't. I take
two pills before I go to bed so that I sleep all through
the night and, each morning, before he goes to work,
Matthew—taking to heart Dr. Deakin's admonishment
that I should rest—brings me another two along with
my breakfast tray. It means that the anxiety I always
feel once he's left for work has dulled by the time I've
showered and dressed. The downside is that, by mid-
morning, I feel so sluggish that it's hard to put one foot
in front of the other. I spend most of my days drifting
between wake and sleep, sprawled on the sofa, the television switched to the shopping channel because I can't
summon the energy to change it. Sometimes, in the
background, I'm vaguely aware of the telephone ringing but it barely pierces my consciousness and, because
I never answer, the calls become less frequent. He still
calls, just to let me know that he hasn't forgotten me,
but I enjoy imagining his frustration at not being able
to get hold of me.

Life is easy. The pills, powerful though they are, allow me to function on some sort of level because the washing gets done, the dishwasher gets loaded and the house gets tidied. I never really remember doing any of it, which should worry me more than it does because it means the pills are playing havoc with my already failing memory. If I were sensible, I would halve the dose. But if I were sensible I wouldn't have needed the pills in the first place. Maybe if I ate a little more the pills wouldn't affect me as much but it seems that I've lost my appetite as well as my mind. The breakfast Matthew brings me goes into the bottom of the bin and I always skip lunch because I'm too drowsy to eat. So my only meal of the day is the one I make in the evening to have with Matthew.

He has no idea how I spend my days. Because the pills wear off about an hour before he gets home, I have time to clear my head, run a brush through my hair, put on a bit of makeup and get something ready for dinner. And when he asks, I invent work that I've done and cupboards I've tidied out.

I want to shut off the whole outside world. I've been getting so many texts—from Rachel, Mary and Hannah, inviting me for coffee, and John, wanting to chat about lesson plans. I haven't answered any of them yet because I don't feel up to seeing anyone, even less chatting about lesson plans. The pressure I'm already feeling increases and I suddenly decide that the best solution would be to misplace my phone. If I've lost it, I won't have to get back to anyone. And as it barely works in the house, it's not as if it's much good to me anyway.

I fetch my mobile. There are a couple of voicemails and another three text messages but I turn it off without opening any of them. I go down to the sitting room and look around for somewhere to hide it. I walk over to one of the orchids, lift it from its pot, place my mobile in the bottom and put the plant back on top.

In case the pills should make me forget that I have dementia, there are always little reminders to tell me that my brain is slowly disintegrating. I can no longer remember how to work the microwave—I wanted to make myself a cup of hot chocolate the other day but had to resort to a saucepan as the various buttons no longer meant anything to me. And things I remember seeing on the shopping channel but have no memory of ordering keep arriving in the post.

Yesterday, another parcel was delivered. Matthew found it on the doorstep when he arrived back from work.

"This was on the doorstep," he said calmly, even though it was the second one in three days. "Have you ordered something else?"

I turned away so that he couldn't see the confusion in my eyes, wishing I'd ordered something that would have fitted through the letter box so that I could have hidden it before he came home. Coming so close on the heels of the spiralizer that arrived on Tuesday was humiliating.

"Open it and see," I said, playing for time.

"Why, is it for me?" He gave the box a shake. "It sounds like some kind of tool."

I watched while he took off the packaging, my brain trying to remember desperately what I had ordered.

"A potato slicer." He looked at me questioningly.

"I thought it looked fun." I shrugged, remembering how a potato had been turned into chips in seconds.

"Don't tell me, it's to go with the vegetable-spiral thing that came on Monday. Where on earth are you getting these things from?"

I told him that I saw them advertised in one of the magazines that come with the Sunday papers because it sounded better than admitting I got them from a shopping channel. In future, to avoid temptation, I'm going to have to leave my bag in the bedroom. I've got into the habit of taking it downstairs with me in the mornings in case I need to make a quick getaway, which means my credit card is easily accessible. But even if my silent caller did turn up, I'd be incapable of going very far. Because of the pills, driving is out of the question, so I'd only get as far as the garden, which wouldn't be much help.

Sometimes I think that he has turned up. I'll start awake, my heart beating furiously, convinced that he's been watching me through the window. Because my instinct is to flee, I half get up from the chair, then sink back down again, not really caring, telling myself that if he is there, well, at least it would be over. I'm lucid enough to know that as well as the pills being my life-line, they'll also be the death of me, one way or another. Or, at the very least, the death of my marriage, because how much longer can I expect Matthew to put up with my increasingly bizarre behavior?

Aware that the pills I took are already making my head a little woolly, I have a quick shower and put on what has become my uniform, loose jeans and a T-shirt, as I've worked out they still look presentable after a day on the sofa. One day, I wore a dress and it was so creased by the time I finished sleeping the day away, Matthew joked I must have spent it crawling through the bushes in the garden.

Leaving my bag where it is, I carry the tray downstairs, tear the toast into tiny pieces and take it into the garden for the birds. I wish I could sit for a moment and enjoy the sun but I only feel safe in the house with the doors locked. I haven't been out since I started taking the pills regularly. I've been relying on food from the freezer for our evening meals and I've resorted to using the cartons of long-life milk that we keep for emergencies. Matthew noticed last night that the fridge was almost empty, so I'm hoping he'll suggest going shopping tomorrow.

My limbs feel heavy as I go back into the house. I rummage in the freezer and find some sausages and then rummage in my brain, searching for something I can do with them to turn them into an evening meal. I know there are a couple of onions hanging around somewhere and there's bound to be a jar of tomatoes in the cupboard. Dinner sorted, I go gratefully into the sitting room and sink onto the sofa.

The presenters on the shopping channel have become like old friends. Today, the goods on offer are watches studded with little crystals, and I'm glad I'm too tired to go and fetch my bag from the bedroom.

The house phone starts ringing; I close my eyes and let sleep take me. I love the feeling of being slowly lowered into oblivion and, when the pills begin to wear off some hours later, the gentle tugging back to reality. Today, as I drowse in the no-man's-land between sleep and wake, I become aware of a presence, of someone nearby. It feels as if he's in the room looking down at me, not on the other side of the window. I lie very still, my senses sharpening as the seconds tick by, my breathing becoming shallower, my body tensing. And when I can bear the waiting no longer, I snap my eyes open, expecting to see him looming over me with a knife in his hand, my heart beating so hard I can hear it thudding in my chest. But there is no one there and when I turn my head toward the window, there is no one there either.

By the time Matthew comes home an hour later, the sausage casserole is in the oven, the table is set, and to make up for the lack of any kind of second course, I've opened a bottle of wine.

"That looks good," he says. "But, first, I need a beer. Can I get you something?" He walks over to the fridge, opens the door. Even I flinch at the empty shelves. "Oh, didn't you do any shopping today?"

"I thought maybe we could go tomorrow."

"You said you'd go on your way back from your meeting," he says, taking out a beer and closing the fridge door. "How did it go, by the way?"

I look surreptitiously at the calendar on the wall and see the words INSET DAY under today's date. My heart sinks.

"I decided not to go," I tell him. "There didn't seem much point when I'm not going back to work."

He looks at me in surprise. "When did you decide that?"

"We talked about it, remember? I said I didn't feel up to going back and you said we could talk to Dr. Deakin about it."

"We also said we'd wait to see how you felt after a couple of weeks on the pills. But if that's what you want . . ." He takes a bottle opener from the drawer and takes the cap off his beer. "Does Mary think she'll be able to find somebody to replace you at such short notice?"

I turn away so that he can't see my face. "I don't know."

He takes a drink straight from the bottle. "Well, what did she say when you told her you weren't going back?"

"I don't know," I mumble.

"She must have said something," he persists.

"I haven't told her yet. I only really decided today."

"But she must have wanted to know why you weren't going to the meeting."

I'm saved from answering by a ring at the doorbell. Leaving him to go and answer it, I sit down at the table and put my head in my hands, wondering how I could have forgotten about the Inset day. It's only when I hear Matthew apologizing profusely to someone that I realize Mary is at the door and, horrified, I pray that he's not going to invite her in.

"That was Mary." I lift my head and see him standing in front of me. He waits for me to react, to say something, but I can't, I don't know how to anymore. "She's gone," he adds. For the first time in our marriage, he looks angry. "You haven't told her a thing, have you? Why haven't you answered any of her messages?"

"I didn't see them. I've lost my mobile," I tell him, sounding worried. "I can't find it anywhere."

"When did you last have it?"

"I think it might have been the night we went out for dinner. I haven't really been using it as much lately, so I didn't notice until now."

"It's probably somewhere in the house."

I shake my head. "I've looked everywhere, and in the car too. I tried calling the restaurant but they haven't got it either."

"Well, what about your computer, have you lost that, too? And why haven't you been answering the house phone? Apparently, everyone from the school has been trying to get hold of you—Mary, Connie, John. At first they thought we must have gone away on a last-minute holiday but, when you didn't turn up for the meeting today, Mary thought she'd better come round and check that everything was all right."

"It's the pills," I mumble. "They knock me out."

"Then we'd better ask Dr. Deakin to reduce the dose."

"No." I shake my head. "I don't want to."

"If you're capable of ordering things from a magazine, you're capable of getting back to your colleagues, especially your boss. Mary was very understanding but she must be angry."

"Stop going on at me!"

"Going on at you? I've just saved your skin, Cass!"

Knowing he's right, I back off. "What did Mary say?"

He retrieves his bottle of beer from where he left it on the counter when he went to answer the door. "There wasn't much she could say. I told her that you'd had a few health problems over the summer and that you were taking medication and she wasn't altogether surprised. Apparently, she was worried about you last term."

"Oh," I say, deflated.

"She didn't say anything at the time because she thought it was just fatigue making you forgetful and that you'd be all right after the summer break."

I give a hollow laugh. "She's probably relieved I'm not going back then," I say, mortified that Mary had noticed my memory lapses.

"On the contrary—she said they would miss you and to let her know as soon as you feel up to going back."

"That was nice of her," I say, feeling guilty.

"Everybody's rooting for you, Cass. We all want you to get better."

Tears blur my eyes. "I know."

"You'll have to get a medical certificate from Dr. Deakin."

"Could you ask him?"

I feel his eyes on me. "All right."

"And could you take me to the supermarket? I don't want to drive while I'm on the pills and we need food."

"Do the pills really affect you that much?"

I hesitate, because if I tell him that they do, he might ask Dr. Deakin to reduce the dose.

"I'd rather not risk driving, that's all."

"Fair enough. We'll go tomorrow."

"You don't mind?"

"Of course I don't mind. Anything I can do to make your life easier, tell me and I'll do it."

"I know," I say gratefully. "I know."

# TUESDAY, SEPTEMBER 1ST

I can hardly wait for Matthew to bring up my break-fast tray so that I can start taking my pills again. I'd forgotten it was bank holiday yesterday so I haven't taken any pills for three days now. I never take any at weekends in case Matthew realizes how much they af-fect me, I just hide them in my drawer. Besides, with him around, I don't really need them to get through the day. I still need them at night though, otherwise I'd lie awake thinking about Jane, about her murder, about her murderer, who still hasn't been caught. And who is still phoning me.

I caught myself a couple of times during the week-end eyeing the pills, wondering if I could take maybe one, just to calm me. The first time was on Saturday morning when we came back with a car full of shopping. We'd had a coffee out and I'd enjoyed being back in the real world, if only for a while. Back home, I was putting the shopping away, marveling at how a fridge full of food could make me feel that I was back in control of my life, when Matthew took out a beer.

"I may as well start as I mean to go on," he'd said cheerfully.

"What do you mean?" I'd asked, wondering if he felt the need to get drunk just to be able to put up with the increasing demands I make on him.

"Well, if Andy makes one of his curries tonight, we'll probably be having beer with it."

I took a long time putting the cheeses we'd bought into the fridge, playing for time. "Are you sure it's tonight we're going to Hannah and Andy's?"

"Bank Holiday Saturday, that's what you told me. Do you want me to phone and check?"

The information meant nothing to me but I didn't want Matthew to guess I'd forgotten. "No, it's fine."

He took a sip of his beer and fished his mobile from his pocket. "I think I'll check, all the same. It won't hurt."

He phoned Hannah, who confirmed that she was definitely expecting us.

"Apparently, you're bringing dessert," Matthew said when he hung up.

"Oh, yes," I said, fighting down panic, hoping I had enough ingredients to at least make a cake of some sort.

"I could go and get something from Bértrand's, if you like."

"Maybe one of their strawberry tarts," I replied gratefully. "You don't mind?"

"No, of course not."

Even though another embarrassment had been avoided, my mood took a dive. I glanced at the calendar hanging on the wall and saw something written in the square for Saturday. I waited until Matthew had left the room and went over to see what it said: HANNAH AND ANDY'S 7 P.M. I tried not to let it get me down but it was hard.

Then, over dinner, Hannah asked if I was looking forward to going back to school. I hadn't thought about what I was going to tell people, so there was a bit of an awkward silence until Matthew stepped in.

"Cass has decided to take some time off," he explained.

Hannah was too polite to ask why but, over coffee, I saw her deep in conversation with Matthew while Andy kept me busy with photos of the holiday they'd just had.

"What were you talking about with Hannah?" I asked on the way home in the car.

"It's normal she's worried about you," he said. "You're her friend." And I was glad that we'd be going to bed when we got in and I'd have a legitimate reason for taking some pills.

I hear Matthew's feet on the stairs so I close my eyes, feigning sleep. If he knows I'm awake, he'll want to chat and all I want are my pills. He puts the tray down and kisses my forehead gently. I pretend to stir a little.

"Go back to sleep," he says softly. "I'll see you to-night."

The pills are in my mouth before he's reached the bottom of the stairs. Then, exhausted by the effort I had to make over the last three days, I decide to stay in bed instead of getting dressed and going down to the sitting room as I usually do.

The next thing I know, a persistent ringing wakes me from a deep sleep. At first I think it's the phone but when it carries on long after the answering machine should have kicked in, I realize that someone is pressing over and over again on the doorbell.

I lie there, unperturbed by the fact that there's someone at the door. For a start, I'm too drugged to care and also, the murderer is hardly going to ring on the bell before coming in to kill me, so it must be the postman with more packages of things I don't remember ordering. It's only when I hear her shouting through the letter box that I realize it's Rachel.

After shrugging on a dressing gown, I go down and open the door.

"At last," she says, looking relieved.

"What are you doing here?" I mumble, aware that I'm slurring.

"We were meant to be meeting for lunch today, at the Sour Grapes."

I look at her in dismay. "What time is it?"

"Hold on a minute." She takes out her phone. "Twenty past one."

"I must have fallen asleep," I say, because it seems politer than saying I forgot.

"When you hadn't turned up by quarter to one, I tried to get hold of you on your mobile but, when I couldn't get an answer, I tried phoning here and, then, when you didn't pick up, I was worried that you'd broken down on the way or had an accident," she explains, "because I knew you'd have let me know if you were going to be late. So I thought I'd better drive over and make sure you were all right. You don't know how glad I was to see your car in the drive!"

"I'm sorry you've had to come out," I say guiltily.

"Can I come in?" Without waiting for an answer, she walks into the hall. "Would you mind if I make a sandwich?"

I follow her into the kitchen and sit down at the table. "Help yourself."

"It's for you, not me. You look as if you haven't eaten in days." She takes some bread from the cupboard and opens the fridge. "What's going on, Cass? I go off to Siena for three weeks and come back to find you looking like someone I don't know."

"It's been a bit difficult," I say.

She puts a jar of mayonnaise, a tomato and some cheese on the table and finds a plate. "Have you been ill?" she asks. She looks so beautiful with her gorgeous tan and white shift dress that I feel self-conscious in my pajamas. I pull my dressing gown around me.

"Only mentally."

"Don't say that. But you do look dreadful and your voice is all over the place."

"It's the pills," I say, lying my head down on the table. The wood is cool beneath my cheek.

"What pills?"

"The ones Dr. Deakin gave me."

She frowns. "Why are you taking pills?"

"To help me cope."

"Why, has something happened?"

I lift my head from the table. "Only the murder."

She looks at me, confused. "Do you mean Jane's murder?"

"Why, has there been another one?"

"Cass, that was weeks ago!"

She looks a bit off-kilter so I blink rapidly. But she's still off-kilter so it's obviously me. "I know, and her killer is still out there," I say, jabbing the air with my finger.

She frowns. "You don't still think he's after you, do you?"

"Uh-huh," I say, nodding.

"But why?"

I slump back on the table. "I'm still getting calls."

"You told me you weren't."

"I know. But they don't bother me anymore, thanks to the pills. I don't even answer them now."

Out of the corner of my eye, I watch her spreading mayonnaise on the bread, cutting the tomatoes and slicing the cheese. "So how do you know they're from him?"

"I just do."

She shakes her head in despair. "You know that there's no foundation for this fear of yours, don't you? You're worrying me, Cass. What about your job? Doesn't school start again tomorrow?"

"I'm not going back."

She stops slicing. "For how long?"

"I don't know."

"Are things really that bad?"

"Worse."

She assembles the sandwich and puts the plate in front of me. "Eat this, then we'll talk."

"It might be better to wait until six o'clock."

"Why?"

"Because the pills will have worn off by then and I might make more sense."

She looks at me in disbelief. "Are you telling me that you spend all day like this? What on earth are you taking? Are they antidepressants?"

I shrug. "I think they're more imagination suppressants."

"What does Matthew think about you taking them?"

"He wasn't too keen at first but he's come round to the idea."

She sits down next to me and picks up the plate, offering me the sandwich, because I've made no move to take it. "Eat!" she demands.

After I've eaten both halves, I tell her everything that's happened over the last few weeks, about seeing the knife in the kitchen, about thinking there was someone in the garden, about barricading myself in the sitting room, about losing my car, about ordering a pram, about the things I keep ordering off the shopping channel and, when I get to the end, I can see that she has no idea what to say because she can no longer pretend that I'm suffering from burnout.

"I'm so sorry," she says, looking upset. "How does Matthew feel about it all? I hope he's being supportive."

"Yes, very. But maybe he wouldn't be if he knew how hard it's going to be for him in the future if I do have dementia, like Mum."

"You don't have dementia." Her voice is firm, stern even.

"I hope you're right," I say, wishing I had her confidence.

She leaves soon after, promising to come back and see me when she gets back from yet another business trip to New York.

"You're so lucky," I say wistfully on the doorstep. "I wish I could go away."

"Why don't you come with me?" she says impulsively.

"I don't think I'd be very good company."

"But it would do you a world of good! You could relax at the hotel while I'm at the conference and we could meet up in the evenings for dinner." She takes my hand, her eyes shining with excitement. "Please say yes, Cass, we'd have so much fun! And I'm taking a few days off after so we could spend those together."

For one tiny moment, I feel as excited as her, I feel as if I could really do it. Then reality comes crashing in and I know that I'll never be able to.

"I can't," I say quietly.

She looks at me determinedly "You know very well that there's no such word."

"I'm sorry, Rachel, I really can't. Another time, maybe."

I close the door behind her, feeling even more miserable than I usually do. Not so long ago, I would have jumped at the chance of a week in New York with Rachel. Now, the thought of getting on a plane, of leaving the house even, is overwhelming.

Craving oblivion, I go to the kitchen and take another pill. It wipes me out so quickly that I only wake up when I hear Matthew calling my name.

"Sorry," I mumble, mortified that he's found me comatose on the sofa. "I must have fallen asleep."

"It doesn't matter. Shall I make a start on dinner while you have a shower to wake yourself up?"

"Good idea."

Getting groggily to my feet, I go upstairs, have a cold shower, throw on some clothes and go back down to the kitchen.

"You smell nice," he says, looking up from where he's unloading the dishwasher.

"Sorry, I didn't get round to doing that."

"It's fine. But did you put the washing machine on? I need my white shirt for tomorrow."

I turn quickly. "I'll go and do it now."

"Having a lazy day, were we?" he teases.

"A bit," I admit.

I go to the utility room, sort the shirts from the rest of the laundry and load them into the machine. But as I go to switch it on, I find my fingers hovering uncertainly over the row of buttons, trying to remember which ones to press because, frighteningly, it has gone from my mind.

"You may as well put this one in as well." Startled,

I whip round and see Matthew standing bare-chested, his shirt in his hand. "Sorry, did I scare you?"

"Not really," I say, flustered.

"You looked as if you were miles away."

"I'm fine."

I take the shirt from him and add it to the machine. I close the door and stand there, my mind a blank.

"Is everything all right?"

"No," I say, my voice tight.

"Is it what I said about you having a lazy day?" he says, contrite. "I was only joking."

"It's not that."

"What then?"

My face burns. "I can't remember how to turn on the machine."

The silence only lasts a few seconds but it seems longer. "It's fine, I'll do it," he says quickly, reaching around me. "There, no harm done."

"Of course there's harm done!" I cry, incensed. "If I can no longer remember how to turn on the washing machine, it means my brain's not working properly!"

"Hey," he says gently, "it's all right." He tries to put his arms around me but I shake him off.

"No!" I cry. "I'm fed up of pretending that everything's all right when it's not!"

I push past him, march through the kitchen and out to the garden. The cool air calms me but the increasingly rapid disintegration of my memory is terrifying.

Matthew gives me a while, then follows me out.

"You need to read the letter from Dr. Deakin," he says quietly.

I go cold. "What letter from Dr. Deakin?"

"The one that came last week."

"I didn't see it." Even as I speak I have a vague rec-ollection of seeing a letter with the stamp of the sur-gery on the envelope.

"You must have—it was lying on the side with all the others you haven't opened yet."

I think of the pile of letters addressed to me that have accumulated over the past couple of weeks be-cause I can't be bothered to deal with them.

"I'll sort through them tomorrow," I say, suddenly scared.

"That's what you said a couple of days ago when I asked you about them. The thing is—" He stops, look-ing awkward.

"What?"

"I opened the one from the surgery."

My mouth drops open. "You opened my mail?"

"Only the one from the surgery," he says quickly. "And only because you didn't seem to be dealing with it. I thought it might be important, that maybe Dr. Dea-kin wanted to see you, or change your medication or something."

"You had no right," I say, glaring at him. "Where is it?"

"Where you left it." Hiding the fear I feel with an-ger, I march into the kitchen and go through the pile of letters until I find it. My fingers shake as I take the single sheet of paper from the already opened envelope and unfold it. The words dance before my eyes: "spo-ken to a specialist about your symptoms"; "like to refer *you for tests*"; "*early-onset dementia*"; "*make an ap-pointment as soon as possible.*"

The letter falls from my hands. Early-onset demen-tia. I roll the words around in my mouth, trying them on for size. Through the open door, a bird picks up the words and begins chirruping, "*Early-onset dementia, early-onset dementia, early-onset dementia.*"

Matthew's arms come round me but I remain rigid with fear. "Well, now you know," I say, my voice shaky with tears. "Satisfied?"

"Of course not! How could you say that? I'm just sad. And angry."

"That you married me?"

"No, never that."

"If you want to leave me, you can. It's not as if I don't have enough money to go into the best home there is."

He gives me a little shake. "Hey, don't say things like that. I've told you before, I have no intention of leaving you, ever. And Dr. Deakin only wants to refer you for tests."

"But what if it turns out I do have it? I know what it's going to be like, I know how impossibly frustrating it's going to be for you."

"If that time comes, we'll face it together. We still have years ahead of us, Cass, and they could be very good years, even if it turns out that you do have de-mentia. Anyway, there'll be medication you can take to slow it down. Please don't start worrying before there's something to worry about. I know it's hard, but you have to stay positive."

I somehow get through the rest of the evening but

I feel so frightened. How can I stay positive when I can't remember how the microwave or the washing machine works? I remember Mum and the kettle, and the hot tears start all over again. How long will it be before I can no longer remember how to make myself a simple cup of tea? How long will it be before I can no longer dress myself? Matthew, seeing how down I am, tells me that things could be worse, so I ask him what could be worse than losing my mind and, when he can't answer, I feel bad for putting him on the spot. I know it's no good being angry with him when he's trying his best to remain positive. But it's that shooting-the-messenger thing: it's hard to feel grateful when he's robbed me of my last bit of hope, that it was something other than dementia that was causing my memory loss.

# SUNDAY,
# SEPTEMBER 20TH

I stand in the kitchen, slowly stirring the risotto I've made for lunch, my eyes on Matthew in the garden pulling weeds from flower beds. I'm not watching him, I'm just using him to focus my eyes while my mind swirls around, a reaction to the weekend and the lack of drugs.

It's two months since Jane's murder and I have absolutely no idea where the last few weeks have gone. Thanks to the pills, they've passed in a painless blur. With difficulty, I count backward, trying to work out when I received the letter from Dr. Deakin referring me for tests, and come up with three weeks ago. Three weeks, and I still haven't come to terms with the fact that I might have early-onset dementia. Maybe one day I'll be able to face up to it—my tests are scheduled for the end of next month—but for the moment I don't want to have to.

Jane floats into my mind. Her face lingers there, her expression as blurred as it was on the day I saw her in the woods and I'm sad that I can barely remember what she looks like. It all seems to have happened so long ago. My silent caller is still around though. During the week, when I'm home alone, I'm aware of the phone ringing at regular intervals throughout the day. Sometimes, through the fog in my brain, I hear Hannah, or Connie, or John, leaving a message on the answering machine. But when a call cuts off before it can be picked up, I know that it's him.

I'm still ordering things from the shopping channel, except that I've upped my game and am now ordering jewelry instead of kitchen gadgets. On Friday Matthew came home from work holding another parcel left by the postman on the doorstep and my heart sank at the thought of playing yet another round of guess the contents.

"That smells like my favorite dish," he'd said, smiling, before coming over to kiss me while I tried to work out what I'd ordered.

"I thought it would be a nice start to the weekend."

"Lovely." He held up the box. "Another gadget for the kitchen?"

"No," I said, hoping it wasn't.

"What is it then?"

"A present."

"For me?"

"No."

"Can I look?"

"If you want."

He took a pair of scissors and cut open the outer packaging.

"Knives?" he asked, drawing out two black flat leather boxes.

"Why don't you open them and see?" I suggested. Suddenly, I knew what they were. "Pearls," I said. "They're pearls."

He flipped open the lid of one of the boxes. "Very nice."

"They're for Rachel," I told him confidently.

"I thought you'd already bought her some earrings?"

"These are for Christmas."

"We're only in September, Cass."

"There's nothing wrong in starting early, is there?"

"No, I suppose not." He drew out the bill and gave a low whistle. "Since when have you spent four hundred pounds on your friends?"

"I can do what I like with my money," I said defensively, knowing I was right in not telling him about the cottage in Ile de Ré I'd bought for Rachel.

"Of course you can. So who are the other ones for?"

All I can think is that I must have forgotten I'd ordered them and ordered another set. "I thought you could give them to me for my birthday."

He frowned, less willing to play along with pretense than before. "Don't you already have some?"

"Not like these," I said, hoping a third set wouldn't turn up.

"Right." I could sense him looking at me curiously. He's doing that a lot at the moment.


The risotto ready, I call Matthew and we sit down to lunch. Just as we're finishing, there's a ring at the doorbell. Matthew goes to answer it.

"You didn't mention that Rachel was coming," he says, bringing her to the kitchen. Although he smiles, I can tell he's not overly pleased to see her. I am, but I'm also caught off guard, because I have no idea if I've forgotten that she was meant to be coming or if she's just dropped in of her own accord.

"Cass didn't know, I just thought I'd drop in for a chat," she says, coming to my rescue. "But if I'm disturbing you, I can always go away again." She looks at me questioningly.

"No, it's fine," I say hurriedly, hating the way Matthew always makes her feel unwelcome. "We've just finished lunch. Have you eaten or can I get you something?"

"An espresso would be lovely."

Although Matthew's on his feet, he doesn't move, so I go over to the cupboard and take out some cups.

"Would you like one, too?" I ask him.

"Please."

I place a cup on the stand and take a capsule from the rack.

"So, how are you?" Rachel asks.

"Fine," I say. "What about you? How was your trip?" I go on, keeping it purposefully vague because I can't remember where she went.

"Same as usual. Guess what I bought at the airport on the way back?"

I put the capsule into the slot but instead of sliding in it stays sticking out of the top.

"What?" I ask, trying to push it in.

"An Omega watch."

I take the capsule out and try again, aware of Matthew's eyes on me. "Wow. It must be gorgeous," I say. The capsule still won't go down.

"It is. I thought I'd treat myself."

I press down on the capsule, trying to force it in. "Dead right," I say. "You deserve it."

"You have to lift the lever first," Matthew says quietly.

My face burning, I do as he says and the capsule slips into place.

"Why don't I take over?" he suggests. "Maybe you and Rachel would like to sit in the garden. I'll bring the coffee out."

"Thanks," I say gratefully.

"Are you all right?" Rachel asks, once we're on the terrace. "Maybe I should have phoned first, but I was in Browbury this morning and thought I'd drop in on impulse."

"Don't worry, it's not you, it's me," I say, making her laugh. "I couldn't remember how to work the coffee machine. First it was the microwave, then the washing machine. Now it's the coffee machine. Next I'll be forgetting how to dress myself." I pause a moment, steadying myself to make the big announcement. "It seems I might have early-onset dementia."

"Yes, you told me a couple of weeks ago."

"Oh," I say, deflated.

"You haven't been for the tests yet, have you?"

"No, not yet."

"What about the pills? Are you still taking them?"

"Yes." I lower my voice. "But I never take any on weekends because I don't want Matthew to know how much they affect me. I just pretend to take them and hide them in my drawer."

She frowns at this. "Cass! Surely, if they affect you that much, you shouldn't be taking them at all! Or at least be taking a smaller dose."

"Maybe, but I don't want to. Without them I wouldn't make it through the week. They make me forget I'm alone in the house, they make me forget about the phone calls."

"Are you still getting them?"

"On and off."

She places a hand on my arm. "You have to tell the police, Cass."

I glance up at her. "What's the point? I don't suppose they'd be able to do anything."

"You don't know that. Maybe they could put a trace on your incoming calls or something. What does Matthew think?"

"He thinks I'm not getting them anymore."

"Here comes Matthew with our coffee," she interrupts loudly, warning me of his arrival. He puts a cup down in front of her and she looks up at him sweetly. "Thank you."

"Just shout if you want a refill."

"We will."

She leaves an hour later, offering to come and pick me up the following Friday and take me out for the evening. She knows I don't trust myself to drive and I hate that I now have to rely on people to take me out and about. The regret I feel for the life I used to have is like a physical pain. But it isn't dementia that has robbed me of my independence, I realize, though that day may one day come. It's the guilt and fear that have riddled my every waking moment since I drove past Jane's car two months ago. It's guilt and fear that have diminished me. If Jane hadn't happened, if I hadn't met her, if she hadn't been murdered, I would have been able to cope with the news that I have early-onset dementia. I would have faced it head-on and would, at this very moment, be looking at my options instead of spending my days asleep on the sofa.

The realization of what I've become, and why I've become as I am, is a massive wake-up call. It snaps me out of my lethargy and makes me determined to take some positive action. I think about what I can do to turn my life around, or at least start getting it back on track, and decide to go back to Heston. If anyone can help me in my quest for peace of mind, it has to be Alex, Jane's husband. I don't expect him to take away the guilt that I feel because it will always be with me. But he had seemed a kind and compassionate man and if he sees that I'm truly sorry for not stopping to help

Jane that night, he might find it in his heart to forgive me. And then maybe, just maybe, I might be able to start forgiving myself. I might even be able to do something about the fear, nurtured oh-so-carefully by my silent caller. I'm not so naïve as to think that all my problems are going to be solved with one trip to Heston. But at least it's a start.

# MONDAY,
# SEPTEMBER 21ST

I add the pills that Matthew brought me this morning to the little pile already in my drawer, because if I'm to drive to Heston today I need a clear head. I spend a long time in the shower letting the water wash over me, and when I eventually get out, I feel mentally stronger than I have for a long time. Almost reborn. Maybe that's why, when the phone starts ringing around ten o'clock, I decide to answer it. For a start, I want to check that the calls weren't just a figment of my imagination and, second, I can't really believe that he would continue to call when I haven't answered the phone in God knows how long.

The sharp drawing in of breath as I take the call tells

me I've taken him by surprise and, delighted that I've wrong-footed him, I'm able to cope with the silence coming down the line better than before. My breathing, normally shaky with fear, remains even.

"I've missed you." The whispered words slide silkily down the line, hitting me like an invisible force. Fear resurfaces, raising bumps on my skin, choking me with its venom. I throw the phone down. *It doesn't mean he's nearby*, I tell myself, trying to regain some of the calm I'd felt earlier. *Just because he spoke to you, it doesn't mean he's watching you.* I take a few breaths, reminding myself that the fact he wasn't expecting me to answer the phone proves that he doesn't know my every move. But it's hard not to feel afraid all over again. What if he decides to pay me a visit, now that he knows I'm back in the land of the living?

I go into the kitchen, my eyes instinctively checking first the window, then the back door. I try the handle; it remains reassuringly unmoveable. No one can get in unless I let them.

I go to make coffee, but remembering the struggles I had with the machine yesterday, I pour myself a glass of milk instead, wondering why my caller chose to speak to me this time when he never has before. Maybe he wanted to destabilize me because, for the first time, he hadn't been able to sense my fear. I feel a surge of triumph at having changed something fundamental between us. I haven't exactly brought him out into the open but I've made him divulge a little of himself, even if it was only a whisper.

I don't want to get to Heston too early so I do a little tidying to take my mind off the fact that I'm alone in the house. But my mind won't settle. I make myself a cup of mint tea, hoping it will calm me, and sit in the kitchen drinking it. Time passes slowly but with a lot of willpower I manage to hang on until eleven and then I leave, putting on the alarm as I go. As I drive through Browbury, I remember the last time I was here, the day I bumped into John, and work out that it must have been about five weeks ago. When I remember how scared I'd been that day because I'd thought that the murderer was in the garden, I feel real anger that someone could instill such fear in me. And where had those five weeks gone? Where had the summer gone?

I arrive in Heston, leave my car in the same road and cross over to the park. There's no sign of Jane's husband or the children but I didn't expect it to be that easy. I don't want to think about the possibility that he might not come to the park at all, or what I'll do if he refuses to listen to me, so I sit for a while on an empty bench, enjoying the feel of the late-September sun on my face.

At around twelve-thirty I make my way to the pub, stopping off at the village shop to buy a newspaper. I order a coffee at the bar and carry it to the garden. There are a surprising number of people already having lunch there and I feel suddenly conspicuous, not only because I'm alone but also because everyone seems to know each other, or at least be regular customers.

I find a small table under a tree, a little away from everyone, and open the paper. The headlines aren't very interesting so I turn to the next page. An article with the title WHY HAS NOBODY BEEN ARRESTED? jumps out at me. I don't have to read it to know it's about Jane's murder.

Alongside the article is a photograph of a young woman, a friend of Jane's, who seems as frustrated as I am by the slowness of the police investigation. *"Some-body must know who the murderer is,"* she is quoted as saying, a sentiment picked up and chewed over by the reporter. *"Two months ago, a young woman was bru-tally murdered,"* the article finishes. *"Somebody some-where must know something."*

I close the paper, my stomach churning. As far as I know, the police had stopped appealing for the person who saw Jane alive in her car that night to re-contact them, but this latest article might stir things up again. I'm too wound up to sit, so I leave the pub and start walking down the street in search of Jane's husband because, now, more than ever, I don't want to go away empty-handed. I have no idea where he lives, if he lives in the village itself or in the new estate that has been built on its outskirts but, as I pass a row of stone cottages, I see two identical tricycles parked in one of the front gardens. Without giving myself the chance to hesitate I walk up the path and knock on the front door.

I see him checking me out through the window but he takes so long coming to the door that I think he's not going to open it.

He looks down at me from the doorstep.

"The tissue lady," he says, his voice neither friendly nor unfriendly.

"Yes," I say, gratified that he's remembered. "I'm sorry to disturb you but could I talk to you for a couple of minutes?"

"Not if you're a journalist, no."

I shake my head quickly. "I'm not a journalist."

"If you're a medium of some kind, I'm not interested either."

I smile a little, almost wishing it was the reason I was there. "No, nothing like that."

"Let me guess—you and Jane go way back and you want to tell me how bad you feel that you lost contact with her."

I shake my head. "Not exactly."

"So why do you want to talk to me?"

"I'm Cass."

"Cass?"

"Yes. I wrote to you a few weeks ago. Jane and I had lunch together just before . . ." I trail off, not knowing what else to say.

"Of course!" A frown crosses his face. "But why didn't you tell me who you were when we bumped into each other in the park?"

"I don't know. Probably because I didn't want you to think I was intruding. I was driving through Heston that day and remembered Jane mentioning the park so I decided to stop. It didn't occur to me that I might bump in to you."

"I seem to spend most of my life there," he says,

grimacing. "The girls never tire of it. They ask to go every day, even when it's raining."

"How are they?"

"They're doing really well." He opens the door wider. "Come in. The girls are asleep so I have a few minutes." I follow him to the sitting room, where toys litter the floor and Jane gazes at me from myriad family photos. "Would you like a cup of tea?"

"No, thank you," I say, suddenly nervous.

"You said you wanted to talk to me?"

"Yes." Sudden tears fill my eyes and I grope in my bag for a tissue, angry at myself.

"Please, sit down. You've obviously got something on your mind."

"Yes," I say again, taking a seat on the sofa.

He pulls up a chair and sits down opposite me. "Take your time."

"I saw Jane that night," I say, twisting the tissue around my fingers.

"Yes, I know, at a party. I remember Jane telling me."

"No, not that night. The night she was . . ." The word "murdered" sticks in my throat. "The night she was killed. I was in Blackwater Lane and I drove past her car in the lay-by."

He doesn't say anything for so long that I think he's gone into some kind of shock.

"Have you told the police?" he asks eventually.

"Yes. I'm the person who phoned in to say that she was alive when I saw her."

"Did you see anything else?"

"No, only Jane. But I didn't know it was her, it was raining too hard for me to make her out, I could see it was a woman but that's all. I only knew it was Jane after."

He exhales heavily, and his breath hangs in the air between us. "You didn't see anybody in the car with her?"

"No. If I had I would have told the police."

"So you didn't stop?"

Unable to meet his eyes, I bow my head. "I thought she'd broken down so I pulled in front of her. I thought she might get out of her car but she didn't—it was pouring—so I waited for her to flash her lights or sound her horn to tell me that she needed help, and when she didn't I presumed she'd already called someone and that they were on their way. I know I should have got out and run back to check she was all right but I was too scared, I thought it might be some sort of trap, so I decided that the best thing would be to phone the police or one of the breakdown services as soon as I got home, because I was only a few minutes away, and ask them to go and check on her. But when I got home, something happened that made me forget to phone them. Then, the next morning, when I heard that a young woman had been murdered, I felt—well, I can't describe how I felt . . . I couldn't believe that I'd forgotten to make that phone call . . . I kept thinking that if I had, she'd still be alive. I felt so guilty that I couldn't tell anyone, not even my husband, because I thought that if it got out, people would point their finger at me and say that I was to blame for her death because I hadn't done anything to help her. And they would have been right. And then, when I heard that it was Jane, I felt terrible." I swallow down tears. "I may not be the murderer but I feel as much to blame for her death as he is."

I brace myself for his anger but he only shakes his head. "You can't think like that," he says.

"You know what the worst thing is?" I continue. "Afterward, I kept thinking that if I had got out of the car, I might have been murdered too. So I was glad that I hadn't. What kind of person does that make me?"

"Not a bad one," he says gently. "Just human."

"Why are you being so kind? Why aren't you angry with me?"

He gets to his feet. "Is that what you want?" he says, looking down at me. "Is that why you've come here? Do you want me to tell you that you're responsible for Jane's death and that you're a terrible person? Because, if you do, you've come to the wrong place."

I shake my head. "That's not why I've come."

"So what is it you want?"

"I don't know how much longer I can live with the guilt I feel."

"You have to stop blaming yourself."

"I'll never be able to do that."

"Look, Cass, if you want my forgiveness, I'll give it to you gladly. I don't blame you for not stopping; if the roles had been reversed, I doubt Jane would have stopped to help you, she would have been too frightened to, just as you were."

"But at least she might have remembered to get someone to check up on me."

He picks up a photograph of the twins, all smiles and blonde curls. "Too many lives have already been ruined by Jane's death," he says softly. "Don't let it ruin yours."

"Thank you," I say, tears filling my eyes again. "Thank you so much."

"I'm just sorry you've been going through so much anguish. Can I at least make you a cup of tea now?"

"I don't want to trouble you."

"I was going to make one when you knocked at the door, so it's no trouble at all."

By the time he comes back with the tea, I've managed to compose myself. He asks about me, so I tell him that I'm a teacher, without mentioning that I'm not working at the moment. We talk about his little daughters and he admits he's finding it hard being a full-time dad, mainly because he misses his job, adding that when his colleagues had asked him to go in for lunch the previous week, it was the first time since Jane's death that he'd felt up to seeing people again.

"And how was it?" I ask.

"I didn't go because I didn't have anyone to look after the girls. Both sets of parents live too far away to pop over at short notice, although they're brilliant at coming over at the weekend. But it's still very difficult for Jane's parents, you know, seeing the girls. They look so much like her."

"Don't you have anyone locally who can help you out?"

"No, not really."

"I'd be happy to babysit any time," I say. He looks

taken aback. "I'm sorry, that's a stupid thing to say—you don't know me so of course you're not going to trust me with the girls."

"Well, thank you for your offer anyway."

I drain my cup, aware of an awkwardness between us. "I'd better go," I say, standing up. "Thank you for allowing me to talk to you."

"As long as you're feeling better about everything."

"Yes," I say, "I am."

He walks me to the door and I have a sudden urge to confide in him about the calls I've been getting.

"Was there something else?" he asks.

"No, it's fine," I say, because I can't intrude on him any longer.

"Goodbye then."

"Goodbye."

I walk slowly toward the gate, wondering if I've missed my chance, because there's no way I can turn up on his doorstep uninvited again.

"Maybe I'll see you in the park someday!" he calls.

"Maybe," I say, realizing that he's been watching me. "Goodbye."

It's around four by the time I arrive back at the house, too late in the day to take a pill, so I decide not to go in but to sit in the garden until Matthew arrives. I'm not going to tell him that I've been out today because if I do I'll have to lie about where I've been and, if I lie, it might come back to bite me if I can't remember what I told him. The heat makes me thirsty so I go reluctantly into the house, remembering to turn off the alarm on the way in, and head for the kitchen. I open the door and find myself pausing on the threshold. My eyes scan the room; a prickle of unease goes down my spine. Everything seems as it should be but I know that it's not, I know that since I left this morning, something has changed.

I move slowly back into the hall and stand as still as I can, listening for the slightest sound. There is nothing, only silence, but I know that doesn't mean there isn't someone there. I take the phone from its cradle on the hall table and slip quietly back through the front door, pulling it shut behind me. I move away from the house, making sure to stay just inside the gate so that the phone is still in range and, with shaking fingers, I dial Matthew's number.

"Can I call you back?" he asks. "I'm in a meeting."

"I think someone's been in the house," I say cautiously.

"Hold on a minute."

I hear him excusing himself and the scrape of his chair and a few seconds later he's back on the line.

"What's the matter?"

"Someone's been in the house," I say, trying to hide my agitation. "I went for a walk and when I came back, I could tell someone had been in the kitchen."

"How?"

"I don't know," I say, frustrated at sounding crazy again.

"Is something missing? Have we been burgled? Is that what you're trying to tell me?"

"I don't know if we've been burgled; all I know is that someone has been in the house. Can you come home, Matthew? I don't know what to do."

"Did you put the alarm on when you left?"

"Yes."

"So how would they have got in without triggering it?"

"I don't know."

"Are there signs of a break-in?"

"I don't know. I didn't stay long enough to find out. Look, we're wasting time. What if he's still there? Don't you think we should call the police?" I hesitate a moment. "Jane's murderer is still on the loose."

He doesn't say anything and I know it was stupid of me to have mentioned it.

"Are you quite sure that someone has been in the house?" he asks.

"Of course I am. I wouldn't make it up. And he might still be in there."

"Then we'd better call the police." I sense his reluctance. "They'll get there quicker than me."

"But you will come?"

"Yes, I'll leave now."

"Thank you."

He phones back a minute later to tell me that the police will be with me shortly. Although they come quickly, they also come quietly, so I know Matthew didn't mention the word "murderer" to them. The police car pulls to a halt in front of the gate and I recognize the policewoman who came the time I set off the alarm.

"Mrs. Anderson?" she says, walking down the drive toward me. "I'm PC Lawson. Your husband asked me to come by. I believe you think there might be someone in your house?"

"Yes," I say quickly. "I went for a walk and when I came back, I could tell that someone had been in the kitchen."

"Did you see any signs of a break-in—glass on the floor, that sort of thing?"

"I only went as far as the kitchen so I don't know."

"And you think they're still there?"

"I don't know. I didn't stay around to find out. I came straight out here and phoned my husband."

"Can I get in through the front door? Do you have a key?"

"Yes," I say, giving it to her.

"Stay here, please, Mrs. Anderson. I'll let you know when it's safe to come in."

She lets herself into the house and I hear her calling out, asking if anyone is there, and then, for the next five minutes or so, everything goes quiet. Eventually, she comes back out.

"I've made a thorough search of the house and I can't find anything to suggest there was an intruder," she says. "There's no sign of a forced entry, all the windows are secure and everything seems to be in order."

"Are you sure?" I ask anxiously.

"Perhaps you'd like to come in and have a look around," she offers. "Check that nothing's missing, that kind of thing."

I follow her back into the house and go through every single room but although I can't see anything out of place I know that someone had been there.

"I can just sense it," I say helplessly when she asks me to explain how I know.

We go back down to the kitchen.

"Maybe we can have a cup of tea," PC Lawson suggests, sitting down at the table.

I go to put the kettle on and find myself stopping in my tracks.

"My mug," I say, turning to her. "I left my mug on the side when I went out and now it's gone. That's how I know someone's been in here. My mug isn't where I left it."

"Maybe it's in the dishwasher," she says.

I open the dishwasher and see my mug sitting on the rack.

"I knew I wasn't going mad!" I say triumphantly. She looks at me doubtfully. "I didn't put it in here," I explain. "I left it on the side."

The door opens and Matthew comes in.

"Everything all right?" he asks, looking at me nervously.

I leave PC Lawson to speak to him, while my mind works furiously, wondering if it's possible that I made a mistake about leaving my mug on the side. But I know that I didn't.

I turn my attention back to PC Lawson, who has just finished telling Matthew that she couldn't find any trace of a break-in or of anyone being in the house.

"But there was someone," I insist. "My mug didn't get into the dishwasher on its own."

"What do you mean?" Matthew asks.

"Before I went out, I left my mug on the side and, when I came back, it was in the dishwasher," I explain again.

He looks resignedly at me. "You probably don't remember putting it in there, that's all." He turns to PC Lawson. "My wife sometimes has problems with her memory, so she forgets things."

"Right," she says, looking sympathetically at me.

"It has nothing to do with my memory!" I say, annoyed. "I'm not stupid. I know what I did and didn't do!"

"But sometimes you don't," Matthew says gently. I open my mouth to defend myself but close it again quickly. If he wanted, he could reel off any number of examples when I haven't been able to remember what I've done. In the silence that follows I know that even if I insist until I'm blue in the face, they'll never believe that I left my mug on the side.

"I'm sorry you've come out unnecessarily," I say stiffly.

"It's no problem. Better to be safe than sorry," PC Lawson says kindly.

"I think I'll go and lie down for a while."

"Good idea." Matthew smiles encouragingly at me. "I'll come up in a moment."

After PC Lawson leaves, I wait for Matthew to come and find me. When he doesn't I go downstairs to find him. He's in the garden, sipping a glass of wine as if he doesn't have a care in the world. A flash of anger hits me.

"I'm glad it doesn't bother you that there was someone in the house," I say, looking at him in disbelief.

"Come on, Cass, if all they did was put a mug in the dishwasher, it's not a threat, is it?"

I can't work out if he's being sarcastic, as he's never shown this side of himself before. A voice inside me warns: *Be careful, don't push him too far!* But I can't stop the anger I feel.

"I suppose you'll only believe me the day you come home and find me with my throat cut!"

He puts his wineglass down on the table. "Is that what you really think is going to happen? That someone is going to come into the house and murder you?"

Something snaps inside me. "It doesn't matter what I think because nobody takes any notice of what I say anyway!"

"Do you blame us? There's absolutely no foundation for any of your fears, none at all."

"He spoke to me!"

"Who?"

"The murderer!"

"Cass," he groans.

"No, he did! And he's been in the house! Don't you understand, Matthew? Everything has changed!"

He shakes his head in despair. "You're ill, Cass, you have early-onset dementia and you're paranoid. Can't you just accept it?"

The cruelty of his words stuns me. I can't find anything to say so I turn my back on him and go into the house. In the kitchen I stop to swallow down two of my pills, giving him time to come after me. But he doesn't, so I go upstairs, peel off my clothes and climb into bed.

# TUESDAY, SEPTEMBER 22ND

When I next open my eyes it's the morning and, all at once, the events of the previous evening come rushing back. I turn my head toward Matthew, wondering if he tried to wake me when he came to bed to apologize for his hurtful words. But his side of the bed is empty. I look at the clock: it's eight-thirty. My breakfast tray is on the table, which means he's already left for work.

I sit up, hoping to see a note propped against my glass of juice but there's only a bowl of cereal, a small jug of milk and my two little pills. I feel sick with apprehension. No matter how much he tells me that he'll never leave me, that he'll stay with me, this new harder edge to his character has thrown me. I understand that it must be frightening for him to have a wife who keeps banging on about being stalked by a murderer but shouldn't he try to get to the bottom of my fears before dismissing them so abruptly? When I think about it, he's never once sat me down properly and asked why I think the murderer is after me. If he had, I might have admitted to seeing Jane's car that night.

Tears of loneliness spill from my eyes and I reach for the pills and the juice to wash them down with, desperate to numb the pain. But I can't stop crying, even when sleep begins to take me, because all I feel is terrible despair, and fear at what the future might hold for me. If I have dementia and Matthew leaves me, all I'll have to look forward to are years in a care home where a few of my friends will visit out of obligation, an obligation that will end the minute I can't remember who they are. My tears increase and become huge sobs of wretchedness, and when I'm woken some time later by a terrible groaning noise, with my head feeling as if it's about to explode, it's as if my emotional pain has manifested itself into physical pain. I try to open my eyes but find that I can't. My body feels as if it's on fire and, when I lift my hand to my head, I find it wet with sweat.

Aware that there's something terribly wrong, I try to get out of bed but my legs won't hold me up and I fall to the floor. I can feel sleep pulling me back but some sixth sense tells me that I mustn't give in to it and I focus instead on trying to move. But it seems impossible and all I can think of, through the fog in my brain, is that I've had a stroke of some kind. My survival instinct kicks in and I know my only chance is to get help as quickly as possible so, heaving myself onto all fours, I make it to the top of the stairs and half fall down them to the hall below. The pain makes me almost lose consciousness but with superhuman effort I use my arms to pull my body along the floor toward the table where the phone sits. I want to call Matthew but I know I have to call the emergency services first, so I dial 999 and, when a woman answers, I tell her that I need help. I'm slurring so much I'm terrified she won't be able to understand what I'm saying. She asks for my name and I tell her it's Cass. She then asks where I'm calling from, and I just about manage to tell her our address when the phone slips from my grasp and clatters to the floor.

"Cass, Cass, can you hear me?" The voice is so faint that it's easy to ignore. But it comes back so insistently that I end up opening my eyes.

"She's here," I hear someone say. "She's waking up."

"Cass, my name's Pat, I want you to stay with me, all right?" A face comes into focus somewhere above me. "We're going to take you to hospital in a minute but can you just tell me, is this what you took?" She holds the box of tablets that Dr. Deakin prescribed for me and, recognizing them, I give a little nod.

I feel hands on me, lifting me, and then cool air on my face for a few brief seconds as I'm carried out to an ambulance.

"Matthew?" I ask weakly.

"You'll see him at the hospital," a voice tells me. "Can you tell me how many you've taken, Cass?"

I'm about to ask her what she means when I start vomiting violently and, by the time we arrive at the hospital, I'm so weak I can't even smile at Matthew as he stands looking down at me, his face white with worry.

"You can see her later," a nurse tells him briskly.

"She'll be all right, won't she?" he asks, distraught, and I feel worse for him than I do for myself.

There's a blur of tests so it's only when the doctor starts asking me questions that I realize she thinks I've taken an overdose.

I stare at her, appalled. "An overdose?"

"Yes."

I shake my head. "No, I would never do that."

She gives me the kind of look that tells me she doesn't believe me and, bewildered, I ask to see Matthew.

"Thank God you're all right," he says, reaching for my hand. He looks at me in anguish. "Was it me, Cass? Was it what I said? If it is, I'm so sorry. If I thought for a minute that you'd do something like this, I'd never have been so harsh."

"I didn't take an overdose," I say tearfully. "Why does everybody keep saying that I did?"

"But you told the paramedic you did."

"No, I didn't." I try to sit up. "Why would I say something that isn't true?"

"Try to stay calm, Mrs. Anderson." The doctor looks severely at me. "You're still very ill. Fortunately, we didn't have to pump your stomach as you brought up most of the pills in the ambulance, but you're still going to need monitoring for the next twenty-four hours."

I clutch Matthew's arm. "She must have misunderstood. The paramedic showed me the pills Dr. Deakin prescribed for me and asked me if they were the pills I took, so I said yes, because they're the pills I take. I didn't mean I'd taken an overdose."

"I'm afraid our tests show that you did," the doctor says.

I look beseechingly at Matthew. "I took the two you brought me with my breakfast but I didn't take any after that, I swear. I didn't even go downstairs."

"These are the boxes the paramedics took from the house," the doctor says, handing a plastic bag to Matthew. "Would you know if there are any missing? We don't think she took a lot, maybe a dozen or so."

Matthew opens the first of the two boxes. "She only started this one a couple of days ago and there are eight pills missing, which is right because she takes four a day, two in the morning and two in the evening," he says, showing the doctor. "As for the other box," he goes on, checking the contents, "it's full, just as it should be. So I don't know where she would have got them from."

"Is there any way your wife could have stockpiled some of them?"

Upset at being dismissed from the conversation, I'm about to remind them that I'm present when I suddenly remember the little pile of pills in my drawer.

"No, I would have noticed if there'd been any missing," Matthew says. "It's usually me that gives them to her, you see, before I leave for work in the mornings. That way I know she's not going to forget to take them." He pauses. "I don't know if you know—I told one of the nurses—but there's a possibility that my wife has early-onset dementia."

While they talk about my possible dementia, I try to work out if I somehow took the pills from my drawer without knowing what I was doing. I don't want to believe that I did but when I remember how wretched, how hopeless I'd felt and how I had craved oblivion, maybe, after taking the two pills that Matthew had brought me, I'd reached into the drawer and taken the others. Had I subconsciously wanted to end the life that had suddenly become unbearable?

Already weakened by what I've been through, the remaining energy I have drains out of me. Exhausted, I lie back on my pillow and close my eyes against the tears seeping from their corners.

"Cass, are you all right?"

"I'm tired," I murmur.

"I think it's best if you leave her to sleep," the doctor says.

I feel Matthew's lips on my cheek. "I'll be back tomorrow," he promises.

# MONDAY,
# SEPTEMBER 28TH

In the end, I had to admit to taking the pills, because the evidence was there in my bloodstream. I admitted that I'd had some pills hidden away in my drawer but insisted that I hadn't stockpiled them with the intention of killing myself, explaining I had simply put them there because on the days when Matthew was at home with me I hadn't felt the need to take them. When they asked why I couldn't have told Matthew that, I found myself explaining that I hadn't wanted him to know that the pills knocked me out to the point where I couldn't do anything. Matthew, looking skeptical, pointed out that what I'd said wasn't strictly true because, as far as he was concerned, I was still able to function at an acceptable level. So I amended it to barely knew what I was doing. The only good thing is that because I took so few, they put it down to a cry for help and not an intention to kill myself.

When Matthew brought me home the following evening, the first thing I did was go upstairs to the bedroom and look in the drawer. The pills had gone. I know that Matthew doesn't believe I took them accidentally even though he hasn't actually come out and said it. But it feels like another nail in the coffin of our relationship. It's not Matthew's fault; I can't imagine what it must be like for him to go from a wife who, at the beginning of the summer, was a little absent-minded to a wife who, by the end of the summer, is demented, paranoid and suicidal.

He insisted on taking the rest of the week off, even though I told him he didn't have to. In truth, I would have preferred him to go to work because I wanted to be able to think about where I was going. My accidental overdose made me realize how precious life was, and I was determined to get back in control of mine while I still could. I started off by refusing to take the new blue pills that had been prescribed for me, telling Matthew I preferred to try to cope without them because I needed to get back to living in the real world.

With everything that had happened, I forgot that I was meant to be going out with Rachel—or maybe I would have forgotten anyway—so I was nowhere near ready when she turned up on the doorstep on Friday evening.

"If you just give me ten minutes . . ." I said, happy to

see her. "I'm sure Matthew will make you a cup of tea while you're waiting."

Matthew looked at me in surprise. "You're not seriously going out, are you?"

"Why not?" I frowned. "I'm not an invalid."

"Yes, but after what happened." He turned to Rachel. "You do know that Cass has been in hospital, don't you?"

"No, I had no idea." Rachel looked shocked. "Why? What happened?"

"I'll tell you over dinner," I said hurriedly. I looked at Matthew, daring him to tell me I couldn't go. "You don't mind looking after yourself tonight, do you?"

"Not at all, it's just . . ."

"I'm fine," I insisted.

"Are you sure, Cass?" Rachel said uncertainly. "If you've been ill . . ."

"A night out is exactly what I need," I told her firmly.

Ten minutes later, we were on our way and I used the journey to Browbury to tell her about my accidental overdose. She was horrified that the pills could subconsciously make me do something so dangerous, but seemed happy when I reassured her that I didn't intend on taking any more medication. Luckily, she understood that I didn't want to talk about what had happened and for the rest of the evening we talked about other things.

Then on Saturday—ten weeks since my life fell apart—Matthew brought me tea in the mug that had caused so much fuss on Monday afternoon and I found myself going over everything again. In my mind I could see the mug standing clearly on the side and, although my mind can't always be trusted, I was pretty sure that I hadn't put it in the dishwasher before leaving the kitchen. So who had? The only person with a key to the house, apart from me, is Matthew, but I knew it wasn't him because methodical as he is, he always stacks from the back and the dishwasher was practically empty. Anyway, if he had popped home in the middle of the day, he would have admitted it. The truth is, I'm the one who stacks from the front. And if I can take an overdose without knowing what I'm doing, it's not too hard to suppose I can put my mug in the dishwasher without remembering about it.

We somehow got through the weekend with Matthew tiptoeing around me as if I was an unexploded time bomb waiting to go off at any moment. He didn't actually sigh with relief this morning when he could escape back to the office but I know he found babysitting me hard work, even though without the pills I'm much more coherent. But my accidental overdose has left him on edge and the thought that I might do something stupid while he's at home means he can't relax around me.

As soon as he's left for work I get up, because I want to be out of the house before my silent caller phones. I could just ignore the call but I know that if I do, he'll only phone back until I pick up, which will end up destabilizing me. And today I need to be calm, because I'm going back to Heston to see Jane's husband.

My plan is to arrive in the early afternoon when I think it's most likely the twins will be asleep, so I stop off in Browbury on the way, where I have a leisurely breakfast and spend the rest of the morning shopping for new clothes, because nothing seems to fit me anymore.

Alex doesn't seem overly surprised to see me standing on his doorstep again.

"I thought you might be back," he says, ushering me in. "I could tell there was something else on your mind."

"You can tell me to go away again, if you like," I say. "Only I hope you don't because if you can't help me, I don't know who can."

He offers me a cup of tea, but suddenly nervous about what I'm going to say, I refuse.

"So what can I do for you?" he asks, taking me into the sitting room.

"You're going to think I'm mad," I warn, sitting down on the sofa. He doesn't say anything so I take a deep breath. "Right, here goes. The day I phoned the police to tell them that I'd seen Jane alive, they made a public announcement asking the person who had called them earlier to contact them again. The next day I received a silent phone call. I didn't think too much about it but when I got another the following day and a couple more the day after, it began to freak me out. They weren't heavy-breather-type calls—I could have coped with that—there was just this silence on the line, except I knew that there was someone there. When I told my husband, he said it was probably a call center trying to get through, but I began to live in dread of the phone ringing because—well, I suspected they were coming from the person who killed Jane."

He makes a noise, a grunt of surprise, but when he doesn't say anything, I go on.

"It wouldn't have been hard for him to trace me from my license plate. When I pulled in front of Jane's car, I stopped for quite a few minutes, so it's possible that he was able to see my registration number despite the rain. The more he phoned me, the more traumatized I became. I presumed he'd thought I'd somehow seen him and was trying to warn me off from telling the police. But the only person I'd seen was Jane. I tried ignoring the calls but, when I did, he would carry on phoning until I picked up and I began to realize that he never phoned when my husband was around, which made me think he was watching the house.

"I was so frightened that I insisted on having an alarm installed but he still managed to get in and leave a calling card in the kitchen, a huge kitchen knife, exactly like in the police photos. The next day, I thought he was in the garden and barricaded myself in our sitting room. I was put on medication, which turned me into a mental and physical wreck, but it was the only way I could cope with the calls. Then, last Monday, after I got back from visiting you, I knew he'd been in the house while I was out. It wasn't that anything was missing or damaged but I could sense he'd been there. I was so sure I called the police, but they couldn't find any trace of a break-in, and when I realized that the mug I'd left on the side before going out had somehow found its way into the dishwasher, I was triumphant. It was proof that someone had been in the house—except that when I said as much, everyone looked at me as if I was mad." I pause to catch my breath. "The thing is, I have early-onset dementia and I forget so many things that people don't believe me anymore. But I know he was in the house last Monday. And now I'm terrified that I'm going to be his next victim. So what I want to know is, what should I do? The police already think I'm imagining things so if I tell them the murderer is after me, they're not going to believe me, especially when I can't prove that I've been getting calls in the first place. I sound crazy, don't I?" I add hopelessly.

He doesn't say anything for a moment and I imagine him trying to work out how he can get rid of me without causing offense.

"I *have* been getting calls," I say. I glance up at him, standing by the bookshelf, leaning against it, contemplating what I've just told him. "I really need you to believe that I have."

"I do believe you," he says.

I look at him warily, wondering if he's just humoring me. "Why? I mean, nobody else has."

"A gut feeling, I suppose. Anyway, why would you make up something like that? You don't seem like an attention-seeker to me. If you were, you'd have gone to the police and to the media by now."

"They could be a figment of my imagination."

"The fact that you're telling me they could be makes it unlikely."

"So you really do believe that I've been getting calls from the person who killed Jane?" I ask, needing him to confirm it.

"No. I believe you're getting calls but they're not coming from the person who killed Jane."

"Don't tell me they're coming from a call center," I say, not bothering to hide my disappointment.

"No, it's obvious that there's more to them than that. Someone is definitely harassing you."

"So why can't they be coming from the murderer?"

"Because it's not logical. Look, what exactly did you see when you drove past Jane's car? If you'd been able to see her clearly, you would have recognized her. Yet you told me you didn't."

"I couldn't make out her features," I confirm. "I had the impression she was blonde, but that was all."

"So if you had seen someone sitting next to her in the car, the most you'd have been able to say was that they were dark or fair."

"Yes, but the killer doesn't know that. He might think that I saw him clearly."

He leaves the bookshelf and comes to sit down next to me. "Even if he was sitting next to Jane, in the passenger seat? The police think she picked him up before she got to the lay-by. Well, if she did, he would hardly have been sitting in the back seat, would he?"

"No," I say, wondering what it must have been like for him to hear all the rumors that his wife had a lover.

"And there's another flaw to your reasoning. If he really thinks that you might go to the police with vital information about him, why would he let you live? Why not just kill you? He's already killed once, so why not again?"

"But if the calls aren't coming from him," I say, be-wildered, "who are they coming from?"

"That's what you need to find out. But, I promise you, they aren't coming from the person who killed Jane." He reaches out and takes hold of my hand. "You need to believe me."

"You don't know how much I want to." My eyes fill with tears. "Do you know what I did on Tuesday morning? I took an overdose. I didn't do it on purpose, I wasn't even aware I had swallowed down a load of pills, but I suppose I did it because, subconsciously, my life had become intolerable."

"If I could have spared you any of it, I would have," he says quietly. "But I had no idea that Jane's murder could impact anyone other than our family."

"It's strange," I say slowly. "I should feel relieved that it isn't the murderer who's been phoning me. But at least I thought I knew who it was. Now, it could be anybody."

"I know this is probably not what you want to hear, but it's more likely to be someone you know."

I stare at him in horror. "Someone I know?"

"Daddy?"

One of his little daughters appears in the doorway dressed in a T-shirt and nappy and clutching a toy rabbit. Getting to his feet, Alex sweeps her into his arms while I dry my tears hurriedly.

"Is Louise still asleep?" he asks, giving her a kiss.

"Loulou sleeping," she says, nodding.

"Do you remember the tissue lady from the park?"

"Is your knee better?" I ask. She holds her leg

straight out so that I can see for myself. "Wonderful," I say, smiling at her. "All gone." I look up at Jane's husband. "I'll let you get on. Thank you, again."

"I hope I've helped."

"Yes, you have." I turn to his little daughter. "Good-bye, Charlotte."

"You remembered," he says, pleased.

He walks me to the door. "Please think about what I told you."

"I will."

"Take care."

There are so many emotions running through me that it's impossible to drive, so I find a bench in the park and sit for a while. Some of the fear that I've been carrying around with me for the past ten weeks, since that first phone call, has disappeared. Even though Matthew and Rachel both told me it wasn't logical to suppose that it was the murderer phoning me, they didn't know that I had seen Jane that night, so they couldn't understand my fears. But Jane's husband had all the facts and when I look at his reasoning—about why the calls can't be coming from the murderer—it's hard to fault it. But what about his other reasoning, that the calls are coming from someone close to me?

Fear comes back, doubling in size, settling inside me, squeezing the breath from me to make more room for itself. It dries my mouth, sends names ricocheting around my brain. It could be anybody. One of my friends' husbands, the lovely man who comes every few months to clean the windows, the man from the alarm company, the new neighbor down the road, a father from school. I go through every man I know and end up suspecting them all. I don't ask myself why any of them would want to do such a thing—I ask myself, why not? Any one of them could be a psychopath.

Not wanting Alex to come along with his little daughters and find me sitting here, like a stalker, I leave the park. I should go home, but what if I find that someone's been in the house again? They've already got past the alarm once, but how? Somebody with the technical knowledge to do so. The man from Superior Security Systems? I remember the window I found open after he left that day. Maybe he fixed it in some way so that he could come and go as he pleased. Is he my silent caller?

Reluctant to go back to the house, I drive back to Browbury and find a hairdresser who can take me without an appointment. It's only when I'm sitting in front of the mirror with nothing to do except look at my face that I realize how much the last couple of months have taken out of me. I look gaunt and the hairdresser asks me if I've had a recent illness, because my hair shows signs of stress. I choose not to tell her that I have early-onset dementia or that I overdosed just a few days before.

I'm so long at the hairdresser's that Matthew's car is already in the drive when I get back. As I pull up outside the front door, it flies open.

"Thank God! Where have you been?" he asks, looking frantic. "I've been worried about you."

"I went to Browbury to do some shopping and have my hair cut," I say mildly.

"Well, next time, leave a note, or phone and tell me you're going out. You can't just wander off, Cass."

I smart at this. "I didn't just wander off!"

"You know what I mean."

"Not really. I'm not going to start telling you my every move, Matthew. I didn't before and I'm not going to start now."

"Before you didn't have early-onset dementia. I love you, Cass, so of course I worry about you. At least get yourself another mobile so that I can contact you."

"All right," I say, putting myself in his shoes. "I'll get one tomorrow, I promise."

# TUESDAY, SEPTEMBER 29TH

When the phone rings the next morning, I think about what Alex said about the calls coming from someone I know and take the call.

"Who are you?" I ask, interested rather than scared. "You're not who I thought you were, so who are you?"

I put the phone down, feeling strangely victorious, but to my dismay he phones straight back. I stand there wondering if I should answer, knowing that if I don't he'll call until I do. But I don't want to give him what he wants, I don't want to stand there submissively silent, not any more. I've lost too many weeks of my life already. If I don't want to lose any more, I need to start standing up to him.

Worried that I'll end up cracking, I go out to the garden to get away from the sound of the phone. I think about taking it off the hook so that he can't get through but I don't want to anger him any more than I already have. The other option is to go out for the day and only come home once Matthew is back. But I'm fed-up being driven from my home. What I need is something to keep me busy.

My eyes fall on my secateurs, which are lying where I left them two months before, the day before Hannah and Andy came round for a barbecue, on the windowsill along with my gloves, so I decide to do a bit of pruning. It takes me about an hour to get the roses in shape and then I weed steadily until lunchtime, marveling that whoever is calling me has so much time to spare on a futile exercise, because he must have guessed by now that I'm not going to pick up. I try to work out the sort of man he is but I know that to stereotype him as a loner who has trouble forming relationships would be a mistake. He could be a pillar of the community, a family man, a man with plenty of friends and interests. The only thing I'm sure about now is that he's someone I know, and this makes me less frightened than perhaps I should be.

It's sobering to realize that if it hadn't been for the murder, I would never have put up with his calls in the first place. I would have laughed at him down the phone, called him pathetic, told him that if he didn't stop annoying me I would call the police. The only reason I didn't was because I thought he was the murderer and I was so paralyzed by fear that I couldn't do anything.

The thought that he has got away with so much for so long makes me determined to bring him out into the open.

Around one o'clock the calls, which have been getting less frequent, suddenly stop altogether, as if he's decided to take a break for lunch. Or maybe he has repetitive-strain injury from dialing my number so often. I take a leaf from his book and make myself some lunch, pleased that I've managed to stay so long in the house by myself. But when two-thirty comes and goes without him calling back I begin to feel uneasy. Although I'm determined to bring him out of hiding, I'm not ready for him yet.

Wanting to be able to protect myself in case he decides to pay me a visit, I go to the garden shed and take out a hoe, a rake and, more important, some hedge cutters, and move to the front of the house where I feel safer. As I'm clearing dead flowers from a bed, the man from up the road—the ex-pilot—walks by and this time he calls hello. I look over at him, weighing him up. I feel so much better after my chat with Alex yesterday, and the man looks sad, not sinister, so I say hello back.

I do about another hour's gardening, keeping an ear out for the phone and when I've finished, I bring one of the sunbeds round to the side of the house to rest until Matthew gets back. But I can't relax. I want to get my life back but I know I'm not going to be able to until I find out who my tormentor is. And to do that, I'm going to need help.

I go into the hall and phone Rachel.

"I don't suppose you could meet me after work, could you?"

"Is everything all right?" she asks.

"Yes, everything's fine, I just want your help with something."

"Sounds intriguing! I can meet you in Castle Wells, if you like, but I can't get there until six-thirty. Will that do?"

I hesitate, because I haven't been back to Castle Wells since I lost my car in the car park. But I can't expect Rachel to always come to Browbury when she only works ten minutes away from Castle Wells.

"The Spotted Cow?"

"See you there."

I leave Matthew a note, telling him I've gone to buy myself a new mobile, and drive to Castle Wells. I don't want to risk parking in the multi-story again so I find a space in one of the smaller car parks and head for the main shopping precinct. As I walk past the Spotted Cow, I look through the window to see if it's already crowded and see Rachel sitting at a table halfway down the room. Just as I'm wondering why she's already there, an hour earlier than she told me she would be, somebody walks over to her table and sits down. And I find myself staring at John.

Shocked, I duck down quickly and hurriedly retrace my steps, going back the way I came, away from the Spotted Cow, glad that neither of them had seen me. Rachel and John. My mind reels, but only because I'd never expected them to get together. And is that what they are? Together? I try to remember the body language

I'd seen and it had definitely looked cozy. But a couple? Yet the more I think about it, the more it makes sense. They are both clever, gorgeous and fun. I imagine them having nights out, filled with laughter and drinking, and a wave of sadness hits me. Why haven't they said anything? Especially Rachel.

I slow my pace, realizing that the thought of the two of them together isn't a nice thought. Although I love Rachel dearly, John seems too much of a gentle soul to be truly happy with her. And too young. I hate that I feel disapproving and I'm glad I've been forewarned in case Rachel decides to tell me later when we meet that she and John are together. They might not be, of course. Maybe they're just meeting as ex-lovers, in which case Rachel will probably never tell me. When I think about it, she's never told me much about the men she goes out with, probably because she never stays with them very long.

I suddenly realize that I'm not likely to find a phone shop in the direction I'm heading so I cross over the road and go back toward the center without passing in front of the Spotted Cow. A little farther along I see the Baby Boutique and I go red with embarrassment when I remember how I had pretended to be pregnant that day. As I draw level, I find myself pushing the door open and I can't believe that I'm actually going to confess that I'd lied about expecting a baby. But if I'm to get my life back I need to get it in order, so I walk over to the counter, relieved that the shop is empty, relieved that the same young woman is there.

"I don't know if you remember me," I begin. She looks at me inquiringly. "I came in a couple of months ago and bought a sleep-suit."

"Yes, of course I remember you," she says, smiling. "We're expecting babies around the same time, aren't we?" She looks down at my stomach and when she sees my lack of a bump she looks up at me in dismay.

"I'm sorry," she falters.

"It's all right," I say hurriedly. "I wasn't actually pregnant. I thought I was but I wasn't."

She gives me a sympathetic look. "Was it one of those phantom pregnancies?" she asks and because I feel I've earned the right to keep a little of my integrity intact, I tell her that it was probably down to a lot of wishful thinking on my part.

"I'm sure it will happen for you soon," she says.

"I hope so."

"If you don't mind me saying so, I did think buying the pram was perhaps a little premature. I'm not sure what exactly we can do but if I ask our manager, I'm sure she'd agree to take it back at a slightly discounted price."

"I haven't come here to try and give the pram back," I reassure her, realizing that's what she thinks. "I'm very happy to keep it. I just wanted to say hello."

"I'm very glad you did."

I say goodbye and walk toward the door, amazed at how good I feel.

"By the way, it was the right pram, wasn't it? The navy-blue one?"

"Yes," I say, smiling.

"Thank goodness for that. Your friend would have shot me if I'd got it wrong."

I go into the street, her words echoing in my ears. *Your friend*. Had I misunderstood? Had she been referring to the couple who'd been in the shop at the same time as me? Maybe, once I'd left the shop that day, she hadn't been sure which pram I'd ordered and had asked them if it was definitely the blue one I'd wanted. But she had said friend and not friends and, anyway, she knew that they were just people who happened to be in the shop at the same time as me. So who was she talking about?

Even though the truth is staring me in the face, I don't want to believe it. The only person who knew I was in the shop that day was John, and I don't want to believe that he arranged to have the pram sent to me because then I'd have to ask, why? My head reeling again, I cross back over the road and head for Costas, where we'd gone after I bumped into him coming out of the Baby Boutique. I order a coffee and sit at the window, my eyes fixed on the shop over the road, trying to work out what could have happened.

It could be fairly innocent. John has always had a soft spot for me so maybe when he went to the shop and mentioned that I'd suggested he buy a sleep-suit for his friend's baby, the assistant had talked about my supposed pregnancy quite naturally and, delighted for me, he decided to buy me a present. But surely he wouldn't have chosen something as expensive as a pram, and if it was a gift, why had he sent it anonymously? And why, when we met a while later in Browbury, didn't he mention either my pregnancy or the pram? Had he been embarrassed about what he'd done? None of it made any sense.

The alternative, that it wasn't innocent at all, makes my heart pound. Had John been following me that day, had he been following me the day he'd knocked on my car window in Browbury? When I think about it now, it was unusual that I bumped into him twice in less than ten days. Had he arranged to have the pram sent to me anonymously to frighten me? He couldn't know that I would think I'd sent it myself because he hadn't known at that point about my dementia. I'd only told him about that over lunch in Browbury. And why would he do any of this? *Because he loves you*, a voice whispers in my mind and my heart thuds painfully. He loves me enough to hate me?

When I realize that everything points to John being my silent caller, I feel sick. He knew how nervous I'd been since Jane's murder and when I'd mention the isolated position of our house, he had pointed out that there were other houses nearby. But he's never been to my house so how would he know? I'm suddenly so angry at him that I have to stop myself from going straight to the Spotted Cow and confronting him in front of Rachel. Because, before I do, I need to be absolutely sure of everything.

I turn it around in my head, looking at it from every angle, but no matter how much I don't want it to be true, all the facts are screaming that I've found my tormentor. I think back to July, when I'd shouted at my silent caller to leave me alone, and John had taken on his real persona and pretended surprise. All along it had been him. And I had apologized and told him that I'd been receiving nuisance calls from a call center. How he must have laughed to himself as he pretended he'd phoned to invite me for a drink with Connie and the others from work. I'd told him that I wasn't sure I'd be able to make it because Matthew had taken the following two days off. And on those days, there hadn't been any calls. Even the timing matches; with school closed, he has had the whole summer to devote to terrifying me. But it seems so insane. If someone had told me this morning that John was my silent caller, I would have laughed in their face.

Then something occurs to me and I feel as if I've been hit by a sledgehammer. On the night of Jane's murder, John didn't go back to Connie's. He and Jane used to play tennis together, he had told me that himself. Is it possible they had been lovers? Had he gone to meet her that night? Is it possible that he murdered Jane? The answer has to be no. And then I remember him saying that his girlfriend, who none of us had ever met, was no longer on the scene.

And what about Rachel? If she and John are together, she could be in terrible danger. But if she and John are together, maybe she knows what he's done. I feel suddenly breathless. There are so many scenarios going round in my head that I'm tempted to go straight back home without going anywhere near the Spotted Cow. I look at my watch; I have five minutes to decide.

In the end, I decide to meet Rachel. I use the walk

there to prepare for every eventuality, that John will be with her, that he won't be, that Rachel will tell me about her and John, that she won't say anything about him at all. If she doesn't, should I tell her my fears about John? But even to my ears they seem nonsensical, far-fetched.

By the time I arrive, the pub is so busy that it's just as well Rachel was there an hour earlier or we wouldn't have gotten a seat.

"Couldn't you have found a quieter table?" I attempt to joke, because we seem to be surrounded by a huge group of French students.

"I've only just arrived," she says, giving me a hug, "so we're lucky to have a table at all."

I hear the lie and something inside me stirs.

"I'll get some drinks," I offer. "What would you like?"

"Just a small glass of wine, please, as I'm driving."

The wait at the bar gives me the chance to work out what I'm going to say when she asks me why I wanted to meet because I no longer need her help in tracking down my silent caller. Unless it isn't John, unless I've taken what the shop assistant told me and have woven a whole intricate story around it.

"So, what do you want to chat about?" she asks once I've sat down.

"Matthew," I say.

"Why, what's the problem?"

"No problem, just Christmas coming up. I'd like to do something really special for him. He's had a lot to put up with recently, one way or another, and I'd like to make it up to him. I just wondered if you had any ideas about what I could do. You're so good at things like that."

"It's not for another couple of months," she says.

"I know, but I'm not exactly good at keeping on top of things at the moment. I thought if you could help me plan something, at least you'd be able to remind me what it is."

She laughs. "All right. What sort of thing were you thinking of? A weekend away? A flight in a hot-air balloon? A sky-diving experience? A cookery course?"

"Any of those sound great, except perhaps the cookery course," I say and, for the next half-hour, she comes up with idea after idea, all of which I say yes to because my mind is elsewhere.

"You're not going to be able to give him all of them," she says, exasperated, "although, as money is no option, I suppose you could."

"Well, you've certainly given me plenty to think about," I tell her gratefully. "What about you? Any news since Sunday?"

"No, same old," she says, pulling a face.

"You never got round to telling me about the chap from Siena, you know, the brother."

"Alfie." She stands up. "Sorry, I need the loo, I won't be long."

While she's away, I decide that I'm going to have to somehow introduce John into the conversation and take it from there. But when she comes back, instead of sitting down she stays standing.

"You don't mind if I abandon you, do you?" she

says. "It's just that I've got a busy day tomorrow and I need to get home."

"No, go ahead," I say, surprised that she's going so soon. "I would leave with you but I need a coffee before driving home."

She stoops and hugs me goodbye. "I'll catch up with you later in the week," she promises.

I watch her curiously as she goes, pushing her way through the throng of French students, because I've never known her to leave in such a hurry before. Has she gone to meet John? Maybe he's waiting for her somewhere, in a different pub. As she reaches the door, a shout goes up from one of the French students and I realize that she's trying to call Rachel back.

"Madame, Madame!" she cries. But Rachel has gone. The student begins to grapple with one of the boys next to her and, losing interest, I turn to a passing waitress and ask her to bring me a coffee.

"Excuse me." I look up to see the French girl standing in front of me, a small black phone in her hand. "I am sorry but my friend took this from your friend's bag."

"No, that's not hers," I say, looking at the phone. "She has an iPhone."

"*Si*," she insists. "My friend there—" she turns and points to the boy she'd been grappling with "—he took it from her bag."

"Why would he do that?" I frown.

"It was a *défi*, a dare. It was a very bad thing to do. I try to give it back to her but he would not give it to me. But now I have it so I give it to you."

I look over to the boy she pointed out. He grins back at me and, pressing the palms of his hands together, gives me a little bow.

"He is very bad, no?"

"Yes," I agree. "But I don't think it belongs to my friend. Maybe he took it from someone else."

She calls over to him and after a quick conversation in French, where everybody around them seems to be nodding in agreement, she turns back to me.

"*Si*," she says again. "Yes. She push past him and he took it from her bag." She looks anxiously at me. "If you want, I give it to the man at the bar."

"No, it's fine," I say, taking it. "Thanks. I'll make sure she gets it. I hope your friend hasn't taken anything of mine," I say, frowning at her.

"No, no," she says hurriedly.

"Well, thank you."

She goes back to her friends and I turn the phone over in my hand, still not convinced it belongs to Rachel. It has to be one of the most basic pay-as-you-go models on the market. Did John give it to her? It feels as if everything's crumbling around me and I don't know who to trust, not even myself. I flip the phone open and go into the list of contacts. There's only one number registered. I hesitate for a moment, wondering if I'm really going to dial it. I feel like a stalker but I'm not even sure it's Rachel's phone and, anyway, I don't need to say anything, all I need is to listen to the voice at the other end.

Feeling sick with apprehension, I call the number. It's answered immediately.

"What the hell are you phoning me for? I thought we agreed only for texting."

Even if I had wanted to speak I wouldn't have been able to. Because suddenly, I find it impossible to breathe.

It's the noise of the French students getting up to leave that brings me back to reality. I look down at the phone in my hand and realize that, in my shock, I've forgotten to hang up. The call has been timed out anyway and, my mind racing, I try to work out if, during those couple of minutes when the line was still open, anything incriminating could have been heard. But the person on the other end would only have been able to hear the sounds of the voices around me, not the frantic beating of my heart. Anyway, maybe he had hung up long before then, because he must have realized something was wrong.

My coffee arrives and I gulp it down quickly, aware that Matthew will be wondering where I am because in my note I hadn't mentioned meeting Rachel, I'd only said that I was going out to buy a phone. I walk quickly to the car and hide Rachel's phone at the back of the glove compartment. I want to get home as fast as possible but nothing in the world will make me go back via Blackwater Lane, so I put my foot down, thinking about what I'm going to say to Rachel when she calls, as she surely will.

"I know you left me a note but I didn't expect you to get back this late," Matthew grumbles as I walk into the kitchen. He gives me a kiss.

"Sorry, I met Rachel for a quick drink." The room is cool compared to outside and smells faintly of toast.

"Ah, that explains it. Did you get yourself a new mobile?"

"No, I wasn't sure which one to buy but I promise I'll get one tomorrow."

"We can look at the different models on the Internet, if you like," he offers. "By the way, Rachel phoned. She asked if you could call her back."

My heart skips. "I'll do it in a minute. I need a shower first, it's so hot out there."

"It sounded pretty urgent."

"I suppose I'd better do it now then."

I fetch the phone from the hall and bring it back to the kitchen.

"Wine?" Matthew asks, as I dial her number. The bottle is already open so I nod, the phone to my ear.

"Hello, Cass." It's the first time I've heard Rachel sound agitated, although she does her best to hide it.

"Matthew said you called," I say.

"Yes, look, do you know if anyone found a mobile after I'd left the pub? I think I might have dropped it somewhere."

"You can't have because I'm phoning you on it," I say reasonably.

"It wasn't my phone, it was a phone that I was look-ing after for a friend. It might have fallen out of my bag or something."

*A friend.* The word sits heavy on my mind. "Have you phoned the Spotted Cow to ask if anyone handed it in?"

"Yes, they don't have it."

"Wait a minute—was it a little black one?"

"Yes, that's it. Do you know where it is?"

"Probably halfway across the Channel by now. You know that group of French students who were sitting near us? Well, after you left they were mucking around with this little phone, throwing it to one another and trying to grab it off each other. I didn't really take much notice because I thought it belonged to one of them."

There's an appalled silence. "Are you sure?"

"Yes. They were making fun of it because it was one of those really basic models. That's why I'm not sure it's the one you were looking after for your friend," I add doubtfully. "Nobody really uses them anymore."

"Do you know if they're still in the pub? The French students?"

The thought of her racing all the way back to Castle Wells is savagely pleasing.

"They were when I left. They looked pretty settled in for the night," I say, safe in the knowledge that they'll be long gone by the time she gets there, as they were already making moves when I left.

"Then I'd better go and see if I can get it back."

"Good luck, I hope you find it."

I put the phone down, relieved that I managed to pull it off.

"What was all that about?" Matthew frowns.

"Rachel lost a phone in the pub and some French students took it," I explain. "She's on her way there now to try to get it back."

"Right," he says, nodding.

"What do you fancy eating tonight? How about some steak?"

"Actually, Andy phoned and asked if I'd like to go to the pub for a pint. You don't mind, do you?"

"No, go ahead. Will you get something to eat there?"

"Yes, don't worry."

I stretch my arms over my head, yawning. "I'll probably go to bed early, in that case."

"I'll try not to disturb you when I come in," he promises, fishing his car keys from his pocket.

I watch him as he walks toward the front door.

"I love you," I call after him.

"I love you more," he says, turning to smile at me.

I wait until the car has pulled out of the drive and then I wait a little longer, just to be sure. And then I run out to my car and get the mobile, the one Rachel told me she was looking after for a friend.

Back in the house, I go into the sitting room and sit down, shaking so much I can hardly open the phone. I go into the text messages and look at the last one she received, just before she left the Spotted Cow.

Tues 19:51
*Hang on in there*
*End in sight, I promise*

I scroll up to the one before, the last one that Rachel sent, probably from the ladies'.

Tues 19:50
*False alarm, she had nothing of interest to say*
*I'm leaving now, really fed up.*
*Beginning to wonder if it will ever end* ☺

And the ones before that, earlier this evening.

Tues 18:25
**Let me know what happens**

Tues 18:24
*Job done, seeds of disrepute planted*
*I asked him to tell the head, so hopefully they'll take root*
*Waiting for her to arrive.*

And then the rest of the messages for today, starting with the first one that morning.

Tues 10:09
**We have a problem**
**When I phoned this morning she said she knew**
**I wasn't murderer**

Tues 10:09
*Wtf?*

Tues 10:10
**Didn't sound frightened either**

Tues 10:10
*What you going to do?*

Tues 10:10
**Phone back**
**Wear her down, like before**

Tues 10:52
*How goes it?*

Tues 10:53
**She's refusing to pick up**

Tues 10:53
*Sure she hasn't gone out?*

Tues 10:53
**Pretty sure**

Tues 10:53
*Keep on trying*

Tues 10:54
**Will do**

Tues 16:17
*Guess what? She just phoned, wants to chat*
*Any ideas?*

Tues 16:19
**Maybe to do with calls I made this morning**
**Find out everything you can**

Tues 16:21
*Have arranged to see her in CW*
*I'll already be there for J so will kill two birds with one*
*stone*

Then I realize I'll get there much faster if I scroll to the very beginning of the messages. And I see that they start on 17 July, the night I drove down Blackwater Lane and saw Jane in her car.

17 Jul 21:31
*Receiving clear?*

17 Jul 21:31
*Yes* ☺

17 Jul 21:31
*Good. Remember, no phoning, only text me at work, or when you know she's not around*
*Important that you keep this phone on you at all times*
*I'll check in with you every evening when she's asleep*

17 Jul 21:18
*It's going to be hard not seeing you for next few months*

17 Jul 21:18
*Think of the money*
*If she had given you some, it wouldn't have come to this*
*Now we get it all*

17 Jul 21:18
*It is going to work, isn't it?*

17 Jul 21:19
*Of course. Look how well it's worked already*
*She already thinks she's forgetting things*
*And that's only small stuff, wait until we really*
*start messing with her head*

17 Jul 21:19
*Hope you're right. I'll send her text about Susie's present*
*later*
*If she falls for it we'll be home and dry*

18 Jul 10:46
*Good morning!*
*Just to let you know she's on way to meet*
*you*

18 Jul 10:46
*Ready and waiting*
*Did she say anything about Susie's present?*

18 Jul 10:47
*No but she seemed on edge*

18 Jul 10:47
*Let's hope my text did the trick*
*Did you hear about local woman murder?*

18 Jul 10:47
*Yes, awful*
*Let me know how it goes*

18 Jul 12:56
*Omg it went like a dream!*
*Thought I should warn you she's on her way home*

18 Jul 12:56
**Already? Thought you were having lunch together**

18 Jul 12:56
*She lost her appetite* ☺

18 Jul 12:57
**It worked that well?**

18 Jul 12:57
*Couldn't have gone better, she had total meltdown*

18 Jul 12:58
**She really believed she forgot about present?**

18 Jul 12:58
*Told her she was the one who suggested it*
*Brilliant watching her pretending she remembered!*
*Is the money ready, because she'll check*

18 Jul 12:58
**160 in drawer**

18 Jul 12:59
*Bingo!*

It takes me about an hour to read through all the messages and get back to where I started, with the last message Rachel sent from the Ladies' toilet in the Spotted Cow. Most of them are read through eyes blurred with tears and some remain seared in my brain long after I've moved on to the next. They alone are enough to start me on the road to the truth, a truth I'm half scared to face because I know it will destroy me. But when I remember what I've been through for the last three months, and that I'm still standing, I realize that I'm stronger than I think.

I close my eyes, wondering when Matthew and Rachel first began their affair. I think back to when they first met, about a month after Matthew appeared in my life. I was already in love with him and was desperate for Rachel to like him, yet they hadn't really hit it off. Or so it had seemed at the time. Maybe there had been an instant connection between them, and they had been cool with each other to hide it. Maybe they had become lovers not long after, before Matthew had even married me. It's terrible to think that my marriage to Matthew might have been nothing more than a sham, a means for him and Rachel to get their hands on my money. What I want to believe is that he truly loved me and that his desire for my money only came after, and that it was Rachel who planted the seed in his head. But for the moment, it's something I don't know.

I get slowly to my feet, feeling as if I've aged a hundred years in the last couple of hours. Rachel's phone is still in my hand and I know I have to hide it before Matthew comes back. He isn't out with Andy, he's out with Rachel, helping her look for the little black mobile that holds so much incriminating evidence. I scan the room and my eyes fall on the orchids lined up on the windowsill. My mobile is still hidden under one of the plants. I walk over, lift a different plant out of its pot, place the phone in the bottom and put the orchid back. And then I go to bed.

It's only when I hear Matthew's car pulling into the drive that I realize the danger I'm in. If Rachel and Matthew have managed to trace the French students, they'll know I have the phone. I throw the covers off me and leap from the bed, hardly able to believe that I came up to bed instead of taking the phone to the police. But I had been in such a daze, and so distraught, that I hadn't been thinking straight. Now it's too late. Without my mobile, and the house phone downstairs, I have no way of calling them.

The sound of the car door slamming propels me into the bathroom, looking for something to defend myself with. I fling open the cupboard; my eyes fall on a pair of nail scissors but they don't seem enough of a weapon. Matthew's key rattles in the lock and, in a panic, I grab a can of hairspray and run back to the bedroom. Climbing into bed, I slide the hairspray under my pillow, easing off the top as I do so. Then, lying down facing the door, I close my eyes and feign sleep, my hand gripping the hidden can tightly. And like ticker tape running through a machine, the text messages hurtle through my brain.

20 Sep 11:45
*I'm bored*

20 Sep 11:51
**Why don't you drop in and see coffee machine
in action
New one in place**

20 Sep 11:51
*Really?*
*Thought you didn't want us meeting up*

20 Sep 11:51
**Willing to make an exception
Also need you to dig**

20 Sep 11:51
*For what?*

20 Sep 11:52
**Why she's OK at weekends when she's crashed
out during the week**

20 Sep 11:52
*OK, what time?*

20 Sep 11:53
**2 p.m.**

20 Sep 23:47
*Big risk kissing me in hall this afternoon*

20 Sep 23:47
**Worth it**
**Find out anything?**

20 Sep 23:47
*She doesn't take her pills at weekends*
*Doesn't want you to know how much they affect her*
*So hides them in drawer*
*Which means she only gets the 2 you put in her orange juice*

20 Sep 23:49
**Did she say which drawer?**

20 Sep 23:49
*Bedside*

20 Sep 23:49
**Hold on, going to check**

20 Sep 23:53
**You're right, found 11**
**Have a brilliant idea**

20 Sep 23:53
*You're getting me excited*

20 Sep 23:54
**Will use them for overdose**

20 Sep 23:54
*No!!! You can't!!!*

20 Sep 23:54
**Make it seem like suicide attempt, make her
seem unstable**

20 Sept 23:55
*What if they kill her?*

20 Sept 23:55
**Our problem would be solved
But they won't. Will research properly, don't
worry**

I hear his soft tread on the stairs, and with each step
he takes, my heart thumps a little louder; the beat of a
drum heralding his arrival. As he comes to a stop at
the foot of my bed, it reaches a crescendo and I can't
believe he can't hear it, or see my body shaking underneath the quilt. Surely he can sense my fear, just
as I can sense him standing there looking down at me.
Does he know I have the phone? Or am I safe, at least
for another night? The waiting becomes unbearable,
then impossible. I stir slightly and half open my eyes.

"You're back," I mumble sleepily. "Did you have a
good time with Andy?"

"Yes, he sends his love. Go back to sleep, I'm going
for a shower."

I close my eyes obediently and he leaves the room.

And as his footsteps disappear down the hall, the ticker tape of messages continues to scroll through my brain.

21 Sep 16:11
*We have problem*
*She knows you were in the house earlier*

21 Sep 16:11
*How?*

21 Sep 16:11
*Don't know, have called police*

21 Sep 16:12
*What? Why?*

21 Sep 16:12
*Because she wanted me to*
*Would have looked suspicious if I refused*
*Going home now, hope I'll be able to cover for you*

21 Sep 23:17
*Can you get back to me asap*
*Really worried, need to know what happened this afternoon*

21 Sep 23:30
*Don't worry, all OK*

21 Sep 23:30
*How did she know I was there?*


21 Sep 23:30
**You put her mug in dishwasher**
**She noticed**


21 Sep 23:31
*Did I? Don't remember*


21 Sep 23:31
**Who has eod now?**


21 Sep 23:31
*You seem very cheerful considering near miss*


21 Sep 23:31
**Everything has worked out for best**


21 Sep 23:32
*How's that?*


21 Sep 23:32
**After police left I told her she was paranoid and**
**eod**
**She stormed off, took 2 pills**


21 Sep 23:33
*So?*

21 Sep 23:33
*So will add 13 in drawer to orange juice tomorrow morning*
*+ 2 she takes*
*Total 15*
*+ 2 already in bloodstream*
*Should be enough*

21 Sep 23:34
*You mean it's really going to happen?*

21 Sep 23:34
*Too good a chance to miss*
*It's now or never*

21 Sep 23:34
*Will it work?*

21 Sep 23:35
*I can attest to row we had*
*You can say she was depressed when you saw her yesterday afternoon*
*Say she told you about pills in drawer but you never thought she'd use them*

21 Sep 23:36
*15 pills won't kill her, will they?*

21 Sep 23:36
*No, just make her ill*

*I'll go home at lunch time, pretend I want to
make up*
*Hopefully will find her unconscious and will
call ambulance*

*

22 Sep 08:08
*Have done it*
*Leaving for work but will go back in couple of
hours*

22 Sep 08:09
*What if she doesn't drink juice?*

22 Sep 08:09
*She will make another suicide attempt*

22 Sep 11:54
*Just got call from hospital*
*On way there now*

22 Sep 11:54
*Does that mean it worked?*

22 Sep 11:55
*Looks like it. She phoned ambulance herself*
*Will let you know*

I suddenly realize that the shower hasn't been turned
on, that Matthew isn't in the bathroom. My heart races
with fear. Where is he? In the dark silence, I strain

my ears and hear the low murmur of his voice coming from the front bedroom. He and Rachel must be terrified that the phone will somehow find its way into the hands of the police and that their game will be up. Are they in enough of a panic to kill me? Or at the very least force-feed me enough pills to make it look as if I've made another suicide attempt, except that this time it succeeds? As I lie in bed, waiting for him to come back, my hand still clutching the can, I feel more frightened than I ever have. Especially now that I know about the knife.

o8 Aug 23:44
*Went like a dream at doctors today*

o8 Aug 23:44
*Medication?*

o8 Aug 23:44
*Yes but says she won't take it*
*Need to get her to change her mind*

o8 Aug 23:45
*I think I may have just the thing*

o8 Aug 23:45
*What?*

o8 Aug 23:45
*A great big kitchen knife*
*Just like the one used in the murder*

o8 Aug 23:46
*??? Where did you get it?*

o8 Aug 23:46
*London*
*Thought I could plant it somewhere for her to find*
*Give her a scare*

o8 Aug 23:46
*Not a good idea, she'll phone the police*
*And what about fingerprints*
*Don't think it will work*

o8 Aug 23:47
*It will if we plan properly*

o8 Aug 23:47
*Will think about it*

o9 Aug 00:15
*Have thought about it*

o9 Aug 00:17
*You there?*

o9 Aug 00:20
*I am now! You have a plan?*

o9 Aug 00:20
*Yes but too difficult to explain by text*
*Will phone you*

09 Aug 00:20
*Thought we agreed phoning too risky?*

09 Aug 00:21
**Desperate times desperate measures and all that**

09 Aug 20:32
**Have left back door open**
**Stick to what we agreed and make sure you get the hell out of it quick**
**Hope we're not making a mistake**

09 Aug 20:33
*Trust me, it will be fine* ☺

09 Aug 23:49
**Hi**

09 Aug 23:49
*Thank God! Heard her screaming, have been dying to know what happened!*

09 Aug 23:50
**Can't actually believe it worked, she was hysterical**

09 Aug 23:50
*Glad police didn't come*

09 Aug 23:51
**Managed to persuade her she was seeing things**

09 Aug 23:51
*Told you*
*Had to leave knife in shed, hope that's ok*

09 Aug 23:52
**No problem—you never know, we might need
it again one day**

What if, at this very moment, Rachel is persuading
Matthew to go down to the shed, take the knife and
use it to kill me? If he were to slit my throat, people
would think that Jane's murderer had struck again.
Matthew would attest to the silent calls I'd been getting
and wring his hands that he hadn't believed me when
I'd told him the murderer was after me. Rachel would
give him an alibi for tonight, saying she had asked him
to go round because after seeing me earlier in the pub,
she'd been worried about me. The knife used to kill me
would never be found, just as the knife used to kill Jane
has never been found. And I would become known as
Cass Anderson, the second victim of the woods murderer.

The door to the spare bedroom clicks open. I hold
my breath, waiting to hear which way he'll go, down
the stairs and out to the garden or along the landing
toward me. If he goes downstairs, will I have enough
time to run to the sitting room, take Rachel's mobile
from under the orchid and leave the house before he
comes back? Should I leave on foot or take the car? If I
take the car, the noise of the engine starting will bring
him running. If I leave on foot, how far would I get

before he notices I'm no longer in bed? When I hear his footsteps padding down the landing toward the bedroom, I'm weak with relief that I don't have to make any decisions. Unless he already has the knife, unless he took it from the shed before coming in.

He comes into the bedroom and it takes all of my willpower not to leap from the bed and spray hairspray into his eyes, to attack before I'm attacked. My finger, poised on the nozzle, is shaking so much I doubt I'd be able to aim properly, and it's only the thought of not being able to disable him before he overpowers me that keeps me where I am. I hear the rustle of his clothes as he undresses and force myself to breathe evenly, like someone in a deep sleep. If he gets into bed and finds me trembling like a leaf, he'll be suspicious. And, tonight, my life depends on staying calm.

# WEDNESDAY, SEPTEMBER 30TH

When morning comes, I can hardly believe that I'm still alive. It seems to take Matthew an agonizingly long time to leave for work and, once he has, I dress hurriedly and go down to the kitchen, waiting for his call to come in, acutely aware that today of all days I need to play it just right. Today, more than ever, I need to be who he wants me to be.

I thought I might not feel scared, now that I know who he is, my silent caller. But knowing what he is capable of makes me more frightened, which serves me well when the phone starts ringing around nine. Because I actually spoke to him yesterday, when I asked him who he was, I know I'm going to have to say something again today or he'll wonder why my newfound confidence has disappeared overnight. So again, I ask him who he is and then, just before hanging up, I ask him to leave me alone with what I hope is the right amount of fear in my voice.

I have a lot to do today if I'm to unravel their web of lies and deceit so I drive straight to Hannah's house, hoping she won't have gone out. Fortunately, her car's in the drive.

She seems surprised to see me so it's only when, looking slightly embarrassed, she asks me if I'm feeling better that I suspect Matthew has told her I tried to commit suicide. I don't have time to ask her what exactly she's heard so I tell her that I'm almost back to my old self, hoping that will cover it. She invites me in for a coffee and, when I refuse, telling her that I'm in a hurry, I know she's wondering why I've called round.

"Hannah, do you remember the barbecue you came to at ours, at the end of July?" I ask.

"Yes, of course," she says. "We had those delicious marinated steaks Matthew bought from the farm shop." Her eyes light up at the memory.

"This might sound a bit of a silly question but was it when we bumped into each other in Browbury that I invited you?"

"Yes, you said you wanted to have us around for a barbecue."

"But did I actually tell you when? I mean, did I say to come on the Sunday?"

She thinks for a moment, wrapping her slender arms around her waist. "Wasn't it the next day that you invited us? Yes, that's right, I remember Matthew saying that you'd asked him to phone as you were busy in the garden."

"I remember now," I say, making myself sound relieved. "The thing is, I've been having problems with my short-term memory and there are several things I'm not sure about, whether I actually forgot, or if they didn't happen the way I think they did in the first place. That probably doesn't make much sense, does it?"

"In a roundabout sort of way," she says, smiling.

"For example, I've been beating myself up over your invitation to dinner a couple of weeks ago, because I didn't remember you inviting us—"

"That would be because it was Matthew I spoke to," she interrupts. "I'd left a couple of messages, one on the house phone and one on your mobile and, when you didn't phone back, I phoned Matthew."

"And then he forgot to tell me you'd asked me to bring dessert."

"I didn't ask," she protests. "He offered."

To give more substance to the questions I've just asked, I tell her that I may have early-onset dementia and ask her not to tell anyone for the moment as I'm still trying to get used to the idea myself. And then I leave.

24 Jul 15:53
*She wants to meet in Bb, sounded upset*
*Any idea why*

24 Jul 15:55
*Man from alarm company made her nervous
maybe it's that
Can you go?*

24 Jul 15:55
*Yes, told her I'd meet her at 6*

24 Jul 15:55
*Let me know if anything we can use*

24 Jul 23:37
*Hi, how did your meeting with her go?*

24 Jul 23:37
*Fine, nothing to report, said the alarm man spooked
her*

24 Jul 23:37
*Did she tell you she bumped into Hannah?*

24 Jul 23:38
*Yes*

24 Jul 23:38
*Said she told them to come for a bbq
Didn't say when so thinking of using it*

24 Jul 23:38
*How?*

24 Jul 23:38
*Not sure*
*Btw told her I'm going to rig*

24 Jul 23:39
*How did she take it?*

24 Jul 23:39
*Not happy, said I'd already told her so she*
*thinks she forgot*
*Wrote it on the calendar in case she checks,*
*I'm a good forger*

24 Jul 23:39
*Good to know!*

25 Jul 23:54
*Hi, how was your day?*

25 Jul 23:54
*Fine, missing you though. It's so hard L*

25 Jul 23:54
*It's only for a couple of months*
*Have come up with great idea for bbq with*
*H&A*
*Need you to phone house at 10 tomorrow, pre-*
*tend to be Andy*

25 Jul 23:54
*?*

25 Jul 23:55
*Just play along*

26 Jul 10:35
*Thanks, Andy!*

26 Jul 10:35
*Haha did it work?*

26 Jul 10:35
*Out buying sausages for bbq at this very moment*

26 Jul 10:36
*She really believes she invited them?*

26 Jul 10:36
*Yep!*

26 Jul 10:37
*Can't believe it's so easy*

26 Jul 10:37
☺

When I leave Hannah's, I drive to the alarm company in the industrial estate and go into the reception. A lady looks up from behind an untidy desk.

"Can I help you?" she asks, with a smile.

"We had an alarm fitted by your company a couple of months ago. Would it be possible to have a photocopy of our contract? I'm afraid I've mislaid ours."

"Yes, of course." She looks at me inquiringly.

"Anderson," I tell her.

She types it into her computer. "Here we go."

The paper whirs out of the photocopier and she reaches over and hands it to me.

"Thank you." I look at it for a moment, noting the installation date for Saturday, 1 August. And Matthew's signature at the bottom.

20 Jul 23:33
**Guess what? She told me over dinner she wants alarm**
**Has already arranged for someone to call around Friday**

20 Jul 23:33
*Sorry! That was me going on about your isolated house*
*Told her you needed alarm, didn't think she'd actually go ahead*

20 Jul 23:34
**If we get one, it will make things more difficult**

20 Jul 23:34
*Not if you give me the code* ☺

27 Jul 08:39
**Good morning!**

27 Jul 08:40
*Thought you might phone. Are you on way to rig?*

27 Jul 08:41
No at industrial estate, waiting for alarm company to open

27 Jul 08:41
*Why?*

27 Jul 08:41
Going to order the alarm and make her think she did

27 Jul 08:42
*How you going to do that?*

27 Jul 8:42
By forging her signature on dummy contract

27 Jul 8:43
*Can you?*

27 Jul 8:44
Piece of cake. Told you, I'm a good forger
Alarm company about to open, will get back to you

27 Jul 10:46
On train to Aberdeen, have arranged to have alarm installed Saturday morning

*I need to be there but need her out, any ideas?*

27 Jul 10:47
*Will have a think*
*Safe journey*

29 Jul 09:36
*The silent calls are really spooking her!*
*Doesn't want to stay by herself so I suggested she go to hotel*

29 Jul 09:36
*Nice for some*

29 Jul 09:37
*You and me one day, I promise*
*Works out well because she'll be out of the way Saturday when alarm installed*
*But need you to do something for me*

29 Jul 09:38
*OK*

29 Jul 09:38
*Phone house later and leave message*
*Pretend to be from alarm company confirming installation Friday*

29 Jul 09:39
*Don't you mean Saturday?*

29 Jul 09:39
*No, Friday. Trust me, I know what I'm doing.*
*Make same call again tomorrow*

29 Jul 09:40
*OK*

31 Jul 16:05
*Hi, are you back from rig yet?*

31 Jul 16:34
*I am now. At house, about to leave for hotel*
*Told her I found alarm man standing on doorstep*
*Taking dummy contract to prove she ordered it*

31 Jul 16:35
*Hope she buys it*

31 Jul 16:35
*She will*

31 Jul 19:13
*She did*

31 Jul 19:14
*Must think she's going mad!*

31 Jul 19:14
*Isn't that the plan?*

I leave the alarm company and drive to Castle Wells. The shop assistant in the Baby Boutique is busy with a customer so I wait, trying to curb my impatience.

"Don't tell me," she says when she sees me standing there. "You've had second thoughts about keeping the pram."

"Not at all," I reassure her. "But there is something I'd like to know. When I came in yesterday, you mentioned my friend would have shot you if you'd sent the wrong pram."

"That's right." She nods.

"So how did it happen?" I ask. "I'm just curious, because it was completely unexpected. It just turned up out of the blue."

"I did suggest having it delivered a bit nearer the time, because—well, anything can happen. But she wanted it delivered straight away."

"How did it come about? Did she say she wanted to buy me a present and ask for suggestions?"

"More or less. She came in a couple of minutes after you left and said she was a friend of yours. She asked if there was anything in particular you'd been looking at so I told her you'd already bought a sleep-suit and the young couple who were here said jokingly that you'd also liked the pram, and she said it was perfect and ordered it there and then." She looks at me anxiously. "I wondered if I'd spoken out of turn because she seemed shocked when I said we were expecting our babies at around the same time but she reassured me that you'd already told her you were pregnant, she was just surprised that you'd told me."

"The thing is, I was so excited about possibly being pregnant that I told two of my friends and I have no idea which one sent the pram because there wasn't a note with it. Would you be able to tell me what her name was? I'd like to be able to thank her."

"Of course. If you hang on a sec, I'll check on the computer. If you can just remind me of your name?"

"Cassandra Anderson."

"Ah, yes, here it is. Oh, there's no name. She didn't fill that part in."

"Then do you remember what she looked like?"

She thinks for a moment. "Let me see—tallish with dark curly hair. I'm sorry, I suppose that's not much help."

"No, on the contrary, I know exactly who it is. Great, now I'll be able to thank her." I pause a moment. "By the way, do you remember speaking to my husband?"

"Your husband? No, I don't think so."

"He called here the day the pram was delivered—it must have been the Thursday—because he thought the pram had been sent by mistake."

"I'm afraid I don't remember that at all. Are you sure he spoke to me? Mind you, I'm the only one here during the week."

"I must have misunderstood." I smile. "Thank you, you've been a great help."


04 Aug 11:43
*She's just asked to meet in CW, sounded upset*

04 Aug 11:50
*I silent called again*
*You going?*


04 Aug 11:51
*Yes but really busy at work so hope it's quick*
*Will let you know what happens*


04 Aug 14:28
*Best news ever—she thinks your calls are coming from murderer*


04 Aug 14:29
*What???*
*Maybe she is mad*


04 Aug 14:29
*Makes our job easier if she gets there all by herself*
*Also managed to back up bbq story*
*Told her she told me she invited H&A on Sunday*


04 Aug 14:30
*Good work*


04 Aug 14:31
*Need to get back to work, speak later*


04 Aug 14:38
*Guess what?*

04 Aug 14:39
*Thought you had to get back to work*

04 Aug 14:39
*On my way back to car park saw her coming out of baby boutique*

04 Aug 14:39
**Baby boutique?**
**What she doing in there?**

04 Aug 14:40
*Don't ask me*

04 Aug 14:40
**Can you find out?**

04 Aug 14:40
*Don't really have time*

04 Aug 14:40
**Make time**
**Why would she go into baby shop?**
**Might be something we can use**
**We need to use every little thing we can against her**

04 Aug 14:41
*OK*

04 Aug 15:01
*You're never going to believe this*

04 Aug 15:01
**At last**
**What took you so long?**

04 Aug 15:02
*Don't be grumpy*
*I bring you good tidings*

04 Aug 15:02
**Go on**

04 Aug 15:02
*You're going to be a daddy!*

04 Aug 15:03
**WTF???**

04 Aug 15:03
*Are you sure about vasectomy?*

04 Aug 15:03
**Of course I'm sure!**
**What's going on?**

04 Aug 15:03
*Search me*
*She told woman in shop she was pregnant*
*So have ordered you a pram*

04 Aug 15:03
*??*

04 Aug 15:04
*She fell in love with it apparently*
*Can make her think she ordered it, like alarm*

04 Aug 15:04
**Not sure it will work twice**

04 Aug 15:04
*Worth a try*
*If it doesn't can blame shop for mix-up*
*But will need you to be home Friday for delivery*

04 Aug 15:05
**Ok will take couple of days off**
**Play concerned husband**
**Need to think how I can work pram thing**

04 Aug 15:06
*Wish you could spend couple of days with me L*

04 Aug 15:06
**Our day will come**
**Btw I nipped back home and changed code on alarm**
**With bit of luck she'll set it off**

04 Aug 15:07
*She's going to have one shit day*

04 Aug 15:07
**Let's hope first of many** ☺

04 Aug 23:37
*How did it go with alarm?*

04 Aug 23:38
**Wish you could have been here to see it**
**Police came out**

04 Aug 23:38
*She really believed she put in wrong code?*

04 Aug 23:38
**Didn't even question it**

04 Aug 23:38
*Taking candy from baby comes to mind*

04 Aug 23:39
**Incredible isn't it?**

06 Aug 23:45
*All set for pram arriving tomorrow?*

06 Aug 23:47
☺

06 Aug 23:47
*Will you use pregnant thing?*

06 Aug 23:47
*If I can*


07 Aug 23:46
*Thanks for the pram*


07 Aug 23:46
*Glad you like it*
*How did it go?*


07 Aug 23:47
*So funny*
*There was massive mix-up*
*She ordered me a garden shed as surprise*
*Thought pram was shed at first so were talking at cross purposes*


07 Aug 23:47
*?*


07 Aug 23:47
*Don't worry, it was fine*
*Said she never ordered pram so I pretended to phone shop*
*Then threw pregnancy thing at her, said woman in the shop had congratulated me*


07 Aug 23:48
*What did she say?*

07 Aug 23:48
*Woman in shop presumed she was pregnant so went along with it*

07 Aug 23:48
*Weird! What about the pram?*

07 Aug 23:49
*Believes she must have ordered it*

07 Aug 23:49
*No way!*
*She's really screwed up*

07 Aug 23:49
*Best thing is managed to get her to agree to see doctor*
*Appt tomorrow*

07 Aug 23:50
*She won't be pleased you already spoke to him about her*
*What if he doesn't put her on medication?*

07 Aug 23:50
*He will. I've told him she's paranoid and highly strung*
*Hopefully her behavior will confirm it*

From the Baby Boutique I head out to the school where I used to work, arriving just as the lunch break is under way. I think of John and my face flushes with guilt at how quickly I'd accused him, even to the point of him murdering Jane. But I still don't know how innocent he is—he met with Rachel, didn't he? Jane's face appears in my mind and the sadness I always feel comes back. But I can't think about her now, not just yet.

I push open the door to the school's reception area. The corridors are empty and as I walk along I realize how much I miss it all. I arrive in front of the staff room door, take a deep breath and go in.

"Cass!" Connie leaps to her feet, knocking her salad onto the floor, and gives me a huge hug. "Oh, my God, how lovely to see you! Do you know how much we miss you?"

Other colleagues crowd round, asking how I've been and telling me how pleased they are to see me. After I've reassured them that I'm fine, I ask where John and Mary are.

"John's on canteen duty and Mary is in her office," Connie says.

Five minutes later, I'm on my way to see Mary. She looks as delighted to see me as everyone else was, which is reassuring.

"I wanted to apologize for letting you all down," I explain. "First of all, over the Inset day."

"Nonsense," she says, smart as ever in a navy suit and pink shirt. "Your husband gave us plenty of notice so it wasn't a problem. I'm just sorry that I couldn't see you when I popped round in the evening with the flowers. Your husband said you were asleep."

"I should have written to thank you," I say guiltily,

because I don't want her to know that Matthew never gave me the flowers.

"Don't be silly." She looks cautiously at me. "I must say, I didn't expect to see you looking so well. Are you quite sure you're not up to coming back? We miss you."

"I'd love to come back," I say wistfully. "But as you know, I've been ill. In fact, I think you noticed there was something wrong with me last term."

She shakes her head. "I never noticed anything at all, I'm afraid. If I'd known you felt under such pressure, I would have tried to help. I do wish you'd spoken to me."

"But didn't you tell my husband that you'd noticed me not being on top of things?"

"The only thing I told your husband, when he phoned to tell me you wouldn't be coming back, was that you were my most organized and efficient member of staff."

"Did my husband tell you why I wasn't coming back?"

She looks at me candidly. "He said you'd had a nervous breakdown."

"I'm afraid he exaggerated a little."

"I thought he might have, especially when your medical certificate only mentioned you were suffering from stress."

"I don't suppose I could see it, could I?"

"Yes, of course." She goes over to her filing cabinet and flicks though the folders. "Here it is."

I take the paper and study it for a moment.

"Could I have a copy of this, please?"

She doesn't ask why and I don't offer any more information. "I'll get it done for you straightaway," she says.

16 Aug 23:52
**Good news**
**I did as you suggested and cut through the woods on the way to Chichester**
**She had complete breakdown**
**Called out doctor, he said she must take the pills regularly**

16 Aug 23:52
*At last!*

16 Aug 23:52
**There's more**
**Says she doesn't want to go back to work**
**Think we're on home straight**

16 Aug 23:53
*Thank God*
*Time to get down to final part*
*Think I can get into house tomorrow?*

16 Aug 23:53
**Will try and knock her out with pills**
**But be careful**

17 Aug 10:45
*I'm at the house, she's completely out of it*
*How many did you give her?*

17 Aug 10:49
**2 in orange juice + 2 prescribed**
**Wondered why she didn't answer phone**
**Where is she**

17 Aug 10:49
*Crashed out in front of television*
*Have ordered couple of things from shopping channel*

17 Aug 10:49
**Why?**

17 Aug 10:50
*Make her think she ordered them*
*You said she already ordered me earrings so why not*

17 Aug 10:50
**Don't overdo it**

17 Aug 10:50
☺

20 Aug 14:36
**You at house?**

20 Aug 14:36
*Yes, have tidied up a bit*
*Hopefully she'll think she did it*
*If not you can say you did before work and make her feel bad*

24 Aug 23:49
*Phoned Head this afternoon and told her about nervous breakdown*
*Said not to expect her back*

24 Aug 23:49
*What did she say?*

24 Aug 23:49
*Feels bad that she didn't see it coming*
*Wants a medical certificate*

26 Aug 15:09
*How's life?*

26 Aug 15:10
*Would rather be in Siena*
*Machine not delivered, they've said Tuesday now*
*Just ironed you some shirts*

26 Aug 15:10
*Thanks*
*Will take you to Siena as soon as all this over*
*Btw thanks for potato thing*

26 Aug 15:11
*Glad you like it*
*You'll get something else in a couple of days*

28 Aug 17:21
*How's it going?*

28 Aug 17:37
*Head wants to come round with flowers*


28 Aug 17:38
*What did you say?*


28 Aug 17:38
Said yes but will tell her C too ill to see her and
bin the flowers
Btw got certificate from Dr., only says stress
though


28 Aug 17:38
*Damn*


28 Aug 17:38
No mention of breakdown either
So will forge letter for eod tests


28 Aug 17:39
*She's so gullible sure she'll believe it*
*Hope you don't mind but I ordered some pearls for my-self*


28 Aug 17:39
You deserve them


31 Aug 23:49
*How was your day?*

31 Aug 23:50
**Same old**
**She didn't mention meeting you for lunch**
**tomorrow**

31 Aug 23:50
*Good, means she's forgotten*
*Have to be at house for washing machine delivery*
*So will pretend I've come to see why she didn't turn up*

01 Sep 15:17
**How did it go?**

01 Sep 15:18
*Machine arrived at 11, she slept all through it*
*Then rang on door to see why she hadn't turned up for*
*lunch*
*Thought she wasn't going to answer door at first*

01 Sep 15:18
**How was she?**

01 Sep 15:18
*Could barely understand her*
*She's so messed up, went on about murder, told me about*
*seeing knife*
*Sounds raving mad*

01 Sep 15:19
**Good**
**Plan to tell her tonight that she is**

01 Sep 23:27
*Did you tell her?*

01 Sep 23:28
**Yes, still completely out of it when I got home**
**So took advantage, asked her to put on washing**
**machine**
**She couldn't, showed her letter from doctor re**
**eod tests**

01 Sep 23:29
*How did she take it?*

01 Sep 23:29
**How do you think?**

I leave Mary soon after, promising to keep in
touch. As I go out of the front entrance, someone
calls my name. Turning, I see John hurrying toward
me.

"Don't tell me you were going without saying hello,"
he reproaches.

"I didn't want to disturb you on canteen duty," I lie,
because I'm still not sure if he's friend or foe.

He searches my face. "How are you?"

"I'm fine."

"Good."

"You don't seem convinced," I say.

"I didn't expect to see you up and about so soon,
that's all."

"Why not?"

He looks embarrassed. "Well, not after all you've been through."

"What do you mean?"

"Rachel told me," he says awkwardly.

"What did she tell you?"

"That you took an overdose."

I nod slowly. "When did she tell you that?"

"Yesterday. She phoned me here at school and asked if I could meet her for a drink when I'd finished for the day. I was about to refuse—I was afraid she was going to proposition me again—but she said she wanted to speak to me about you. So I agreed to meet her."

"Go on," I say.

"We met in Castle Wells and she told me that last week you took an overdose and were rushed to hospital. I felt terrible, and wished I hadn't taken no for an answer when Matthew told me I couldn't call round to see you."

"When was that?" I frown.

"After Mary told us that you'd decided not to come back to work. I couldn't believe it because, when we'd bumped into each other in Browbury, you hadn't mentioned anything at all about giving up your job and I felt there was something not quite right. It didn't seem to add up. Mary said you were suffering from stress and I knew Jane's murder had been on your mind, but I thought—stupidly, maybe—that I could talk you into changing your mind. But Matthew said you were too ill to see anyone and, when Rachel told me you'd taken an overdose, I couldn't understand how you'd gone downhill in such a short space of time." He pauses a moment. "Did you take an overdose, Cass?"

I shake my head quickly. "Not on purpose. I took too much of my medication without realizing what I was doing."

He looks relieved. "Rachel asked me to tell Mary. She felt that she should know you overdosed."

"Did you?"

"No, of course not, it's not my place to." He hesitates a moment. "I know Rachel is a good friend of yours but I'm not sure she's such a good friend to you. I thought it was really disloyal of her to tell me about your overdose. You need to watch your back, Cass."

"I will," I say, nodding. "If she phones you again over the next couple of days, don't mention that you've seen me, will you?"

"I won't," he promises. "Take care, Cass. Will I see you again?"

"Definitely," I say, smiling at him. "I owe you lunch, remember."

I drive away from the school, happy with everything I've achieved so far. I think about going to see Dr. Deakin but I doubt whether I'll get an appointment at such short notice and, anyway, it's enough to know that in his opinion I'm only suffering from stress. That might have changed if he's been informed of my recent overdose but at least I have Rachel's phone to prove that it was Matthew's doing and not mine.

For the moment, I can't allow myself to think about what would have happened to me if I hadn't been handed the phone, or to think about how the two people I loved best in the world have betrayed me. I'm scared that I'll be so overcome with grief that I'll be incapable of doing what I'm determined to do, what I've been determined to do ever since I heard Matthew's voice at the other end of the line in the Spotted Cow, which is untangle their web of deceit. I didn't need to go and see Hannah this morning, or the woman from the alarm company, or the one from the Baby Boutique or Mary, because everything is there on the phone. But when I woke up I still couldn't quite believe what they'd done, and because they've played so much with my head over the last couple of months, I began to wonder if I'd imagined it, or had maybe misunderstood what I'd read. I didn't dare read the messages again in case I deleted them by accident or in case Rachel or Matthew came by unexpectedly and found me with the phone. My trip out has allowed me to confirm that it really is as I thought.

It has also made me realize how easy I made it for them. It seems incredible now that I didn't question anything at all, not the alarm I supposedly ordered, or the pram, or the washing machine I couldn't use. Everything that happened, I put down to my failing memory. Even losing my car in the car park.

12 Aug 23:37
*We need to up our game*

12 Aug 23:39
*Why?*

12 Aug 23:39
*She opened champagne earlier*

*Says she feels a whole lot better, talked about having a baby*

12 Aug 23:39
*Poor cow*
*I'll phone her tomorrow, see what she says*

13 Aug 09:42
*Just phoned her, she didn't answer*
*Have you silent called yet?*

13 Aug 09:42
**Not yet, just about to**
**Hopefully it will send her back to where we want her to be**

13 Aug 09:42
*Do you want me to go to house later?*

13 Aug 09:43
**Yes but be careful**

13 Aug 09:43
*I always am*

13 Aug 14:31
**Anything happening?**

13 Aug 14:32
*No. She's crashed out in front of telly*

13 Aug 14:32
*Good, means my phone call spooked her*

13 Aug 15:30
*Can I leave? Need to go to Castle Wells*

13 Aug 15:54
*Sorry, was in meeting*
*You may as well*
*Make sure no one sees you as you're meant to*
*be in Siena*

13 Aug 15:54
*I have blonde wig and jogging pants, remember*

13 Aug 15:54
*Wish I could see you*

13 Aug 15:54
*No. You don't*

13 Aug 16:48
*Guess who's come to Castle Wells?*
*Was just about to leave when she arrived in multi-story*
*Following her now, I have an idea*
*Is there spare key for her car?*

13 Aug 16:49
*Yes, at home, why?*

13 Aug 16:50
*You know she has phobia about not finding her car*
*We could make it happen*


13 Aug 16:51
**How?**


13 Aug 16:51
*If you can get away, you could come here and move her*
*car to another floor*
*She's parked on 4th*


13 Aug 16:51
**You're a genius**
**Leaving now, hope I get there in time**


13 Aug 16:51
*I'll keep you posted*


13 Aug 17:47
**I'm here, where is she?**


13 Aug 17:47
*Wandering around town*


13 Aug 17:47
**Shall I move car?**


13 Aug 17:48
*May as well. Can't imagine she'll stay much longer*
*Put it on top floor*

13 Aug 17:48
*OK*


13 Aug 18:04
*She's on her way back, have you moved it?*
*She just bumped into that girl from her work, Connie I*
*think*


13 Aug 18:04
**Yes, sitting in car on top floor**
**Keep an eye on her so I can move it if she comes**
**up here**
**Let me know what's happening**


13 Aug 18:14
*So funny to watch*
*She's looking everywhere for it*
*On 5th floor at moment*
*Feel almost sorry for her*


13 Aug 18:14
**Do you think she'll come up here?**


13 Aug 18:16
*No, going down again*


13 Aug 18:19
**What's happening?**


13 Aug 18:21
*On ground floor, think she's going to office to tell them*
*she can't find car*

13 Aug 18:21
*Shall I move it back to 4th*

13 Aug 18:21
*Yes!*

13 Aug 18:24
*Have you done it?*
She's on way up with attendant, waiting for lift

13 Aug 18:25
Yes, not in exactly same place though, couple
of spaces along

13 Aug 18:25
*Don't think it will matter*
*You better get going*

13 Aug 18:26
Already gone
I'm going to call her to ask where she is, pre-
tend I'm at home

13 Aug 23:48
*Hi, how did it go?*

13 Aug 23:49
Put it this way
She won't be opening champagne again any
time soon

13 Aug 23:49
☺


Suddenly hungry, because I haven't eaten since lunchtime yesterday, I stop at a service station and buy myself a sandwich and something to drink. I eat quickly, impatient to be home. I get back onto the dual carriageway, intending to stay on it all the way home but, five minutes later, without really knowing why, I find myself turning left, down the road to the woods, the one that will take me home via Blackwater Lane. I don't worry too much about it, deciding to let fate take me where it will. After all, it had allowed me to find the phone. What were the chances of the French student taking it from Rachel's bag as she pushed past him? What were the chances of one of his friends having a crisis of conscience and handing it to me? I've never thought of myself as particularly spiritual but, yesterday, somebody somewhere was looking out for me.

Blackwater Lane looks nothing like it did the last time I drove down it. The trees that line the road are a riot of autumnal colors and the fact there are no other cars around make it peaceful, not threatening. When I get to the lay-by where Jane's car was parked, I slow down and pull in. After turning off the engine, I wind down my window and sit for a while, letting the light breeze fill the car. And I feel that Jane is with me. Even though the murderer still hasn't been caught, for the first time since her death, I feel at peace.

I'd intended to go back to the house, take Rachel's phone from under the orchid and hand it to the police, but if I've been brought to this spot it must be for a reason. So I close my eyes and think of Jane, and of how Matthew and Rachel, without conscience, used her murder to get to me.

18 Jul 15:15
*How are you?*

18 Jul 15:16
*Fine. How come you're calling at this time?*

18 Jul 15:16
**I'm out. Told her I was going to the gym**
**Need to keep up appearances**
**Don't want her to question why I'm not going anymore**

18 Jul 15:16
*Wish you were on your way to me, like before*

18 Jul 15:16
**Me too. Do you know how much I miss you?**

18 Jul 15:16
*I think I can guess ☺*
*And we're not going to be seeing each other tonight*

18 Jul 15:16
**Just as well, would want to kiss you**
**But why not?**

18 Jul 15:17
*Susie's canceled her party*
*You know the woman who was murdered? She worked in our company*

18 Jul 15:17
**Seriously?**

18 Jul 15:17
*Just phoned C to tell her, she went into meltdown*
*Turns out she had lunch with her recently*

18 Jul 15:18
**What? Are you sure? The murdered woman?**

18 Jul 15:18
*Yes. She met her at that leaving party I took her to a month back*
*And they arranged to have lunch*
*Jane Walters*

18 Jul 15:19
**I remember! I met Cass at the restaurant after the lunch**
**She said she was meeting a new friend, Jane**

18 Jul 15:19
*That was her*

18 Jul 15:19
**God, she'll be even more upset now**

*She's really nervous about murderer on the loose*

18 Jul 15:20
*Good maybe we can use it*

18 Jul 23:33
*Didn't know you had argument with murdered woman*
*Cass told me*

18 Jul 23:34
*She nicked my parking space*

18 Jul 23:34
*She got what she deserved then*

18 Jul 23:35
*God, you really are a cold-hearted bastard!*

18 Jul 23:35
*Not where you're concerned*
*You do know you're the one for me, don't you?*

18 Jul 23:35
☺

24 Jul 23:40
*The murder has really got to her, she doesn't want to be on own while I'm away*
*Told her to invite you round*

24 Jul 23:40
*Thanks!*

24 Jul 23:40
**Need to keep it genuine**
**You refuse, of course**

24 Jul 23:41
*Can't believe she's so frightened*

24 Jul 23:41
**Good for us that she is**

28 Jul 09:07
**Good morning!**

28 Jul 09:07
*You sound chirpy. What's up?*

28 Jul 09:08
**C phoned to ask me if I'd just called her**
**She sounded jittery so said no for the fun of it**

28 Jul 09:08
*Is that it?*

28 Jul 09:08
**Same thing happened yesterday except it wasn't me**
**Played it down, told her probably a call center**

28 Jul 09:08
*Still don't get it*

28 Jul 09:09
**Thought I could do it again tomorrow. And day after**
**Make her think she has stalker**

28 Jul 09:09
*Brilliant!*

28 Jul 09:09
**Thought you'd be pleased**

05 Aug 23:44
**Had a good day?**

05 Aug 23:57
*Sorry, was in shower*

05 Aug 23:57
**Lovely thought**

05 Aug 23:58
☺ *Day not bad, how about you?*

05 Aug 23:58
**Nothing exciting but just thought**
**Do I silent call tomorrow as I'll be at home**

05 Aug 23. 58
*If you don't she'll guess it's you*

05 Aug 23:59
**Or could think she/house is being watched**

05 Aug 23:59
*Paranoia is good so go for it*

Thinking of those text messages makes me so angry I'm determined to find a way of avenging Jane. I go back over every little thing that has happened since that fateful night. And, suddenly, I know exactly what to do.

I leave the lay-by and drive home quickly, praying that I won't find Matthew or Rachel's car parked in the drive. There's no sign of anyone but I look around carefully as I get out of the car. I let myself into the house. As I'm turning the alarm off the phone starts ringing. I see from the number that it's Matthew, so I pick up.

"Hello?"

"At last!" His agitation is clear. "Have you been out?"

"No, I've been in the garden. Why? Have you been calling?"

"Yes, I tried to get you a few times."

"Sorry, I decided to clear the far end of the garden, by the hedge. I've just come in for a cup of tea."

"You're not going out again, are you?"

"I hadn't intended to. Why?"

"I thought I might take the afternoon off, spend a bit of time with you."

My heart rate speeds up. "That will be lovely," I say calmly.

"I'll see you in an hour then."

I hang up, my mind racing, wondering why he's decided to take the afternoon off. Maybe he, or Rachel, has managed to trace the group of French students who were in the pub last night and know I have the phone. If the students are staying at the college in Castle Wells it wouldn't be difficult to find out their whereabouts today. I've been lucky so far but, despite what I told Rachel, I can't count on them being already on their way back to France.

I hurry out to the garden, hoping Matthew won't have moved the knife from where Rachel left it that day. The cushions from the garden chairs have already been put away for the winter, stacked in a neat pile at the back of the shed. I move them aside and find myself face to face not with a knife, but with an expresso machine. It takes me all of five seconds to work out that it's the one that used to stand in our kitchen, the one where the capsule slotted in without the need to lift a lever. I search a little farther and, under an old garden table, covered with a sheet, I find a box with a picture of a microwave on the front and, when I open it, I find our old microwave inside, the previous model of the one that now stands on our kitchen counter. I want to howl with rage at how easy it was for Matthew to dupe me but I'm scared that I won't be able to stop, that all the emotions I've been keeping inside me since

Rachel's phone was handed to me yesterday afternoon will come spilling out, leaving me incapable of carrying on. So I take my anger out on the microwave, kicking it over and over again, first with my right foot and then with my left. And when my anger has gone and all that is left is immense sorrow, I set it aside for another day, and get on with what I have to do.

It takes me a few minutes more to find the knife, stuffed into a flowerpot at the back of the shed, wrapped in a tea towel that I recognize as belonging to Rachel, because I have an identical one, brought back from a trip to New York. It might not be the knife used in Jane's murder but I still feel sick looking at it. Without touching it, I wrap it up again quickly and put it back where I found it. *By tonight it will be over*, I tell myself, *by tonight it will all be over.*

I go back into the house and stand for a moment, wondering if I'm really going to be able to do it. And because there's only one way to find out I go to the hall, pick up the phone and dial the police.

"Could you come please?" I say. "I live near to where the murder took place and I've just found a large kitchen knife hidden in my garden shed."

They arrive before Matthew, which is what I wanted. There are two of them this time: PC Lawson, who I've already met, and her male colleague, PC Thomas. I make sure I look shaken but not hysterical. I tell them where the knife is and PC Thomas goes straight out to the garden shed.

"You don't think it's the murder weapon that you've been looking for in connection with Jane Walters' murder, do you?" I ask PC Lawson anxiously, in case it hasn't occurred to her that it might be. "It hasn't been found yet, has it?"

"I'm afraid I can't say," she says.

"It's just that I sort of knew her."

She looks at me in surprise. "You knew Jane Walters?"

"Only a little. We got chatting at a party and then we had lunch together."

She gets out her notebook. "When was that?"

"Let me think—it must have been about two weeks before she died."

PC Lawson frowns. "We asked her husband for a list of her friends but your name wasn't on it."

"As I said, I was a new friend."

"And how did she seem when you met her for lunch?"

"Fine. Just normal."

We're interrupted by PC Thomas coming back with the knife, held gingerly in his gloved hands, still partly wrapped in the tea towel.

"Is this what you found?" he asks.

"Yes."

"Can you tell us how you found it?"

"Yes, of course." I take a deep breath. "I was gardening and I needed some flower pots to plant some bulbs in. I knew I'd find some in the shed because that's where Matthew—my husband—keeps them. I picked up a big one and there was a tea towel in the bottom and as I took it out I could feel there was something wrapped inside. I started to unwrap it and, when

I saw the serrated blade and realized it was a knife, I was so scared that I quickly wrapped it up again—it reminded me of the one I'd seen on television in relation to the Jane Walters murder, you see. So I put it back and phoned you."

"Do you recognize the tea towel?" he asks.

I nod slowly. "A friend brought it back from New York for me."

"But you've never seen this knife before."

I hesitate. "I think I might have."

"Other than on the television," PC Lawson says kindly.

I don't blame her for thinking I'm a bit thick after the fiasco with the alarm and the mug. And for the moment it suits me to let her think that I am because if I let slip certain pieces of information which might—well—incriminate Matthew, it won't seem malicious. "Yes, other than on the television," I say. "It was about a month ago, on a Sunday. I went into the kitchen to stack the dishwasher before going to bed and it was lying on the side."

"This knife?" the policeman asks.

"Possibly. I only saw it quickly because by the time I called Matthew to come and see it, it had gone."

"Gone?"

"Yes, it wasn't there anymore. Instead, there was a small kitchen knife lying in its place. But I knew I'd seen a much bigger knife and I was really frightened. I wanted to phone you but Matthew said it was just my mind playing tricks."

"Can you run through exactly what you saw that

night, Mrs. Anderson?" PC Lawson asks, going back
to her notebook.

I nod. "As I said, I went to the kitchen to load the
dishwasher and, as I bent down to put the plates in, I
saw a huge knife lying on the side. It wasn't one I'd
seen before—we don't have any like that—and I got
such a fright that all I could think of was getting out of
the kitchen as quickly as possible so I ran into hall and
began screaming for Matthew—"

"Where was your husband at this point?" she interrupts.

I wrap my arms around my body, pretending ner-
vousness. She smiles at me encouragingly so I take a
deep breath. "He'd gone up to bed before me so he was
upstairs. He came running down and I told him there
was a huge knife on the side in the kitchen. I could see
that he didn't believe me. I asked him to call you because I'd seen a photograph of the knife that was used
in the murder and it looked exactly the same, so I was
terrified the murderer was somewhere in the garden, or
even in the house. But Matthew said he wanted to see
the knife first so he came down to the kitchen and then
he called me to come and look. And when I looked, the
big knife had gone and there was a little kitchen knife
lying in its place."

"Did your husband go all the way into the kitchen or
did he stay in the doorway?"

"I don't really remember. I think he stayed in the
doorway but I'm afraid I was a little hysterical at that
point."

"What did your husband do next?"

"He made a show of looking round the kitchen for the knife but I knew he was just humoring me. And when he didn't find it, he said I must have been mistaken."

"And did you think you were mistaken?"

I shake my head vigorously. "No."

"So what did you think had happened?"

"I thought that the big knife *was* there but that someone had come in through the back door while I was telling Matthew about it and swapped it for a kitchen knife. I know it sounds stupid but that's what I believed and that's what I still believe."

PC Lawson nods. "Can you tell us where you and your husband were on the night of the seventeenth of July?"

"Yes, it was the last day of term—I'm a teacher at Castle Wells High—and I went to a wine bar with some of my colleagues from the school where I worked. There was a storm that night."

"And your husband?"

"He was here, at home."

"By himself?"

"Yes."

"What time did you get back?"

"It must have been about eleven forty-five."

"And your husband was here?"

"He was asleep in the spare bedroom. He phoned me as I was leaving Castle Wells to tell me he had a migraine and was going to sleep in the spare room so that I wouldn't disturb him when I came in."

"Did he say anything else?"

"Just that I wasn't to come home by Blackwater Lane. He said there was a storm coming and I should stick to the main road."

She exchanges a glance with PC Thomas. "So when you got home, your husband was asleep in the spare room."

"Yes. I didn't go and check on him because the door was closed and I didn't want to disturb him but he must have been there." I put a puzzled look on my face. "I mean, where else would he have been?"

"How was your husband the next day, Mrs. Anderson?" PC Thomas takes over.

"Just his normal self. I went shopping and when I came back he was in the garden. He'd had a bonfire."

"A bonfire?"

"Yes, he'd been burning something. He said it was branches, which I thought was a bit strange as with the storm and everything they would have been too wet to burn. But he said they'd been under tarpaulin. He doesn't usually burn branches on the bonfire though, we usually keep them for the chimney. But he said they were the wrong sort."

"The wrong sort?"

"Yes, too smoky or something." I pause. "I thought maybe that was why the air smelled a bit funny."

"In what way?"

"I don't know. It just wasn't the normal bonfire smell, you know, when you burn wood. But maybe it was the rain."

"Did he talk about the Jane Walters murder at all?"

"All the time," I say, hugging myself tighter. "It really upset me, especially as I felt I'd known Jane." PC Thomas frowns and PC Lawson shakes her head imperceptibly, a warning not to interrupt me. "He seemed obsessed by it. I had to ask him to turn off the television on more than one occasion."

"Did your husband know Jane Walters?" PC Lawson asks, studying my face. She looks over at PC Thomas. "Mrs. Anderson had lunch with Jane Walters two weeks before she died," she explains.

"No, he only knew of her, from what I'd told him about her. The day Jane and I had lunch, he came to pick me up but they didn't meet. Jane saw him through the window though. I remember how surprised she looked," I say, smiling at the memory.

"What do you mean?"

"Just that she looked sort of shocked. A lot of people have that reaction because he's . . . well, quite good-looking."

"So your husband didn't know Jane Walters?" PC Thomas says, looking disappointed.

"No, but my friend Rachel Baretto did. That's how I met Jane. Rachel took me to a leaving party for someone who worked at Finchlakers and Jane was there." I pause. "Rachel felt really bad when she heard about Jane because she had a row with her on the day she died."

"A row?" PC Thomas perks up. "Did she say what it was about?"

"She said it was over a parking space."

"A parking space?"

"Yes."

"If she worked with Jane Walters, she must have been interviewed," interrupts PC Lawson.

"She was." I nod. "I remember because she told me she felt bad that she didn't tell you about the row. She was worried you might think she was guilty."

"Guilty?"

"Yes."

"Of what?"

"I presume she meant the murder. So I told her that nobody would murder someone over a parking space." I look at her nervously. "Unless the row wasn't over a parking space."

PC Lawson gets out her mobile and taps something into it. "Why do you say that?"

I look out of the kitchen window to the garden beyond, bathed in the late summer sun. "Well, if it was over a parking space, why didn't she tell you about it?" I shake my head. "I'm sorry, I shouldn't have said that, it's just that I'm not feeling very happy with Rachel right now."

"Why's that?"

"Because she's been having an affair." I look down at my hands. "With my husband."

There's a small silence. "How long has it been going on?" PC Lawson asks.

"I don't know, I only found out about it recently. A couple of weeks ago, Rachel came over unexpectedly and I saw Matthew kissing her in the hall," I say, glad to be able to use something from their text messages against them, even if it means I've just lied to the police.

The two police officers exchange glances again.

"Did you tell your husband what you'd seen?" PC Thomas asks. "Did you confront him?"

"No, he would only have dismissed it and say my mind was playing tricks on me like he did with the knife I saw in the kitchen." I hesitate a moment. "Sometimes I wonder if . . ." I stop, wondering how far I should go in paying Matthew back for what he's done.

"Yes?" PC Lawson prompts.

A pleasing image of handcuffs snapping around Matthew's wrists comes to mind. "Sometimes I wonder if Jane knew about their affair," I say. "Sometimes I wonder if, when she saw him through the restaurant window, she looked shocked because she recognized him. I don't know, maybe she'd seen him and Rachel together." Wanting to be sure they're thinking what I want them to think, I spell it out for them. "When I found the knife in the shed just now I didn't know what to think. At first, I thought the murderer had hidden it there and I was going to phone Matthew to ask him what I should do. And then I remembered that he didn't believe me when I told him about the knife in the kitchen so I phoned you instead." I let tears fill my eyes. "But now I don't know if I did the right thing because I know what you're thinking, I know you think that Matthew is the murderer, that he killed Jane because she knew about him and Rachel and was going to tell me, but he can't be, he can't be!"

With perfect timing, Matthew arrives home.

"What's going on?" he says, coming into the kitchen. He looks over to where I'm standing. "Did you set the alarm off again?" He turns to PC Lawson. "I'm sorry you've been called out again. It's very probable that my wife has early-onset dementia."

I open my mouth to tell them that all I've been diagnosed with is stress but close it quickly, because at this point it isn't really important.

"We're not here for the alarm," PC Lawson explains.

He puts his bag down on the floor, frowning. "Well, if you're not here because of the alarm, can I ask what this is about?"

"Have you seen this before?" PC Thomas holds out the tea towel, the knife clearly visible.

We all hear the tiny hesitation. "No, why, what is it?"

"It's a knife, Mr. Anderson."

"Good grief." Matthew sounds shocked. "Where did you find it?"

"In your garden shed."

"In the garden shed?" He manages to look incredulous. "How did it get there?"

"That's what we're here to find out. Perhaps we can all go and sit down?"

"Of course. If you'd like to come through."

I follow everyone to the sitting room. Matthew and I sit down on the sofa and the two officers draw up chairs. I don't know if they do it on purpose but they place the chairs right opposite Matthew, hemming him in, leaving me out of their claustrophobic triangle.

"Can I ask who found the knife?" Matthew asks.

"Your wife did," PC Lawson says.

"I needed some flower pots to put some bulbs in," I explain. "It was in one of the big ones, wrapped in a tea towel."

"Do you recognize this tea towel?" PC Thomas shows it to Matthew.

"No, I've never seen it before."

I give a nervous laugh. "That shows how often you dry the dishes," I say, pretending I'm trying to break the tension. "We have one exactly like it. Rachel brought it back from New York for us."

"What about this knife, Mr. Anderson?" PC Thomas asks again. "Have you seen it before?"

"No." Matthew shakes his head firmly.

"I was just saying that it looks exactly like the one I saw lying on the side that Sunday evening," I tell him earnestly.

"We've been through all this before," Matthew says wearily. "It was our kitchen knife that you saw, remember?"

"No, it wasn't, it was a much bigger knife."

"Can I ask where you were on the night of Friday the seventeenth of July, Mr. Anderson?" PC Thomas asks.

"I'm not sure I can remember that far back," Matthew says with a little laugh. But nobody laughs with him.

"It was the night I went out with the people from school," I say helpfully. "The night of the storm."

"Oh, yes." Matthew nods. "I was here, at home."

"Did you leave the house at all?"

"No, I had a migraine and went to bed."

"Where did you sleep?"

"In the spare room."

"Why did you sleep there, why not in your own bed?"

"Because I didn't want Cass to disturb me when she came in. Look, what's going on? Why am I being questioned like this?"

PC Lawson studies him for a few seconds. "Just trying to establish a few facts, that's all," she says.

"What facts?"

"A possible murder weapon has been found in your garden shed, Mr. Anderson."

Matthew's mouth drops open. "You're not seriously suggesting that I had anything to do with that young woman's murder?"

PC Thomas looks at him thoughtfully. "What young woman would that be, Mr. Anderson?"

"You know very well who I mean!" His veneer begins to crack and I watch him dispassionately, wondering how I could ever have loved him.

"As I said, we're trying to establish facts. Mr. Anderson, how well do you know Rachel Baretto?"

The mention of Rachel surprises him. He looks up sharply. "Not very well. She's my wife's friend."

"So you're not in a relationship with her."

"What? No! I can't stand the woman!"

"But I saw you kissing her," I say quietly.

"Don't be ridiculous!"

"The day she came over unexpectedly, the day I couldn't remember how to work the coffee machine, I saw you kissing her in the hall," I insist.

"Not again," he groans. "You can't keep making things up, Cass." But doubt has wormed its way into his eyes.

"I think it might be better to continue this down at the station," PC Thomas interrupts. "Would that be all right, Mr. Anderson?"

"No, it would not!"

"Then I'm afraid I'll have to caution you."

"Caution me?"

I turn to them, looking anguished. "You don't really think he killed Jane Walters, do you?"

"What?" Matthew looks as if he's about to pass out.

"It's my fault," I say, wringing my hands. "They were asking me questions and now I'm scared that every little thing I told them is going to be used against you!" He stares at me, horrified, while PC Thomas reads him his rights. When he gets to the end, I start sobbing as if my heart is broken, and I realize that I'm not pretending anymore, because my heart has been broken, not only by Matthew but also by Rachel, who I had loved like a sister.

They lead him away and, once I've shut the door behind them, I dry my tears, because I haven't finished yet. Now it's Rachel's turn.

I dial her number. I was only going to speak to her over the phone but as I wait for her to answer I decide to ask her to come round because it will be much more fun telling her what I have to tell her face to face, much more satisfying to actually see her reaction rather than just hear it.

"Rachel, can you come round?" I ask, tearfully. "I really need to talk to someone."

"I was just about to leave work," she says, "so I can be with you in about forty minutes, depending on traffic." For the first time, I'm able to detect a hint of boredom in her voice and I know she thinks I'm going to start banging on about the murderer being after me again.

"Thank you," I say, sounding relieved. "Please hurry."

"I'll do my best."

She hangs up and I imagine her texting Matthew, as she'll have bought a new phone by now. But with him in custody, she's not going to be able to get hold of him.

She arrives an hour later, perhaps because of traffic, perhaps because she wanted to let me stew a little longer.

"What's happened, Cass?" she asks as soon as I open the door. "Is it to do with Matthew?" She looks worried, which means that I was right, that in the time since I phoned she's been trying to get hold of him.

"How do you know?" I ask, looking surprised.

"Well, you said you needed to talk so I presumed something had happened," she says, flustered. "And I thought maybe it was to do with Matthew."

"You're right, it is," I say.

"Has he had an accident or something?" She can't hide her panic.

"No, nothing like that. Can we sit down?"

She follows me into the kitchen and sits down opposite me. "Just tell me what's happened, Cass."

"Matthew's been arrested. The police came and took him away for questioning." I look at her hopelessly. "What am I going to do, Rachel?"

She stares at me. "Arrested?"

"Yes."

"But why?"

I wring my hands. "It's my fault. They wrote down every little thing I said and now I'm scared they're going to use it against him."

She gives me a sharp look. "What do you mean?"

I take a deep breath. "This afternoon, while I was doing some gardening, I found a knife in the shed."

"A knife?"

"Yes," I say, happy to see she's gone pale. "I got such a fright, Rachel, it was horrible. It looked exactly like the one in the photo—you know, the one that was used to kill Jane. I don't know whether I told you, you know what my memory is like, but one evening, when you were in Siena, I saw a huge knife lying on the side in the kitchen. But when I called Matthew to come and look, it had disappeared. So when I found the knife in the shed, I thought the murderer might have hidden it there, so I called the police—"

"Why didn't you call Matthew?" she interrupts.

"Because he didn't believe me last time and I was worried he wouldn't believe me this time. Anyway, he was already on his way home."

"So what happened? Why did they arrest Matthew?"

"Well, the police came and they started asking me all sorts of questions, about where he was on the night of the murder . . ."

She looks suddenly frightened. "You're not seriously suggesting that they think he's guilty of killing Jane?"

"I know, it's mad, isn't it? The thing is, he doesn't really have an alibi for that night. I was out in Castle Wells—it was our end-of-term dinner—and he was here by himself. So he could have gone out. At least that's the way the police seem to be looking at it."

"But he was here when you got back, wasn't he?"

"Yes, but I didn't see him. He had a migraine and went to sleep in the spare room so that I wouldn't disturb him when I came in. But listen, Rachel, there's something I need to ask you. You know the tea towel you brought me back from New York, the one with the picture of the Statue of Liberty on it? You said you bought one for yourself too." She nods. "Who else did you give one to?"

"No one," she says.

"You must have done," I insist. "It's really important that you remember because it will prove Matthew's innocence."

"What do you mean?"

I take a deep breath. "When I found the knife this afternoon, it was wrapped in a Statue of Liberty tea towel, and when the police asked me if I recognized it, I had to say, yes, that it was ours. I felt terrible because it made Matthew look even guiltier. But after the police left, I found my tea towel in the cupboard—which means that whoever killed Jane is someone who has the same tea towel. So, think, Rachel, because it will prove that Matthew is innocent."

I can see her mind racing, looking for a way out. "I don't remember," she mumbles.

"You bought one for yourself, didn't you? Are you sure you didn't give it away to someone?"

"I don't remember," she says again.

I sigh. "It would make the police's life easier if you could remember but, don't worry, they'll get there in the end. They're going to test the knife for fingerprints and DNA—they said there's bound to be some. So Matthew will be in the clear because they won't find any of his. But it might take a couple of days and, apparently, they can keep him in for twenty-four hours, and if they really suspect him of being involved in Jane's murder, it can be for longer." I let tears fill my eyes. "I can't bear the thought of him sitting there in a prison cell being treated like a criminal."

She takes her car keys from her pocket. "I'd better go."

I watch her face. "Don't you want to stay for a cup of tea?"

"No, I can't."

I go to the door with her.

"By the way, did you find your friend's phone? You know, the one you lost in the Spotted Cow?"

"No," she says, flustered.

"Well, you never know, it might still turn up. Someone might have handed it in to the police by now."

"Look, I've really got to go. Bye, Cass."

She hurries to her car and gets in. I wait until she's started the engine then go over and knock on the window. She winds it down.

"I forgot to tell you—the police asked me if I knew Jane and I said I'd first met her at that leaving party you took me to. So they asked me if you knew her and I said, no, but that you'd had an argument with her over a parking space on the day she died but that was all. But they didn't seem to believe it was over a parking space. So try and remember about the tea towel, won't you? When I phoned them earlier to tell them that I'd found mine in the cupboard, so it couldn't be the one the knife was wrapped in, I said that the only other one I knew of was yours." I pause for effect. "You know what they're like, they'll use every little thing against you if they can."

It feels good to see her eyes dart around, looking for somewhere to run. She rams her car into gear and tears out of the gate.

"Bye, Rachel," I say softly as her car disappears down the road.

Back inside, I phone the police to tell them that the tea towel the knife was wrapped in isn't mine because I've just found it in the cupboard. I remind them that it was Rachel who bought it for me and that she also bought one for herself. I ask about Matthew and pretend to be distressed at the news that they're keeping him in overnight. And once I've hung up, I go to the fridge, take out the bottle of champagne we always keep there for unexpected guests and pour myself a glass.

And then I have another.

# THURSDAY, OCTOBER 1ST

The next morning, when I see that it's the first of October, it seems like a good omen, the right day to make a fresh start. The first thing I do is check the news and when I hear that a man and woman are helping the police with their inquiries in relation to the Jane Walters murder, I can't help feeling a grim satisfaction that Rachel too has been arrested.

I never thought I was a vindictive person but I hope she spent a terrifying few hours being grilled by the police about her relationship with Matthew, about the row she had with Jane and about the tea towel containing the knife. She must be dreading her fingerprints being found on the knife. Of course, once I hand in her secret mobile, both she and Matthew will be released because the police will realize that neither of them killed Jane, that the knife they have is simply one Rachel bought in London to scare me with, not the murder weapon. And then what? They'll live together happily ever after? It doesn't seem right, and it certainly doesn't seem fair.

I have a busy day in front of me but first I have a leisurely breakfast, marveling at how good it feels without the threat of a silent call hanging over me. I want to take out a court order to prevent Matthew, and Rachel, from coming anywhere near me once they're released, so I search on the computer and find that I can apply for a restraining order. Knowing that I'm going to need legal advice at some point, I phone my solicitor and make an appointment to see him at the end of the morning. And then I phone a locksmith and arrange to have the locks changed.

While the locksmith changes the locks, I put Matthew's belongings into bin bags, trying not to think too much about what I'm doing, about what it means. But it's still emotionally draining. At twelve o'clock, I drive into Castle Wells with Rachel's little black phone in my bag and spend an hour and a half with my solicitor, who tells me something I hadn't realized: thanks to the text messages, Matthew can be charged in relation to my "overdose." When I leave, I drive to Rachel's and dump the bin bags containing Matthew's clothes outside her front door. And then I drive to the police station and ask to speak to PC Lawson. She isn't available but PC Thomas is, so I hand him Rachel's mobile and tell him what I told my solicitor, that I found it in my car that morning.

Physically and mentally exhausted, I drive home. I'm surprised at how hungry I am so I find a tin of tomato soup and have it with some toast. Then I wander around the house, feeling at a loss, wondering how I'm going to be able to move on when I've lost both my husband and my best friend. I feel so low, so depressed, that the temptation to sink to my knees and cry my eyes out is overpowering. But I don't give in to it.

I turn on the television to catch the six o'clock news. There's nothing about Matthew and Rachel having been released but when the phone starts ringing shortly after, I realize that nothing has changed, that the same crippling fear is still there. As I walk through to the hall I remind myself that this can't be a silent call but when I lift the receiver and see that the number is withheld, I feel numb with disbelief.

My fingers fumble as I take the call.

"Cass? It's Alex."

"Alex?" Relief washes over me. "You gave me a fright! Did you know your number comes up as withheld?"

"Does it? I'm sorry, I didn't know. Look, I hope you don't mind me phoning you—I got your number from the card you sent me after Jane died—but I've just had a call from the police. They have Jane's murderer in custody. It's over, Cass, it's finally over." His voice is heavy with emotion.

I try to find the right words but my mind is reeling with shock. "That's wonderful, Alex, I'm so pleased for you."

"I know, I can't believe it. When I heard yesterday that two people were helping the police with their inquiries I didn't dare get my hopes up."

"So is it one of them, then?" I ask, knowing that it can't be.

"I don't know, the police didn't say. They're sending someone round to see me. I'm probably not meant to be telling anyone but I wanted you to know. After what you told me on Monday, I thought it might put your mind at rest."

"Thank you, Alex, it's great news, it really is. Will you let me know what happens?"

"Yes, of course. Well, goodbye Cass. I hope you'll be able to sleep easier tonight."

"You too."

I hang up, stunned at what he's just told me. If the police have Jane's murderer in custody, Matthew and Rachel must have been released. So who has confessed? Did the murderer have a crisis of conscience when he heard that two people had been arrested? Maybe someone was harboring him—his mum, his girlfriend—and they decided to turn him in. It seems the most logical explanation.

I'm so on edge that I can't sit still. Where are Matthew and Rachel? Are they back at Rachel's flat, have they found the bin bags with Matthew's clothes inside? Or are they on their way here, to collect the rest of his things? His laptop, work bag, toothbrush, razor— they are all still here. Glad to have something to do, I go around the house gathering them together, putting everything in a box, wanting to be prepared in case they do turn up, because I don't want to have to let them in.

Night falls but I don't go upstairs to bed. I wish Alex had phoned back to tell me who killed Jane. He must know by now. I should feel safer with the murderer in custody but there are too many doubts clouding my mind. The air reeks of unease. It shrinks the walls of the house; they close in around me and squeeze the breath from my lungs.

# FRIDAY, OCTOBER 2ND

I wake to find myself on the sofa, the lights still on because I hadn't wanted to be in the dark. I have a quick shower, nervous about what the day will bring. The doorbell rings, making me jump. My first thought is that it's Matthew, so I keep the new chain in place as I open the door. When I see PC Lawson standing there, I feel as if I'm looking at an old friend.

"Can I come in?" she asks.

We go into the kitchen and I offer her a cup of tea. I presume she's come to warn me that Matthew and Rachel have been released, or to quiz me over how I came to be in possession of Rachel's secret mobile. Or to confirm what Alex told me last night, that they have Jane's murderer.

"I've come to keep you up to date," she says as I take mugs from the cupboard. "And to thank you. Without your help, we would never have solved Jane's murder so quickly."

I'm too busy trying to look surprised to make sense of her words. "You know who killed Jane?" I say, turning to face her.

"Yes, we have a confession."

"That's wonderful!"

"And you led us there," she says. "We're very grateful."

I look at her in confusion. "I don't understand."

"It was just as you said."

*Just as I said?* In a daze, I walk over to the table and sink onto a chair. *Matthew killed Jane?* I feel a rush of fear.

"No, it's not possible," I say, finding my voice. "I dropped a mobile off at the station yesterday. I found it in my car when I was on my way to see my solicitor and when I opened it I realized that it was a phone Rachel was using to communicate with Matthew. If you read the text messages between them—"

"I have," PC Lawson interrupts. "Every single one of them."

I watch as she pops a tea bag into the mugs that I abandoned. If she's read them, she should know that Matthew is innocent. But she told me that it was *just as I said*. My stomach churns at the thought of having to tell her the truth: that I implicated Matthew in

Jane's murder in retaliation for what he did to me. I'm going to have to retract everything I said and I'll probably be charged with perverting the course of justice. Yet what is there to retract? I didn't actually tell any lies. I didn't see Matthew when I got home that night so it *is* possible that he wasn't in his room. But out murdering Jane? He didn't even know her. Why would he confess to Jane's murder if he wasn't guilty? And then I remember the look on Jane's face when she saw him through the restaurant window. I was right, it had been a look of recognition. He did know Jane.

"I can't believe it," I say weakly. "I can't believe that Matthew killed Jane."

PC Lawson frowns. "Matthew? No, Matthew isn't our murderer."

My mind spins. "Not Matthew? Then who?"

"Miss Baretto. Rachel has admitted everything."

The breath goes out of me and the room swims before my eyes. I feel the blood draining from my face, then PC Lawson's hands on the back of my head as she pushes it gently to the table.

"You'll be all right," she says, her voice calm. "Take a couple of deep breaths and you'll be all right."

Shock shudders in and out of me. "Rachel?" I say hoarsely. "Rachel killed Jane?"

"Yes."

I feel panic surge. Despite everything I know she's capable of I don't believe this. I know I'd told the police things to implicate her, as I had with Matthew, but I had only wanted her to be frightened.

"No, not Rachel, she can't have. She wouldn't have,

she's not like that, she wouldn't kill someone! You've got it wrong, you must have . . ." Despite my hatred for Rachel, for what she's done to me, I feel so scared for her that I can't go on.

"I'm afraid she's confessed," PC Lawson says, pushing a mug toward me. Obediently, I take a sip of hot, sweet tea, my hands shaking so much that some of it slops over the side and scalds me. "When we questioned her about it last night, she just caved in. It was incredible—for some reason she thought we were on to her. You were right when you said the row between her and Jane wasn't over a parking space. Of course, we'll have both of their DNA all over the knife—hers and Jane's . . ."

I feel as if I'm caught up in a nightmare. "What— the knife I found in the shed—it's actually the murder weapon?"

"She cleaned it up, of course, but blood residue has been found in grooves in the handle. We've sent it to Forensics but we're certain it's Jane's."

"But . . ." It's a struggle to keep up. "She said she bought it in London."

"She probably did, but before the murder, not after. She couldn't very well tell Matthew that she already had a knife, so she pretended she'd bought it to frighten you with. Leaving it in your shed afterward was a way of hiding it."

"I don't understand." My teeth are chattering with shock so I circle the mug with my hands, craving some warmth. "I mean, why? Why would she do such a thing? She didn't really know Jane."

"She knew her better than you think." PC Lawson sits down next to me. "Did Rachel ever tell you about her private life, introduce you to her partners?"

"No, not really. I met one or two over the years but she never seemed to stay with any of them for very long. She always said she wasn't the marrying kind."

"It's been a bit of a marathon trying to piece everything together," says PC Lawson. "Some things we knew from when we interviewed Jane's colleagues at Finchlakers and, once she confessed, we were able to get the rest from Rachel. It's a bit of a sordid story, I'm afraid." She looks at me, wanting to know if she should go on and I nod, because how can I ever come to terms with it if I don't know the reasons behind it? "OK, here goes. About two years ago, Rachel had an affair with someone at Finchlakers. He was married with three young children. He ended up leaving his wife for Rachel and, once he had, she lost interest. So he went back to his wife, and Rachel started up the affair again. He left his wife for a second time and it was catastrophic for the family." She pauses. "Again, the affair ended but this time, his wife wouldn't take him back. It was especially difficult for the wife as she also worked for Finchlakers, so she saw him every day, and she spiraled into depression."

"But what does this have to do with Jane?" I ask, trying to hold the pieces of the puzzle up in my mind.

"She was Jane's best friend, so Jane got caught up in it all. Naturally, she hated Rachel with a vengeance for breaking up her friend's family, not once but twice."

"I can understand that."

"Quite. But as they worked in different departments their paths didn't cross very often. However, her opinion of Rachel fell even lower when she came across her having sex in the office late one evening. She confronted Rachel the next day, basically telling her to get a hotel in future otherwise she would report her."

"Don't tell me that's why Rachel killed her," I say, with a hollow laugh. "Because she was worried about being reported."

"No, things only became difficult for Rachel when Jane realized the man she'd seen her with in the office was Matthew. Sorry," she says, catching sight of my face. "If you need me to stop for now, just say."

I shake my head. "It's all right, I need to know."

"If you're sure. Do you remember you told us that you thought Jane had recognized Matthew through the restaurant window? Well, you were right, she had."

It seems unfathomable that something I'd made up has turned out to be true. It's so absurd I want to laugh.

"It's easy to imagine how Jane must have felt when she realized that the man she'd seen Rachel having sex with was the husband of her new friend," PC Lawson goes on. "Outraged on your behalf, she sent an email to Rachel, who was away in New York at the time. She reminded Rachel that she'd already broken up one marriage, and said she wasn't going to let her do the same to you, especially as you were meant to be her best friend. Rachel told her to mind her own business but when she went into work on her return from New York, Jane confronted her in the car park. She threatened to tell you about their affair if she didn't break it off with Matthew immediately. So Rachel promised to break things off with Matthew that evening. But Jane didn't trust her and when she returned to the restaurant after her friend's hen party, to use the phone there, she not only phoned her husband, but also Rachel—when Jane confronted her in the car park earlier that day, she had demanded Rachel's business card and had jotted her mobile number on the back. We found lots of business cards in Jane's bag, most of them from people who worked at Finchlakers, so Rachel's didn't stand out. Anyway, Jane asked Rachel if she'd broken things off with Matthew and when Rachel admitted that she hadn't, saying that she needed more time, Jane told her that since she'd be passing by Nook's Corner on her way home, she was going to stop off and tell you about their affair."

"What, at eleven o'clock at night?" I say. "I doubt that she would have."

"You're right, she probably only said it to threaten Rachel. Anyway, Rachel panicked. She told Jane that before she said anything to you, there were certain things she needed to be aware of—hinting at your fragile state of mind, saying that she couldn't just tell you brutally. She suggested that they meet in the lay-by and that once Jane had heard her out, if she still wanted to go ahead and tell you, they would do it together. Jane agreed to listen to what she had to say, so Rachel drove to a track off Blackwater Lane and ran to the lay-by on foot. And, well, we all know the outcome. Jane didn't buy what Rachel told her about you having mental problems, and they began arguing. Rachel maintains that she had no intention of killing Jane, that she only took the knife to frighten her with."

Slowly, things fall into place. When I stopped in the lay-by on the night of the storm, Jane hadn't needed any help because she was waiting for Rachel to arrive. She hadn't known it was me in the car; if she had, she would have run to me through the rain, climbed in beside me and told me that, strangely enough, she'd been on the way to see me. And, sitting in the car, she would have told me that Rachel and Matthew were having an affair. Would I have driven straight to the house to confront Matthew, passing Rachel's car on the way? Or would Rachel have arrived as I was trying to come to terms with the devastating news, and killed us both? It's something I will never know.

"I can't believe it," I mumble numbly. "I still can't believe that Rachel would do such a thing. Even if Jane had told me, so what? Their affair would have been out in the open and Rachel would have got what she wanted, which was Matthew."

PC Lawson shakes her head. "As you know from the text messages, this wasn't just about Matthew, it was also about money. Your money. She felt very strongly that your father should have made some kind of provision for her in his will—she kept saying that your parents used to call her their second daughter—so she felt cheated when everything was left to you."

"I didn't know about the money, not until Mum died."

"Yes, Rachel told us. And while you remained single, she felt that she would be able to have some sort of share of it. But when you got married, and she could see she wasn't your top priority anymore, resentment toward you built up and she decided that the only way to get her hands on what she felt was her due was through Matthew. I'm afraid she deliberately set out to have an affair with him, and once he was in love with her, they concocted their plan to have you certified as mentally unstable, so that Matthew could get control of your money. The day Jane confronted her, they were about to start their campaign against you—it was bad timing, if you like. If Jane had told you about Rachel and Matthew, all her carefully laid plans would have been for nothing."

Tears spill from my eyes. "I bought her a house in France. She fell in love with it and I bought it for her. I was going to give it to her for her fortieth birthday, it was to be a surprise. I didn't tell Matthew about it because I thought he would disapprove. He didn't really like Rachel—at least, that's what I believed back then. If only she had waited—her birthday is at the end of the month."

I feel terrible. I should have understood how devastated Rachel felt at being left out of Dad's will. How could I have been so insensitive? Yes, I had bought her the cottage, but only because I'd been there when she'd fallen in love with it. Would I have thought of gifting her some of the money if she hadn't seen the cottage? Maybe. I hope so.

And why hadn't I given her the cottage straight away, the minute I bought it, instead of keeping it for her birthday so that I could make a big thing out of it? For the last eighteen months, the cottage has stood empty, unused. If I had given it to her, she would have been so happy. I might still have Matthew, and Jane would still be alive. At the very least, I should have told Matthew about the cottage. If I had, and if he and Rachel had already embarked on their affair, he would have told her about it. She would then have waited patiently for her fortieth birthday, and then, once she had her cottage, Matthew would have divorced me and, more likely than not, tried to get some money out of me in settlement. I would have lost Matthew—but Jane would still be alive.

I don't know what it was that made me stumble unwittingly on the truth about Jane's murder. Maybe it was my subconscious—maybe the look of surprise on Jane's face when she saw Matthew outside the restaurant window that day had registered in my brain as a flash of recognition. Maybe her invitation to have coffee at hers had registered as something more than just a casual suggestion to meet up again. Maybe, somewhere deep down, I had known that Matthew and Rachel were having an affair, maybe, somewhere deep down, I had known that Jane was going to tell me. Perhaps it was just pure and simple luck. Or maybe, when I'd sat in the lay-by yesterday and had felt Jane's presence, she had led me to the truth.

It's almost another hour before PC Lawson stands up to leave.

"Does Matthew know?" I ask, as we walk to the front door together. "About Rachel?"

"No, not yet. But he soon will." She turns on the doorstep. "Will you be all right?"

"Yes, thanks, I'll be fine."

As I close the front door behind her, I know that I won't be, not yet. But one day, I will be. Unlike Jane, I have my whole life ahead of me.

# Read on for a sneak peek at
# B. A. Paris's next novel

## *Bring Me Back*

# TWELVE YEARS BEFORE

*Interview: Finn McQuaid*
*Date: 15/03/2006*
*Time: 03.45*
*Location: Fonches*

We were on our way back from skiing in Megève. I decided to stop in Paris on the way up as a surprise for Layla, because she had never been there before. We had dinner in a restaurant by the Notre-Dame cathedral and then went for a walk along the Seine. We could have stayed the night there—now, I wish we had—but we were both eager to get home to our cottage in St. Mary's, in Devon.

It must have been around midnight by the time we left Paris. About an hour and a half into our journey I wanted to go to the toilet so I pulled off the motorway, into the picnic area at Fonches. It's not a service station, you can't get petrol there or anything but I knew it had toilets because I'd stopped there before, on previous skiing trips to Megève. The place was deserted apart from the car I told you about, the one parked directly outside the toilet block. I think there were a couple of lorries in the lorry bay on the other side; there must have been at least two, the one I saw leaving and the other one, the one whose driver we spoke to after.

There was an empty bottle of water rolling around the car and we'd been eating snacks on the way up from Megève so I drove past the toilet block and down to the end of the car park where there was a rubbish bin, so that I could get rid of the wrappers. I—I should have just parked outside the toilet and walked down. If I had, then I would have been nearer. I should have been nearer.

Layla was asleep—she'd fallen asleep as soon as we'd hit the motorway, and I didn't want to wake her so I sat for a while, just to relax a bit. She woke up when I started gathering up the stuff to throw away. She didn't want to use the toilet there, she said she'd rather wait until we stopped at a proper service station, so as I got out of the car I told her to lock the doors behind me, because I didn't like leaving her there in the dark. She really hates the dark, you see.

On my way into the toilets, I passed a man coming out and a minute or so later, I heard a car drive off. He was shorter than me, maybe six foot? I think he had dark hair, he definitely had a beard. I was quick in the toilet, I didn't like being in there, I felt unnerved, as if someone was watching. Maybe it was because one of the stall doors was closed.

As I made my way back to the car, I heard a lorry pull out of the parking bay and I watched it as it headed along the slip road to the motorway. He was driving fast, as if he was in a hurry, but I honestly didn't think anything of it at the time. In the distance I could see the silhouette of our car, it was the only one left because the other one, the one that had been parked in front of the toilet block, had gone. It was only when I got closer that I realized Layla wasn't in the car and I thought she must have changed her mind about going to the toilet. I remember looking behind me, expecting to see her hurrying after me—I knew she'd be as creeped out by the whole place as I was— but she wasn't there, so I got into the car to wait. But the darkness began to get to me so I started up the engine and moved it in front of the toilet block, where there was at least a modicum of light, so that Layla wouldn't have to walk all the way back in the dark.

It must have only been a couple of minutes before I began to worry. It didn't feel right that she hadn't appeared yet so I got out of the car and went into the Ladies' side of the block to look for her. There were three stalls, two were empty but the other one had the door closed so I presumed she was in there. I called to her and when there was no answer I put my hand on the door and pushed against it. It swung open easily and when I saw that Layla wasn't there I hurried back outside and began calling for her, thinking that maybe, after I left the car, she'd decided to go for a short walk to stretch her legs or get some fresh air. But even as I was thinking it, I knew she would never have wandered off, not at night, not when it was pitch-black because, as I said, she hated the dark.

I ran round to the back of the block, in case she was there, and when I couldn't find her I got a torch from the boot and widened my search, taking in the whole picnic area, shouting her name. There was still one lorry in the bay so I went over and called out, hoping to find someone to help me look for her. But there was no one in the driver's cabin and when I hammered on the door no one answered, so I assumed the driver was asleep in the back. I tried hammering on that door too but nobody came and when I took out my phone and realized that I didn't have a signal, I didn't know what to do. I didn't want to leave in case Layla had fallen and was lying injured somewhere, but I knew I wasn't going to be able to find her with only the light from my torch. So I got back into the car and drove as fast as I could to the next petrol station and ran in shouting for someone to help me. It wasn't easy to get them to understand me because my French isn't very good but they finally agreed to phone the local police. And then you came and you spoke good English and you took me back to the picnic area to help me look for Layla, because I really needed to find her.

That was the statement I gave to the police, sitting in the police station somewhere off the A1 in France. It was the truth. But not quite the whole truth.

# ONE

## NOW

My phone rings as I'm walking through the glass-walled foyer of Harry's impressive offices on London Wall. I turn and check the time on the digital display above the receptionist's desk; it's only four thirty, but I'm impatient to get home. It's taken months of perseverance to get Grant James, the famous business magnate, to invest fifty million pounds in Harry's new fund and I'm ready for a celebration. As a thank-you, Harry has booked dinner for me and Ellen tonight at The Hideout, the best restaurant in Cheltenham, and I know she's going to love it.

I glance impatiently at my phone, hoping it's a call I don't have to take. The caller name comes up as Tony

Heddon, a police detective based in Exeter. We first met twelve years ago when I was arrested on suspicion of Layla's murder, and we've become good friends since. There's a curved steel bench to the left of the reception area so I walk over and put my briefcase down on its metallic seat.

"Tony," I say, taking the call. "Good to hear from you."

"I'm not disturbing you, am I?"

"Not at all," I say, noting that he sounds serious, the way he always does when he calls to tell me that an unidentified woman's body has been found by the French authorities. Guessing how awkward he must feel, I decide to plow straight in. "Has another body been found?"

"No, nothing like that," he says reassuringly in his soft Devonshire accent. "Thomas Winter—you know, your ex-neighbor from St. Mary's—came into the station yesterday."

"Thomas?" I say, surprised. "I didn't think he'd still be alive after all these years. How's he doing?"

"Physically he's pretty good, but he's quite elderly now. Which is why we don't want to give too much importance to what he said," he adds, pausing. I wait for him to carry on and while I wait, my mind analyzes what Thomas could have told them. But then I remember that before Layla and I left for our holiday in France, before she disappeared, Thomas only knew us as the happiest of couples.

"Why, what has he said?" I ask.

"That yesterday, he saw Layla."

My heart misses a beat. I lean my free hand on the cold metal back of the bench, trying to process what he's just told me. I know he's waiting for me to say something, but I can't, so I leave him to fill the silence.

"He said he saw her standing outside the cottage and that when he went to speak to her, she ran off," he goes on.

"Because it wasn't her," I say, my voice neutral.

"That's what I suggested. I reminded him that twelve years have passed since he last saw her but he said he'd know her after fifty. She was wearing a hood thing over her head but he was adamant it was Layla. Something about the way she was standing, apparently."

"But he didn't speak to her."

"No. He said, and I quote, "I called her name and she turned her head, but when she saw me, she ran off." He said she went toward the station but the ticket office was closed at that time and we can't find anyone who saw a woman waiting for a train. There's no CCTV so we're none the wiser."

I search for the right response. "You don't really think it was Layla, do you? Not after all these years."

Tony sighs heavily. "I'm inclined to put it down to Mr. Winter's overactive imagination. I thought you should know, that's all."

"Well, thanks, Tony." I want to hang up but it seems too soon. "When are you retiring? September, isn't it?"

"Yes, just another couple of months to go. Not too sure what I'll do with myself, though."

I grab onto this. "You can start by coming down to see us. I know Ellen would love to see you."

"I will, definitely."

Maybe he understands that I'm not up to speaking because he tells me that he has another call to make. I stand for a moment, trying to get things in perspective, wondering why Thomas thought he saw Layla. I make a quick calculation; we had celebrated his eightieth birthday just before leaving for that fateful holiday in France in 2006, which means Thomas is ninety-two now, an age at which people get easily confused, an age where it's easy to dismiss what they say, or what they think they saw. It can only be the ramblings of an old man. Confident, I take my keys from my pocket and carry on to the car park.

The journey home is unbelievably slow, which isn't unusual for a Friday afternoon. As I drive past the "Welcome to Simonsbridge. Please drive slowly" sign at the entrance to the village, my earlier excitement over the new deal starts to come back. It was good of Harry to book The Hideout; he said I should go for the venison steak, and I probably will.

A minute later I'm pulling up in front of the house, nothing much to look at from the outside maybe, but once inside it's my haven, and the garden, my sanctuary. In a normal world Ellen would be standing on the doorstep, as impatient to see me as I am to see her. More often than not, roused from whatever illustration she's working on by the sound of the tires scrunching on the gravel, she opens the door before I'm out of the car. But not now. And today, it seems ominous.

I tell myself not to be stupid, that she doesn't always open the door, that if I'd phoned ahead to tell her the good news, of course she'd be waiting. But I'd wanted to tell her face-to-face, I want to see her telling me how clever I am rather than just hearing it. I know how it sounds but it isn't that I have a huge ego, more that pulling off this deal is a career highlight. A result like Grant James is such an adrenaline rush. It even beats the high I get from outsmarting the markets.

The sound of my key in the lock doesn't bring her to the door. It doesn't bring Peggy, our red setter, either, which is even more unusual. Instead of calling out, I go in search of Ellen, a flicker of worry making itself felt. As I push open the door to the sitting room I see her curled up in one of the armchairs, wearing my blue denim shirt, which she continually pinches from my wardrobe. I don't mind, I love to see her in it. She has her knees pulled up to her chest and the shirt pulled down over them, like a tent.

My silent sigh of relief at finding her there is checked by the way she's staring unseeingly out of the window, her eyes on a distant past. It's a look I haven't seen for a while but a look I know only too well. It explains why Peggy—always sensitive to Ellen's mood—is lying silently at her feet.

"Ellen?" I say softly.

She turns her head toward me and as her eyes come into focus, she scrambles to her feet.

"Sorry," she says ruefully, hurrying over to me, Peggy following more sedately behind her, her age showing. "I was miles away."

"I can see that."

She reaches up and kisses me. "How was your day?"

"Good," I say, putting my news about the contract on hold for a moment. "What about yours?"

"Good too." But her smile is just a little too bright.

"So what were you thinking about when I came in?"

She shakes her head. "Nothing."

I put my finger under her chin and tilt her head upward so that she can't avoid my eyes. "You know that doesn't work with me."

"It really is nothing," she insists.

"Tell me."

She gives a small shrug. "It's just that when I came back from taking Peggy for a walk this afternoon, I found this"—she puts her hand into the front pocket of the shirt and takes something out—"lying on the pavement outside the house."

I look down at the painted wooden doll sitting in her palm and a jolt of shock runs through me, quickly followed by a flash of anger, because for one mad moment I think she's been rummaging around in my office. But then I remember that Ellen would never do such a thing, so I concentrate on chasing the red mist away. Anyway, hadn't she said that she found it on the pavement outside the house?

"Someone must have dropped it," I say, as casually as I'm able. "A child, on her way back from school or something."

"I know. It's just that it reminded me—" She stops.

"Yes?" I prompt, preparing myself mentally, because I know what she's going to say.

"Of Layla." As always, her name hangs suspended in the air between us. And today, because of Tony's phone call, it feels heavier than usual.

Ellen laughs suddenly, lightening the moment. "At least I have a full set now." And of course, I know what she's referring to.

It was Layla who first told me the story, of how she and Ellen both had a set of Russian dolls, the sort that stack one inside the other and how one day the smallest one from Ellen's set had gone missing. Ellen had accused Layla of taking it but Layla denied that she had, and it had never been found. Now, thirteen years after I first heard that story, the irony strikes me because, like Ellen's little Russian doll, Layla went missing and has never been found.

"Maybe you should put it on the wall outside, like people do with dropped gloves," I say. "Someone might come looking for it."

Her face falls and I feel bad, because it's only a Russian doll. But coming on the back of Tony's phone call, it feels a bit too much.

"I hadn't thought of that," she says.

"Anyway, I'll be able to buy you as many Russian dolls as you like now," I say, although we both know that isn't what this is about.

Her eyes grow wide. "Do you mean . . . ?"

"Yes," I say, lifting her into my arms and spinning her around, noting—not for the first time—how much lighter she is than Layla was. Tendrils of chestnut hair escape her short ponytail and fall around her face. Her hands grip my shoulders.

"Grant James invested?" she squeals.

"He did!" I say, pushing thoughts of Layla away. I stop spinning and lower her to the ground. Dizzy, she stumbles a little against me and I enclose her in my arms.

"That's wonderful! Harry must be over the moon!" She wriggles out of my embrace. "Stay there, I'll be back in a minute."

She disappears into the kitchen and I sit down on the sofa to wait. Peggy pushes herself between my legs and I take her head between my hands, noting with a heavy heart how gray she's getting. I pull her ears gently, as she loves me to do, and tell her how beautiful she is. It's something I often tell her, too often maybe. But the truth is, Peggy has always represented more than just Peggy to me. And now, because of the Russian doll, it seems wrong.

I feel restless, too full of kinetic energy to sit. I want to go to my office—a bespoke outhouse in the garden—and make sure that my Russian doll, the one Ellen doesn't know about, is there, in its hiding place. But I force myself to be patient, reminding myself that everything is good in my world. Still, it's difficult, and I'm about to go and find Ellen when she comes back, a bottle of champagne in one hand, two glasses in the other.

"Perfect," I say, smiling at her.

"I hid it at the back of the fridge a couple of weeks ago," she says, putting the glasses down on the table and holding the bottle out to me.

"No," I say, grasping the bottle and using it to pull her toward me. "I mean you." I hold her tight for a moment, the champagne trapped between our bodies. "Do you know how beautiful you are?" Uncomfortable with compliments, she drops her head and plants a kiss on my shoulder. "How did you know that Grant would come through?" I go on.

"I didn't. But if he hadn't, the champagne would have been to commiserate."

"See what I mean about you being perfect?" Releasing her with a kiss, I untwist the wire and ease the cork from the bottle. Champagne bubbles out and Ellen quickly grabs the glasses from the table. "Guess where I'm taking you tonight?" I say as I fill them.

"McDonald's?" she teases.

"The Hideout."

She looks at me in delight. "Really?"

"Yes. Harry booked it as a thank-you."


Later, while she's upstairs getting ready, I go out to my office in the garden, sit down at my desk and slide open the top right-hand drawer. It's a large antique walnut desk and the drawer is so deep I have to reach a long way in to find the wooden pencil box, hidden at the back. I take out the little painted doll nestling there. It looks identical to the one that Ellen found outside the house and as my fingers close around its smooth, varnished body I feel the same uncomfortable tug I always do, a mixture of longing and regret, of desolation and infinite sadness. And gratitude, because without this little wooden doll, I might have been tried for Layla's murder.

It had belonged to her. It was the smallest one from her set of Russian dolls, the one she'd had as a child, and when Ellen's had gone missing, Layla had carried this one around with her for fear that Ellen would take it and claim it as hers. She called it her talisman, and in times of stress she would hold it between her thumb and index finger and gently rub the smooth surface. She had been doing exactly that on our journey from Megève, huddled against the car door, and the next morning, when the police returned to the picnic area, they'd found it lying on the ground next to where I'd parked the car, by the rubbish bin. They also found scuff marks, which—as my lawyer pointed out—suggested she'd been dragged from the car and had dropped the doll on purpose, as some kind of clue. As there was insufficient evidence to prove either way, I was finally allowed to leave France, and to keep the Russian doll.

I put it back in its hiding place and go and find Ellen. But later, when we're lying in bed, our hunger sated by the exquisite dinner we had at The Hideout, our bodies knotted together, I silently curse the little Russian doll she found earlier. It's another reminder that no matter how many years go by, we will never be completely free of Layla.

Barely a month goes by when we don't hear her name—someone called out to in the street, a character in a film or book, a newly opened restaurant, a cocktail, a hotel. At least we don't have to contend with supposed sightings of Layla anymore—Thomas's yesterday was the first in years. There'd been hundreds after she first disappeared; it seemed that anyone who had red hair was put forward as a possible candidate.

I look down at Ellen, snuggled in the crook of my arm, and wonder if she's thinking of Layla too. But the steady rise and fall of her chest against me tells me she's already asleep and I'm glad I didn't tell her about Tony's phone call. Everything—all this—would be much easier if Ellen and I had fallen in love with other people instead of each other. It shouldn't matter that Ellen is Layla's sister, not when twelve years have passed since Layla disappeared.

But, of course, it does.